Remembrance of Things I Forgot

Remembrance

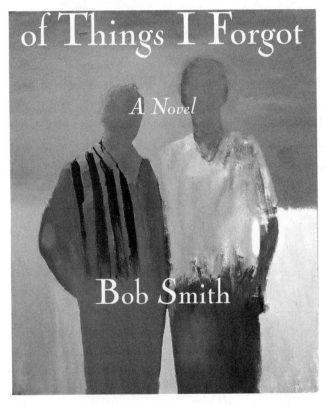

of Things I Forgot

A Novel

Bob Smith

Terrace Books

A trade imprint of the University of Wisconsin Press

Terrace Books
A trade imprint of the University of Wisconsin Press
1930 Monroe Street, 3rd Floor
Madison, Wisconsin 53711-2059
uwpress.wisc.edu

3 Henrietta Street
London WCE 8LU, England
eurospanbookstore.com

3   5   4   2

Printed in the United States of America

Library of Congress Cataloging-in-Publication Data
Smith, Bob, 1958–
Remembrance of things I forgot: a novel / Bob Smith.
    p.   cm.
ISBN 978-0-299-28340-7 (cloth: alk. paper)
ISBN 978-0-299-28343-8 (e-book)
1. Time travel—Fiction.   2. Interpersonal relations—Fiction.
3. Dysfunctional families—Fiction.   4. Gay men—Fiction.
5. New York (N.Y.)—Fiction.   I. Title.
PS3619.M5535R46   2011
813'.6—dc22
2010046335

Title page illustration by Kevin Bean; used courtesy of the artist.

For my family

Mother

Jim

Greg

Elvira

Chloe

Madeline

Xander

Michael

Bozzie

In nature there's no blemish but the mind;
None can be called deformed but the unkind.

Twelfth Night, 3.4

Remembrance of Things I Forgot

1

I T'S SAFE TO SAY your relationship is finished if the only way you can imagine solving your problems is by borrowing a time machine.

Snow was falling on Avenue B, and for months my thoughts had been growing darker each day. I'd been going back and forth on whether to break up with Taylor, my partner of fifteen years, and that morning had decided to leave him. Blizzards in Manhattan usually cheer me up. They blanket the city with a sedative, allowing everyone to cancel plans and stay home, but on that day in December of 2006, I was glumly thinking about my life when Taylor called me at the store.

"Would you make your turkey meatloaf?" he asked. "And pick up a bottle of Veuve Clicquot."

"Meatloaf *and* champagne?" I asked, thinking the weird combination sounded like we were celebrating being broke. He also knew I didn't drink, and envisioning him tipsy on the one night I needed him sober increased my irritation. "What's the occasion?"

"Today I proved time travel is possible."

"Really?"

"I sent a condom back to 1979."

"For *real*?"

"Yes. For real."

I knew I'd said the wrong thing. If I could select one superpower, it would be the ability to predict that I was about to say the wrong thing. It's not a power that would save the world, but it might rescue my relationships.

"I'm just . . . surprised." "Flabbergasted" and "incredulous" were actually more accurate terms. For the past five years, Taylor had been working on this government-sponsored time machine project—which I kept hearing about, even though it's supposed to be top secret. (You'd think the Feds would understand national security is never going to trump the need for two gay men to complain about their jobs.) I'd tried to be supportive, but the truth is I'd always thought building a time machine was more in my line of work. I'm a comic book dealer and spend every day with grown men who inhabit fantasy worlds. It was fine with me that Taylor believed time travel was possible, but I thought the chances of him building a functioning time machine were about as likely as my chances of being bitten by a radioactive spider and being transformed into a wall-climbing, web-shooting hunk.

Honestly, I'd thought the charming Taylor had just suckered the government into giving him a well-paying job where he could play around with their billion-dollar toys for the next twenty years. No one expects his boyfriend to call and say, "Hey, I was out walking today and found a ring. It's hallmarked 'Made in Mordor'" or "I hung your sweater in the wardrobe and now it's being dry-cleaned in Narnia." I was still trying to wrap my head around the idea that Taylor had built a time machine, but it was like trying to wrap my head around the Big Bang. I also felt envious that his dream of a lifetime had come true on the same day my dream disappeared into a black hole. His announcement confirmed my belief that I was about to be unhappy for a long period of time.

"Jesus Christ, John. Try not to sound so thrilled. You ruin everything."

"I'm sorry."

"I'm sure on the day Edison came home with his bulb, the missus didn't bemoan all the candles and kerosene she'd recently bought."

"You're right. I'm proud of you. It's incredible."

My apology was heartfelt, but it was hard to feel happy for Taylor's success while mourning the failure of our relationship. I felt more anxious about telling him "it's over" than when I first said "I love you." He might not even be surprised by my announcement, which would only reinforce my conviction we were finished. I'd had doubts about whether I was making the right decision, until I sadly realized it would be almost like telling a stranger, "I don't love you anymore."

It would have been easier to boot Taylor if he'd done something conventionally unforgivable. He wasn't violent or abusive and hadn't cheated on me with another man; a fickle heart or wayward penis might have caused me to give him a second chance, but it was his brain that had strayed. One of the few smart decisions made by our dumb president was putting Taylor Esgard in charge of the Chronos Project. The Department of Defense had been trying to build a time machine ever since President Kennedy started the program in 1962. Their machine never worked. It was tested in 1965, 1977, and 2003, but each time they threw the switch, New York City suffered a major blackout.

On 9/11 Taylor had been working at the old laboratory next to the World Trade Center, trying to ascertain whether the dud machine was fixable. He and his crew barely escaped before the towers came down. Once history crashed into the Bush administration, time travel became a priority for them, and Taylor insisted on starting over with his ideas in a new location in SoHo. On that traumatic day, I was thankful that Taylor had escaped physically unharmed, but after the attack, he became a Republican, proving that a national calamity can transform a bona fide genius into an idiot.

"I'll be home at seven," he said. "There's still a few phone calls I have to make."

At 9:30, he still wasn't home and still hadn't called. I was furious. He was always late and needed a fucking time machine to be punctual for once. The meatloaf had congealed in its pan and the ice in the champagne bucket had melted. There'd be a sincere apology followed by some lame attempt at humor. "Oh," he'd say, playing the absentminded physicist card. "Time is relative everywhere in the universe, except in my office, where it's constant. Constantly late." It was fortunate the MacArthur Foundation never heard any of his science-whiz jokes before they awarded him their so-called genius grant.

I sat on our boomerang sofa, drinking a glass of mineral water. I wanted a glass of red wine, but had boarded the AA train in my early thirties and wasn't about to let Taylor derail me. Our apartment was filled with vintage '50s pieces that Taylor began collecting when they were still cheap. Figures a gay Republican would collect furniture from the McCarthy Era, I thought. Our dog, Bartleby, was lying at my feet, and I bent down to pet him. We called him Bart for short—he was a beagle/basset rescue—and Taylor always greeted him each morning with "Hello, delicious!" His delight in talking to our dog always made me feel momentarily charmed even when Taylor and I weren't speaking to each other.

After fifteen years together, most of our bickering took place entirely within our own heads. We were a typical long-term couple and had established a comfortable routine where we liked to argue and have sex once a week. The fundamental difference between our temperaments was that Taylor could wake up and become angry with me before he'd had coffee, while I needed two cups to feel bright-eyed and hateful.

On our Noguchi coffee table sat an unopened letter from the New York chapter of the Log Cabin Republicans. They were a group of gay men whose political platform advocated big dicks and small-minded government. The previous year Taylor had joined their board.

Taylor called himself a libertarian. He claimed to want Americans to be free of the authority of the state, while I retorted that Republican libertarianism meant preserving the right not to care about other people or the planet, being ruled by corporations, in addition to being publicly opposed to the legalization of pot.

For a while, I tried to accept Taylor's divergent political views as if he were a family member who was mentally ill; I kept telling myself schizophrenics hear voices, and right-wing conservatives listen to the real crazies on talk radio and cable news. It didn't help. My attempt to tolerate his intolerable beliefs was only driving me insane.

I'm sure many people would argue my primary reason for breaking up with Taylor was inconsequential. Plenty of couples have opposing political views and seem to get along fine. Taylor and I had other disagreements, but they never imperiled our relationship. We argued about what color to paint the kitchen—the red/blue-state divide was an Eggshell/Canvas White split in our house—but our political differences revealed a schism in our values that I found unacceptable.

My life had also changed after 9/11. Two women I'd been friends with for years, Elena and Sonia, had asked me to be their sperm donor, and we had a two-year-old named Isabella. They lived in Santa Fe, and I visited them three or four times a year, often with Taylor. It enraged me that he supported policies that would make Isabella's world less free, less safe, and less inhabitable. Over time, I began to believe I was sleeping with the enemy of my daughter. I'd discussed this with Taylor, and we had many bitter blowups. His sarcastic response was that if lefty do-gooders can only coerce people to do the right thing by incessant nagging, then his side would win every time. We tried couple's counseling, but there were sessions where our therapist seemed like the moderator at an especially vicious presidential debate. Taylor's failure to recognize how important these issues were to me had slowly made me feel I was sleeping with my enemy also.

While getting more mineral water, I passed a picture of the two of us taken the previous year on a rafting trip down the Copper River in Alaska. We were standing in front of the snow-capped Wrangell–St. Elias Mountains amid a field of magenta fireweed. I still felt the tug of my attraction to him. Taylor was tall and handsome with thinning brown hair. He looked like a Y chromosome, broad shoulders tapering down to a narrow waist. He'd rolled up his shirtsleeves and I noticed, for the thousandth time, his thick forearms ivied with veins. Powerful forearms always get me; there's something irresistibly attractive about a man who looks as if he could break my heart with his bare hands.

My cell rang. It was him.

"I'm sorry," he said, before I could speak. "I know I fucked up. There's a car waiting for you. Come down and meet me at my office. I'll show you around and then we'll go out to Chanterelle for dinner."

Taylor's "office" was the site of the time machine at the Singer Building at Broadway and Prince. I'd never been allowed inside before. I was curious to see it, but I was also pissed.

"It's late and now I'm tired. I'll see you when you get home." It wasn't entirely animosity that made me want to stay home; I had been on my feet all day.

"Please just do this for me," Taylor asked. "I know I fucked up dinner. I'm sorry. It was beyond my control and I should've called. But it got crazy here. This has been the biggest day of my life. I think if I was busy that's a reasonable excuse."

One of the unheralded benefits of middle age was that it had convinced me that everyone's heartbeat is a distress signal. I didn't want to go, but could hear Taylor's SOS. Ignoring his cry for help would make me feel Republican.

"I'll be there in a few minutes."

"Thank fucking God," Taylor said before hanging up.

Downstairs no town car was waiting. I had to call Taylor and then wait in the blowing, wet snow—each flake was the size of a snot-drenched handkerchief—for him to call me back. By the time the car arrived fifteen minutes later I was as nasty as the weather. As we drove to the Singer Building, I began regretting my decision to go, leading to the inevitable questioning of my own life. For the most part I enjoyed what I did for a living, but since it wasn't exactly what I set out to do, it felt like happiness once removed. I'd once dreamed of drawing and writing comic books, but was afraid to find out if I was talented enough. I'd failed to even try to be a failure, which is the real definition of a loser. I'd always thought that the one choice I'd made that I'd never regret was picking Taylor for a boyfriend. But when he became a Republican he proved to be my biggest blunder.

I wanted back the guy I fell in love with—the one who didn't confuse being tough with being mean or charity with weakness. He used to make me laugh, a skill you never fully appreciate until someone makes you cry or yawn. He was extremely intelligent, at least in areas other than politics. He was never cheap except for unpredictable outbursts of frugality that were more comical than distressing: "Will you please close the door on the refrigerator? The bulb's going to burn out." And for my late December birthday, he always celebrated what he called "Johnukkah," eight nights of birthday gifts and treats.

The driver stopped in front of the green cast-iron and red terra-cotta building. It was hard to believe a multibillion-dollar project was head-quartered inside. From the outside it appeared to be a clothing boutique closed for the night. Taylor was waiting on the sidewalk.

"Thanks for coming," he said while hugging me.

"You could have called," I grumbled, unable to see that the same impulse that compels boys to burn ants alive with a magnifying glass drives boyfriends to make remarks that do nothing but cause pain.

"My boss is here and he asked to meet you. We'll make it quick and then go to dinner."

"Why's he want to meet me?" I snarled. "I don't care about meeting some nerd who won first prize in his high school science fair for splitting an atom with a Swiss Army knife."

Taylor stopped and turned toward me quickly. "That's it!" he shouted. "I can't take your constant hostility. This should be one of the happiest days of my life. I built a time machine. It's not some science fiction story, but a real working time machine. Something all my physics professors scoffed at, something that might even someday save our species' collective asses. But, no. What will go down in history today is that John Sherkston's fucking meatloaf got cold and his car was late. You know what you should try building? A full-length mirror. So you can see what a self-absorbed fuck you are. I'm really starting to think we're incompatible and should reassess our relationship."

During the ten-second stare-down between us, I noted several snowflakes landing and melting on his dark-stubbled cheeks, and ignored that Taylor always discussed "reassessing" our relationship as if he were an anthropologist observing us. It was a linguistic ploy to make him seem like the more rational of the two of us. Breaking the silence, I said, "I've been thinking that for a long time."

His dark eyes became colder than the wind as he turned away from me and walked to the entrance of the Singer Building. I was stunned and irritated that he had beaten me to the breach. The happiness advantage in a breakup always goes to the dumper not the dumpee. Now Taylor would always be able to claim he'd initiated our split. It was another example of why I couldn't blame all of my dissatisfaction with my life on Taylor. I'd made up my mind to leave him months ago, but I didn't follow through, since the only surety in my life is my perpetual ambivalence. (That's the perfect relationship that keeps eluding me: having someone in my life whom I can blame for *all* of my problems.)

I followed behind Taylor as he put his palm on a gleaming rectangle of stainless steel next to an intercom and a red laser shot out and scanned his retina. Within seconds, two armed soldiers opened the door. "Good evening, Mr. Esgard," said the taller of the pair. We walked through a women's clothing store and followed Taylor into one of the fitting rooms. He placed his palm against the mirror and a doorway was revealed.

"Your secret entrance is in a dressing room?" I asked.

"It wasn't my idea," Taylor snapped and turned away from me as we entered an elevator and rode up three floors. He was right to be angry. For years, I'd treated him horribly due to my concern for the future of humanity. That's one thing liberals don't like to admit: we want a better world and we're determined to make everyone miserable until we get it. The chilling thought occurred to me that breaking up with someone you love to criticize might be the only way to save yourself from becoming unlovable.

We were scanned, frisked, stripped of our clothes, scanned again buck-naked, then allowed to dress, and scanned once more before we were allowed to get near the time machine. Taylor rubbed his earlobe before we entered the final steel door. It was a nervous habit that I'd first noticed when he asked me to move in with him. That tiny gesture always softened me. I was excited and proud of Taylor. He'd done what he set out to do. He looked at me and grinned. I hadn't seen him this gleeful in months. Actually in years, which made me feel like shit.

"Here's my time machine," Taylor announced as we walked into a control room. He pointed to a plate-glass window. "We call it the Finney Room!"

I'd expected a gleaming machine of some sort, humming with blinking lights, but behind the window was a studio apartment, furnished in the steampunk style that Taylor loved. Steampunk's a retro-sci-fi homage to high-Victorian interiors where modern appliances are made to look as if Jules Verne used a rosewood-and-ivory-inlaid microwave (sitting on brass legs with pawed feet) to warm his cognac. Taylor had once seriously suggested steampunking our apartment, but I told him it was too close to dressing up as Gandalf on the weekends.

Our heads turned when the steel door opened and six men in gray suits wearing ear jacks walked in. The last man had a German shepherd on a leash. The dog methodically sniffed the room, and when he finished the lead man said, "All clear for Angler." The steel door opened again, and a balding, gray-haired schlub wearing wire-rimmed glasses scurried in. It took me a second to believe I was seeing Vice President Dick Cheney. Was Taylor insane? I couldn't bear him on TV in my living room, let alone tolerate him standing next to me. I glared at Taylor and he shrugged. "He wanted to meet you." He was trying to deflect my fury by behaving like a cute boy who'd spilled his milk. It didn't work. This was an unforgivable betrayal. I wanted to vomitboard both of them.

"This is my partner, John," Taylor said before sitting down at his desk to check his e-mail. He checked his e-mail obsessively to the point where I fantasized about e-mailing him six times a day, "Talk2meUahole."

"Nice to meet you," Cheney responded as he offered me his hand. He was shorter and friendlier than I'd imagined. On television he seemed mean and imposing. Yet in person he appeared grandfatherly—granted, a grandfather who'd cut you out of the will—but still that was a step up for him. There was an awkward moment as I decided what to do. I shook his hand. This is how people end up as accomplices to murder, I thought. They just wanted to be supportive or they're overly polite and don't want to cause a scene.

Cheney ordered the agents to wait outside, and they departed.

"I've heard a lot about you," he said. "Taylor speaks about you in the same way I talk about Lynne. Someone indispensable to his life and happiness who's always busting his balls. Has it ever occurred to you that if you were more successful, and made more money, you might start partying with us? And if you did, you might make Taylor's and my life easier."

I assumed he was trying to be funny. His lips parted on the right side as if joy were leaking from his head.

"You don't want me to become a Republican," I said. "I'd be the one elephant who'd never let you forget anything."

"You're right," Cheney said. "There's nothing worse than a bleeding-heart Republican. They're in favor of gun rights, but then want a bullet stamp program for poor people who can't afford ammo. Right, Taylor?"

Taylor looked up from his laptop. "You're right, Mr. Vice President."

"Call me Dick."

You're both dicks, I thought.

Cheney peered through the plate-glass window. "So this is it? It looks a lot like my grandmother's house."

It was impossible to determine if Cheney was joking. From his expression, I couldn't tell whether he was smiling or had a toothache. He walked over to address me.

"Taylor said you have your own business, right? Selling funny books?"

"People in my business don't refer to them as 'funny books.'"

Cheney shrugged. "That's what we called them when I was a kid."

I sell new, used, and rare comic books and graphic novels at my shop. Sherkston's Comics isn't large—it's a storefront with a bathroom. I'd once dreamed of owning a gallery devoted to selling the rarest and most valuable comic books, but most of my clientele were hard-core comic collectors with thick heads and thin wallets. Loud argumentative guys from Jersey or Queens who can distinguish correctly between "mint" and "gem mint" but use invented terms like "staple fatigue" in order to get me to shave ten bucks off the price of *X-Men* #44. These guys can gasbag for hours about how *Batman* peaked in '83, and don't get them started on issue #214 of *Superman*, where some hack writer with a sloppy editor let Clark Kent use his heat vision to warm up a TV dinner without removing his eyeglasses, impossible because the lenses would melt. Most days I eagerly commiserated with embittered gray-haired men who lamented the always in perfect condition, nearly complete run of *Ironman* or *The Silver Surfer* that their mothers threw out. My responses always had to be diplomatic since many of them still lived with their mothers. One day as I opened up the store, I found myself proudly thinking, I get by, which later depressed me for weeks when I thought that's exactly what someone on a respirator would say if his mouth wasn't filled with plastic.

"What are you going to use this for?" I asked Cheney. The thought of him and Bush rewriting history was as horrifying as the thought of them rewriting Proust. They'd turn a complex seven-volume literary masterpiece about memory into a series of Post-it notes.

"We don't know yet," said the vice president. "Change history, I guess."

His nonchalance revealed the guiding principle of his administration: lack of concern.

"It's not that simple," Taylor said. "It's possible that the past might allow for multiple timelines that still achieve the same result. Just as you can add six plus three or two plus seven and either way, you get nine."

"Well, we just have to make sure time travel is used for the good of the country," Cheney said. "I don't want it used for personal gain.

Although I have to admit it would be tempting to go back and *ka-ching*. You could make real money with a time machine. Go back and buy Wyoming for a nickel."

"Changing history shouldn't be done lightly," Taylor said. "I mainly built this out of scientific curiosity, to see if time travel was possible. And I hope it may clear up some historical mysteries: what happened to the Anasazi? Did Shakespeare write his plays? But I also hope this time machine is never used. It's more of a backup system in case we fuck up the world completely."

"Sort of an 'In Case of Emergency Break Time Barrier'?" I asked.

"Exactly."

"I change history every day," Cheney said. "You get used to it."

His casual disregard for his life-and-death responsibilities was disgraceful.

"You're running the country like it's a . . . a hobby," I said.

"So? I like to fish and I'm good at it."

"No," I replied. "You've run the country like your other hobby: hunting. You let bin Laden shoot us in the face, after you'd been warned."

Cheney didn't react at all, but Taylor's eyes locked on mine.

"That's disrespectful to him and me," he said.

I didn't apologize to the vice president or Taylor. I didn't care if I was rude. It was my one chance to say what had been burning inside me for six years.

"What have you ever done to change the world?" Cheney asked. "Have you ever done one thing to make the world a better or safer place? Liberals jabber on about problems but you never do anything to solve them. You're like car alarms that no one can shut off. You know, you can actually try to solve problems without waiting for the government. Global warming? Get your carbon footprint out of your ass and invent a solar car. You actually have to take action. It might not work out, but at least you fucking tried."

He shut me up. Once a month I volunteered for an AIDS group, but I didn't confuse my hiccups of charity for virtue. On the street or subway, I repeatedly said "Sorry" to homeless panhandlers, a comment that was more of an apology to my troubled conscience than an actual response to someone else's suffering. I told myself I wasn't indifferent: I was in a hurry, or I was in a bad mood, or I had my own anxieties and problems. Every now and then I did hand out some spare change, but you can't solve real problems by nickel and diming them.

Cheney turned to Taylor. "How's this thing work?"

"It's super easy to operate," he said while waving him over to the window again. "You see those switches on the wall? The green switch starts the process while the red switch stops it. You just type in the date you want to travel to on one of the keyboards." There were two sets of switches and keyboards. One set was inside the Finney Room and the other was in the outer control room. The keyboards appeared to have been manufactured by an early typewriter company with round keys raised by intricately incised bronze stems, while the flat screen looked like a gentleman's dresser mirror being held in place by elaborate nickel-silver clasps. Sitting next to the computer was an old-fashioned candle-stick telephone and a wooden case lined with black velvet. It held a dozen gunmetal-colored bracelets or cuffs.

"What are the bracelets for?" Cheney asked.

"They're portable time machines. They'll allow time travel to any year, whereas the Finney Room can only go back as far as 1904, when this building was built."

"A straight guy would've made key chains," Cheney observed with a chuckle.

Taylor's put-on smile was more a show of teeth than an expression of happiness. I suppressed the urge to say, "It's because he loved Wonder Woman as a kid. It's his one chance to design super-powered accessories."

"I was told to make them as small and portable as possible." Taylor spoke each word with an unnaturally deliberate precision, a sign he was enraged. He pointed to a large Anglo-Indian style chifforobe standing against a wall.

"Those drawers are filled with old money. Tens of thousands of dollars from each decade for the past hundred years."

A cell phone buzzed and Cheney fished it out of his jacket pocket. He answered the call. "Hello, Mr. President. I am. He's right here. Sure." Cheney handed his phone to Taylor. "It's for you."

Taylor accepted the cell like a beauty queen being handed a dozen roses. His delight in talking to the world's most famous incompetent ended my desire to protect his feelings.

"I'm surprised he's calling now," Cheney said. "He hates doing business after six. I always thought that it was a good thing the terrorists attacked in the morning. If they'd chosen evening flights, the country wouldn't have had his full attention until the next day."

"Tell him, 'Mission Accomplished!'" I shouted, shaking my head in disgust. "We should break up. Why would anyone build a time machine that puts history in the hands of a president who's a complete failure at navigating the present? You must be as stupid as he is. It's the most dangerously moronic thing anyone's ever done."

Taylor covered the cell with his hand. "Go fuck yourself!"

Cheney scratched his nose. "Guys," he said. "Don't say things you'll regret later. Lynne and I have a fight rule. Always say the second meanest thing you can think of, not the first. It's why we've been together for forty-two years."

Taylor glared at me, his expression a mixture of bewilderment and fury, the look that asks, "Why do I love *you*?" Then he shook his head in sorrow and walked into the next room.

"I don't know why Kennedy started this thing in New York," Cheney said as he studied a keyboard. "It makes more sense out west." He shrugged. "New York probably gave him more opportunities to get laid."

Cheney rubbed his hands together. "I don't suppose Taylor would mind if we have a look inside." He opened the door of the Finney Room and with his other hand invited me to enter. Once inside I had to admit the steampunk furnishings looked better than I would have supposed. Less theme-parky and more like a luxurious Edwardian men's club.

"I'd heard you two are going through a rough patch," Cheney said as he opened an empty desk drawer. His comment made me angrier. If Taylor was discussing our relationship with him, that was reason enough to end it.

"You should try to work things out. New York's a pricey place to be single."

A rush of panic about my lack of money made my stomach feel like an empty purse. I'd fully considered that if I broke up with Taylor, I wouldn't be able to afford to live in Manhattan and would have to move to Brooklyn. When you break up with someone in New York the odds are high that one or both of you will end up paying more to live in a much crappier apartment. It's why the residents of New York think of the Statue of Liberty as the symbol of the city. After a hundred years of looking for love, she's still single, lives alone, and probably can't afford to move. The prospect of making easy money with a time machine was tempting.

"Too bad you can't use this thing." Cheney gestured to the computer keyboard. "Go back and buy Microsoft stock in 1986."

His comment made me want to use the time machine to change my history of bad financial decisions. Go back to 1994 and scream at myself: "Buy real estate!" Instead, I said to Cheney, "I'd go back to 1963 and buy twenty gem mint copies of *The Amazing Spider-Man* #1." I was amazed to be discussing my personal life with Dick Cheney. Of course, right then talking with anyone would have felt easier than speaking with Taylor.

"They're worth thirty grand apiece," I added.

Cheney looked at me. "That much?"

I nodded. "And the first issue of *Fantastic Four* came out in 1961. I could probably pick up the entire series in secondhand bookstores. It might even be possible to go to Marvel headquarters and buy the original artwork for both issues!" I said, lost in my dollar-sign daydream. "Back then no one thought about preserving that stuff. Original drawings from the first issue of *Spider-Man* would be worth a fortune."

With that money, I could afford to buy an apartment in Manhattan instead of having to move to Brooklyn or, God forbid, Astoria.

"You need to think big," Cheney said. "I didn't get to be vice president by thinking small." The sound of another buzzing cell began to emanate from somewhere on his body. I wondered why he would have two cells. "That's my family line," he explained before grabbing it and checking the screen.

"I have to take this," he said. "It's my daughter Mary. She's having girlfriend problems and calls Dad to complain." Cheney put the phone to his ear and said, "Hi, Honey . . ." as he stepped out of the Finney Room. While he talked, I noticed a group of framed sepia photographs hung on a wall. They were clearly not old, as one was a picture of a smiling straight couple standing in front of a Ford Taurus. I forgot their names but recognized them from Taylor's office holiday party. The guy was one of his colleagues. Next to it was a photo of Taylor, our dog, Bart, and me taken in Provincetown one Christmas. Taylor and I had our arms around each other's shoulders, and Bart was caught in mid-stride. You could even see a few flakes of snow falling. It made me feel miserable that all three of us looked happy.

Suddenly I heard a gentle whirring sound like wind rattling a house. I looked out the plate-glass window and saw Cheney throw the green switch in the control room. His lips moved as he stared directly at me. I couldn't hear what he said but I think it was "Mission Accomplished."

The window and Cheney disappeared and an exposed brick wall replaced them. The room abruptly shook and then there was silence. This was bad; my entire body uh-ohed. My hands started to tremble as I rapidly typed in the time and date that I'd traveled from, mistyping it twice, before throwing the switch again. Nothing happened.

Why would Dick Cheney send me back in time? It made no sense. You'd think he'd side with Taylor in our breakup. He was the one who gave him his time machine. I was the one who had insulted him. Maybe this was his way of getting back at me. "Yeah, liberal homo, you want to change the world? Well, first, let's see if you can change your fucking life."

I opened what had been the door to the control room, but didn't see Taylor or any computers, just a dingy hallway. Two greasy-looking pink upholstered chairs sat on either side of a small table that held an issue of *Paper or Plastic: The Official Trade Journal of the Packaging Industry* and an issue of *Time* magazine. The cover caption read, "Ain't She Sweet" and then, in a smaller font, "Teen Actress Molly Ringwald."

The date on the cover was May 26, 1986.

Something had obviously gone wrong. I didn't want to travel back to the '80s. The '80s were a cultural wasteland. It's a decade that should be remembered for the debuts of liposuction, stonewashed jeans, and twenty-four-hour news channels. It seemed unfair. There were so many other exciting and romantic periods that I would rather have visited: the Gay '90s, the Roaring '20s, the Swinging '60s. The '80s are called "The Reagan Era," and there's a good reason those ten forgettable years are named after a president who died from Alzheimer's. I'd lived through the '80s and didn't feel any compelling need to revisit that decade. I recalled it as a time when our country and I still had a lot to learn, and there wasn't any evidence that either of us had grown appreciably wiser since then. Instead of drinking absinthe with Oscar Wilde or playing bongos with Allen Ginsberg, I'd be lucky to meet the man who coined the word "Infomercial."

I walked back into the Finney Room and retyped the date 2006 repeatedly to see whether I could get the time machine working again. A light blinked once but the digital readout remained unchanged. "Fuck!" I shouted. Perhaps I'd caused a blackout. Then it occurred to me that I might be stuck in the past. What the hell was I going to do? I'd first moved to New York in 1984, and the thought of reliving my youth as a middle-aged man was depressing. (And this would be depressing one year before Prozac was first introduced in the United States.)

I considered going outside, curious about what it would be like to walk around New York again in 1986, but I was afraid that while I played time-tourist I'd miss Taylor, who, I was sure, would rescue me. Unless Dick Cheney lied and told Taylor I'd used the time machine to go back and earn some breakup money. Anything was possible with Cheney. Perhaps he was getting rid of me to make it easier to manipulate Taylor. I soon decided speculation was fruitless. I'd been reading and thinking about Cheney for six years and still had no idea what motivated his behavior. It was like trying to ascribe volition to a Venus flytrap.

According to the digital clock on the control panel it was 1:37 a.m. I was exhausted and there was a comfortable-looking double-sized brass bed in the Finney Room. I went back outside and grabbed the issue of *Time* magazine and fell asleep while reading about Molly Ringwald. When she was six, she recorded a blues album called *Molly Sings*, and the last thing I recall thinking was, The Blues? Wait till she sees what happens to her acting career.

2

THE NEXT MORNING I woke up and realized that I hadn't been rescued. Taylor was late. Then I thought about that. Can you be late if someone's waiting for you in the past? It sounded like a lame Zen koan. I shoved the thought aside as a new worry appeared. Perhaps Taylor had no idea what year I ended up in; maybe I would be stuck here forever. Suddenly all of my imprisoned internal organs started banging on the bars of their cage. I tried to subdue my panic and feel confident that Taylor would figure out some method of tracing my whereabouts. Even if Cheney lied, Taylor was smart enough not to be hoodwinked for long. Then I recalled that he'd believed in Cheney's policies for the past six years. I repeatedly told myself, "He's a MacArthur fellow who received their 'genius grant,'" ignoring the fact that he could never keep track of his wallet and keys.

Lying in bed, I felt like a hypocrite. I'd been complaining about the greediness of the Republicans, and now I was just as disgusting as them. I hadn't thought about using the time machine to help humanity but only to make money for myself. It served me right to be sent back to 1986. (I tried in vain to suppress the thought of how much money I could make if I took Cheney's advice and bought Microsoft stock.) Then, with almost trembling disbelief, it dawned on me that my sister, Carol, was alive. In 1986 she lived in Crescent City, California. Carol had committed suicide in 2001. She put a bullet through her head. For a year she'd been severely depressed, but I'd never dreamed that she would kill herself. The blow of her death had been so painful that the next morning, I woke up crying uncontrollably, almost as if I'd been sobbing in my sleep, something that seemed to be physiologically impossible. Bartleby had licked the tears from my face, something he'd never done before. Carol had been the first person I came out to, the first person I called when something hilarious happened, and the first person I called when something horrible occurred. Her death made my life less interesting, a loss of sustaining joy that had been as everyday as eating. I confronted the bitter paradox that the only person who could have possibly comforted me about Carol's death was Carol. Then I had to accept that since she was gone forever, I would always remain bereft.

Of course, I also remembered my father was alive in Buffalo in 1986. In a few years, he'd be forced to retire from the state police and discover that losing his job felt as if he had retired from living. Soon, he began drinking heavily at beer-and-shot bars where if a man ordered a White Russian, that commie would be shown the door. Six years after his retirement my father was dead from congestive heart failure due to alcoholism. Drinking yourself to death is a patient form of suicide that, though never a surprise, is nevertheless always shocking.

Suddenly time travel seemed like the biggest guilt trip. I thought it was grossly unfair that I had to deal with two suicides. It made me feel like we should change our family name to the Lemmings. There wasn't any way I could spin this—and believe me, I tried—as some *Sophie's Choice* moment where I had to choose one family member over another. We had tried to get my father to quit drinking after he became an alcoholic, and it hadn't worked. But what was I going to do, take a pass on trying to save him a second time out of cynicism or laziness?

The thought of being able to see and talk to them again seemed providential. I sat up, feeling jittery and confused, knowing that I needed to do something immediately. I should call Carol—no, I should go and see her. I could prevent her death. I could warn her about her impending depression, possibly readying her to deal with the crisis when it came.

With my father, it was less clear-cut. Once he started drinking heavily he couldn't stop. Should I go to Buffalo and warn him? Call him now? Would a one-man intervention from the future be more convincing than the attempt by his entire family to stop him from drinking? I didn't know. The future in the past was just as much an unknown as it was in the present. It occurred to me that trying to save them might cause me to be stuck in the '80s, but that was a punishment I'd willingly endure.

I considered that by altering the past, I might change the future. Someone's good fortune could become bad, but didn't that also suggest that someone's misfortune might change for the better? I'd already changed the past just by showing up there. And is there such a thing as destiny or fate? In my own life, I could think of examples of what at the time had seemed like bad luck that had turned out to be a lucky break. In 1977 I'd applied to NYU's undergraduate film school and to my astonishment had been accepted, but even with scholarships and financial aid, I couldn't figure out how to pay for the tuition and the cost of making a film. The numbers didn't add up in a way that someone from a middle-class family, one generation away from farmers, could justify. Instead, I'd gone to SUNY Buffalo, which had felt like a huge failure at the time. Years later, it hit me that if I had come out in New York City in 1977, the odds were that I would probably have become infected with HIV and died sometime in the '80s. Not going to NYU had probably saved my life. It's always made me wonder what other close calls in my life had gone unrecognized.

I ultimately decided that every action has unforeseen consequences and that I wasn't altruistic enough to let my sister die just to possibly avoid World War III. Sorry, Future! At any moment Taylor could show up and whisk me back to the present, but I vowed then that I wouldn't go back until I'd tried to save Carol. I didn't want to return to the future shouldering a double load of should-haves: things I should have done differently in my life, along with the things I should have done differently when time travel gave me a second chance to do them again.

My stomach was growling and I needed coffee badly. It was six a.m. on the West Coast: too early to call Carol. The Finney Room had a small kitchen area, and a quick survey revealed an empty refrigerator and bare cupboards. It made sense. Taylor never did any grocery shopping in our time, so why should I expect him to do it in the past? I decided to go out, but it felt eerie. It's unsettling when your youth recaptures you. In case Taylor showed up while I was having breakfast—I had no doubt that he was trying to find me—I wrote him a note asking him to wait for me. I left it prominently placed on a table near the front door. Even easily distracted Taylor would spot it. Then I recalled that I didn't have the right kind of money for that era. My colorized tens and twenties would look counterfeit. Taylor had said the dresser was filled with cash. Opening a drawer, I found a treasure chest brimming with silver dollars, double eagles, and large denomination bills going back each decade until the 1890s. If I'm stuck here, at least I'll live well, I thought, before grabbing a thick stack of hundred dollar bills that had been printed in 1982.

In the bottom drawer were four Glock 22 semiautomatic pistols with enough ammo to start my own war with Iraq. There was also a key for the apartment that was attached to a Gore-Lieberman key chain, a goofball joke of Taylor's. He had thought of everything. I looked out the window and saw a man on the sidewalk, wearing a T-shirt and shorts. I removed my sweater. My sartorial style is Standard Gay Guy (take ten years and ten pounds off Standard Straight Guy), and my usual black Izod shirt (in summer) or sporty zip-up sweater (in winter) and blue jeans were always accessorized with a good haircut and the latest sunglasses.

If you're going to time travel, New York's the first place you should visit. It's always been a jumble of past, present, and future; a nineteenth-century brownstone stands next to an Art Deco office building, built across the street from an undistinguished apartment tower thrown up in the early '70s, a real eyescraper whose blunt ugliness makes even atheists pray that it will be torn down. I'd left on a snowy day in December and had arrived two decades earlier on the first hot, muggy day in June. The day when New York goes from balmy to brutal overnight and you notice even the pigeons have sweat stains under their wings.

Outside on the street, I marveled at the SoHo I remembered. There were relatively few people walking the sidewalks. Back then the area was still primarily known for the cast-iron facades of its buildings instead of the vacant faces of tourists. Then I noticed the automobiles; they were all boxy and uniformly ugly, more carton than car, especially compared to the more curvaceous models that would supplant them. I walked down Prince Street to Wooster, taking stock of businesses that had moved or closed. In 1986, SoHo barely clung to its bohemian identity and was still marginally more interested in Andy Warhol's paintings of dollar bills than real cash. I felt strangely disoriented. It's one thing to contemplate the roads not taken in your life, but it's another, more outlandish experience to actually walk those boulevards again. It was scary, but also exhilarating. I'd deliberately broken a law of physics and was driving in the wrong direction on a one-way street.

I craved a Starbucks double-shot skim latte but understood I'd have to fly to Seattle to place my order, since caffeine hadn't yet become America's favorite recreational drug. Fortunately, I remembered the Cupping Room was a block away and went there for breakfast after buying the *Times* at the Korean deli on Spring Street. I placed my order of poached eggs, sausage, and dry wheat toast, then looked at the front page of the paper. The date: June 12, 1986. I scanned the headlines: a Solidarity leader in Poland . . . Thatcher . . . Gorbachev . . . President Reagan appointed someone to the Federal Reserve. I tried to remember when Reagan had died. Was it in 2003 or 2004?

As I hurried back to the Singer Building, I spotted the Sylvia Gallen Gallery on West Broadway and stopped walking. I was stricken with a mixture of astonishment and disbelief. Sylvia had given me my first job in New York. I looked at my watch. It was after ten and my twenty-six-year-old self was working the front desk. I was wildly curious to talk to myself, something no other sane person in history had ever done. But it would have to wait. I could be returned to my own time at any minute and my mission was to talk to my sister. Of course, Carol might not even be home, and my message for her was not one you could leave on an answering machine. Then I realized I could tell Junior about Carol's suicide. Whatever happened to me, he'd be here. Junior could be her guardian.

I saw movement in the front window of the gallery. The shutters that blocked the interior space from the unwanted intrusion of sunlight opened and a tall, dark-haired young man stepped inside the window, carrying a placard. There was a moment of uncanny confusion similar to unexpectedly catching your own reflection in a mirror.

It baffled me that back then I didn't think I was handsome. In New York I'd always thought other young men's beauty towered over me in the same manner that the Chrysler Building would have dwarfed my parents' house in Buffalo.

Junior still had a spiky head of black hair, the sudden reappearance of which overjoyed me, as if I had been reunited with a long-dead childhood pet. At that point in my life, I'd joined a gym and like a holistic Dr. Frankenstein creation began the noninvasive operation of exchanging my weakling body parts for those of a muscle man.

He wore a black and gray vertically striped shirt that looked ridiculously like stylish prison-wear—perhaps from the Bastille. The short sleeves were cut high on Junior's newly muscular arms, which he showed off with the Look-What-I-Made pride of a kid who's built a go-cart. I'd mercifully deleted that shirt from my memory. Striped apparel had been banished from my wardrobe long ago. After a certain age, no one needs to add more lines to his body.

His skin was smooth and unblemished, without my crow's feet or laugh lines or sun-damaged spots or the occasional broken blood vessel or weird brown spot that had appeared on my neck sometime after I turned forty. One of the many problems with aging is that you begin to think of yourself as a slob because your birthday suit can never be cleaned or pressed no matter how spotted or wrinkled it gets. He also wasn't wearing eyeglasses. My eyesight had been perfect until I turned forty-two.

Junior and I quickly exchanged the almost imperceptible third-eye wink of recognition that two strange gay men give each other when they meet or pass on the street, the mutual acknowledgment that your private parts are public knowledge to other members of the cognoscenti.

It upset me terribly when I read the sign Junior placed in the gallery window:

Gary Wright
Maps
June 11th–July 11th

Gary was the only artist on Sylvia's roster who became a friend of mine. He made beautiful, intricate ink-and-watercolor maps that included finely detailed roads, croplands, and forests, even tiny railroads. I still owned one of Gary's drawings of the Galapagos Islands. Gary was a polymath and possessed the seemingly effortless conversational flair that had impressed me about New Yorkers when I first moved to the city. He could talk about anything, from the extinction of Haast's eagle to explaining that Diane Arbus's name was properly pronounced Dee-Anne—the estate is very picky about that. It had been a revelation to discover that people who could talk about anything didn't always have to be unbearable. Sometime during the early '90s, Gary had moved to Florida, where he later died—of cancer, not AIDS. It was impossible not to feel bleak, recalling his death and all my other friends who had died. Junior checked to see whether the sign was centered properly, glanced at me, seemed to almost smile, and then stepped back inside the gallery and closed the shutters.

I stood frozen at the doorway. I should call Carol, but the temptation to meet myself was irresistible. I could afford to spare half an hour, but still waited on the sidewalk. The prospect of meeting myself made me feel awkwardly shy and embarrassed. I tried to think of how I would introduce myself: "I'm you, only with less hair and problems you can't imagine!" That would win him over. Would he even recognize me? He would have to be disappointed by my appearance. I still had muscular arms and a firm chest, but had reached the age where every time I was photographed there was a fifty–fifty chance of a slight double chin vandalizing my portrait. I'd also added two inches to my waistline over the past two decades, but didn't feel as bad about transitioning from slim-fit to relaxed-fit jeans. The extra weight didn't bother me, since I didn't require other men to have washboard abs in order to think they were sexy. What if he hates my looks? That was stupid, I thought. Not every relationship in my life has been based upon physical appearance. I have a great personality; however, my charm is contingent on not being dissatisfied with my job, unhappy with my appearance, or in the midst of ending a fifteen-year relationship.

Once inside the gallery, it almost felt as if I were stalking myself. I was disappointed to see that I wasn't seated behind the reception desk. As usual, Sylvia was in her office talking on the telephone; she always left the door open. It was impossible not to listen inadvertently to conversations that I thought I shouldn't be hearing—an art collector's ex-nanny poked a number 9 knitting needle through his Miró, and where could he get it surreptitiously and expertly repaired before it went to auction at Sotheby's? After Sylvia hung up, she would stroll out of her office and discuss with me—a nobody from Buffalo—what she had just been talking about, almost as if she considered it part of my job to eavesdrop.

Sylvia stood up. She was much younger than how I remembered her. Her hair was still mostly black—she hadn't gone completely silver yet—and I'd forgotten how she used to gently twine her fingers through a lock of it when trying to solve a problem. She began flipping through a file drawer, peering intently through angular black eyeglasses whose severe modernity said "art dealer" in the same way bejeweled turbans signaled fortune-tellers. She wore an up-to-the-minute designer black suit—Sylvia always wore black—and her signature Calder silver brooch. (She claimed it was her "forged signature look" after she'd swiped the idea from Georgia O'Keefe.)

The gallery had a small kitchen area, and I must have been in back getting a cup of coffee. I'd started drinking coffee under Sylvia's tutelage. "John," she'd say while filling each of our mugs, "drinking coffee is how adults face the day; the ritual of turning an initially repellent bitter brew into something more palatable each morning—by adding milk and Sweet and Low, or, since you're still young and distressingly slender, real sugar—and then actually convincing yourself that you not only look forward to it, but actually relish it, is a daily lesson in how to live."

I was startled to see my Galapagos drawing hanging on a wall and walked over to admire it. I'd been able to purchase the drawing after Sylvia generously sold it to me for half price, letting me pay her in installments. Next to the drawing was a small painting titled *Tenochtitlan, Mexico, 1521*, that had a red dot posted next to its catalog number. It was a map of the Aztec capital on the day Cortez and his troops burned the city to the ground. Billowing smoke and flames were painted in minute detail, and somehow the delicacy of the small artwork movingly evoked the destruction of an entire civilization.

I heard someone walking behind me, and from over my shoulder came a familiar and yet alien voice. "Isn't it amazing how he captures that moment in history?" Junior waited for me to respond to his comment about Gary's drawing, but when his eyes met mine, an upwelling of tenderness overwhelmed me and I became flustered.

"I, uh, love that his work reminds us that all maps tell a story," I finally managed to say.

"I love that too!" Junior gushed, then his face reddened as if he was ashamed of his own enthusiasm. It was easy to see that his heart was as unwrinkled as his face. "Did you know he's visited all the places he draws?"

"No," I lied, amused by Junior's sincerity.

"I think that's one of the things that gives his maps such an intimate quality," he explained. "He makes the world look handcrafted."

Sylvia had encouraged me to try my hand at selling artworks, and I'd always been nervous about doing it. Junior seemed slightly hyper, and I thought a joke might allow him to relax.

"Maybe God's name is written somewhere at the South Pole?" I suggested. "Like a potter signing a bowl."

"With his ego?" Junior said. "I'm sure his signature would be the size of Brazil. In fact, it might be Brazil."

"God does have an artistic temperament. He's become a bitter recluse since he thinks his work hasn't been properly appreciated."

"His best work's behind him," Junior declared. "He's been living off his reputation for years."

Junior smiled as his eyes butterflied around my arms and chest. It took me a second to figure out I was being cruised by myself, which was the most unsettling compliment I'd ever received. My smile widened slightly, wordlessly signaling that I appreciated the compliment while also reassuring him that I thought he was attractive as well.

This was getting weird, but I was relieved that Junior liked me. (Of course if he disliked me, what could I do? My only recourse would be to stop talking to myself.) I wanted to stand there all day chatting with him about art, but I needed to talk to him privately. I still had no idea what I was going to say. I needed to prove to Junior that I was him from the future and to tell him about our sister's death. And it had to be done quickly and persuasively. I couldn't disclose what I had to reveal here at his job. I had no idea how he'd react, which struck me as strange. Making any one of those statements would brand me as nuts, but telling him both at once would make even Dee-Anne Arbus say, "You're too fucking weird for *me*." On Junior's desk was an exhibition catalogue for the Van Gogh show at the Met, and I used it to stall for time.

"Did you see the Van Gogh exhibition?" I asked.

I felt dishonest leading him on with questions whose answers I already knew; it made me feel like God talking to Abraham or Job.

He grinned. All of my life people had told me that I had a great smile, but this was the first time I could verify it. "Oh, yes. We had tickets for my best friend Michael's birthday on January 22nd."

Michael Adams was my best friend then and would still be my best friend twenty years later.

"It turned out to be the perfect day to go. There was a snowstorm—everyone here kept calling it a blizzard—that shut down the city. But I grew up in Buffalo and Michael's from Olean, and western New York boys don't think six inches of snow is a reason to stay home. When we got to the Met, the galleries were empty. We had the whole exhibit to ourselves! I was especially moved by his last paintings: the seventy he did in seventy days before he shot himself; they're one of the greatest achievements of any artist."

I stopped smiling and felt distraught that someday Junior would bitterly understand the horror of seeing someone you love die from a self-inflicted gunshot wound. I'd always regarded Van Gogh's suicide as a sad fact of art history without fully grasping that it was also a family tragedy. People make jokes about Vincent cutting off his ear—I probably had myself—but his brother, Theo, must have been devastated by Vincent's increasingly self-destructive behavior. I suddenly felt a kinship with Theo's plight.

Junior seemed to have read my mind. "His brother, Theo, died six months later. He had syphilis but he was never able to come to terms with his grief."

"Come to terms with his grief," I said with unexpected sharpness. "That phrase makes it sound as if there will be some sort of negotiation about the depth of your sorrow. There isn't. Every death is an unconditional surrender."

Junior appeared to be understandably disturbed by my outburst and became subdued. We moved to another of Gary's intricately beautiful drawings; it was an overhead view of the East Village, centered on St. Marks Place, where he lived, reminding me again that Gary would be dead in ten years.

"So much for the ability of art to console us," I said. "For Theo, even owning every Van Gogh painting and drawing was inadequate compensation for the loss of his brother."

Junior listened attentively as we came to the next picture in the gallery, a map of Venice.

"Art makes life better, but it doesn't necessarily make it enjoyable," he said. "Cezanne's apples aren't much help when you're hungry."

"Or Andy Warhol's soup cans for that matter."

We walked over to the last map, an overhead view of the cities of Niagara Falls and the lower Niagara River. Finely drawn plumes of spray obscured the cataracts.

"I recognize that view," I said emphatically. Niagara Falls was the setting for many of the most memorable moments of my childhood.

"Me too," Junior said. "My grandparents had an apartment right there." He pointed to a spot overlooking Goat Island and the American Falls. "And my cousins lived right there," he added, pointing to a spot on the gorge in Lewiston on the lower river.

Junior's mouth quivered as if he were on the verge of laughing.

"My sister . . ." He began but immediately stopped himself. He appeared to regret mentioning Carol, and I wondered why.

"What?" I asked.

"Well, it sounds really negative but I think it's funny."

"Tell me."

"My sister says, 'Niagara Falls has the most beautiful view of the two ugliest cities in North America: Niagara Falls, Ontario, and Niagara Falls, New York.'"

I chuckled because that sounded like something Carol would have said. Unfortunately, that's true, I thought, thinking of the hideous gambling casinos that would be built on both sides of the border in the next twenty years.

Junior frowned. "That's not a very good sales pitch." He nodded toward the painting.

"I don't know. The painting is beautiful; it's the cities that are ugly."

Hearing him talk about Carol revealed how much he loved her. There's a subtle change in register in someone's voice when they speak about someone they love, when for an instant vocal cords are plucked like harp strings.

It was a gratifying to see that I was someone whom I'd like to know. My recollection of myself as a young man had focused almost entirely on my callowness, errors of judgment, fiascos, and romantic ineptitude. Our mistakes would be easier to accept if we'd actually been *complete* idiots; you can't really blame someone who's wrong about everything. But I actually possessed several virtues: I was curious and intelligent, and steadfast to the people I loved. (Taylor was another story—he deserted me by becoming a Republican.) I decided that I could entrust Junior with preventing Carol's suicide. If I unexpectedly returned to my present, he would watch out for her. I needed someone I could rely on, someone I could trust, and, like most people, deep down, I believed I could only depend on myself.

We walked back to the reception desk, but our attention remained more focused on each other than the art. Junior introduced himself, and when I couldn't choose a name, I just blurted out "John" also. I looked for a flicker of recognition but he took it in stride: there were a lot of Johns in the world. He asked, "What do you do?"

I was unprepared for his question and considered lying. I was afraid that everything I revealed to him about his future would somehow lead to Armageddon. Then I blew off the future again and admitted, "I'm a comic book dealer." If he asked to see my inventory or shop, I'd claim I dealt privately with high-end comic book collectors. All twenty of them.

"Really?" he said, sounding pleased. "I deal a little part time and I've thought about that as something to fall back on. But I want to write and draw comic books."

It wouldn't be until two years later that I'd give up trying to become a comic book artist and settle for becoming a full-time comic book dealer. It had been a difficult decision, and while I'd convinced myself it was the right one, hearing Junior's virgin ambition revived a series of long-submerged regrets.

Junior noticed the rapid change in my demeanor. "Are you all right?"

I pushed my face into a grin. "Oh, yeah," I replied. "Are you working on something?"

"Uh, yeah," he said. "I'm working on a new character, Dark Cloud."

I'd spent several years working on Dark Cloud, the mentally ill, severely depressed, sexually confused, and totally hot superhero, but after Marvel and DC rejected him so did I.

Junior stopped talking and his twinkling eyes indicated he was eager for me to ask about his character.

"What's his story?"

"Starting when he was a teenager, Dark Cloud began to be troubled by feelings of melancholy. Whenever he saved someone's life, he'd find himself wondering whether they wouldn't just be better off dead. He finally sought the help of a therapist. It turned out Dark Cloud suffered from debilitating survivor's guilt after his father had sent him to Earth in a rocket ship when their home world was destroyed."

"A depressed, mentally ill superhero?" I asked. "One of his superpowers should be that he can actually suck all of the oxygen out of a room." It seemed unfair to use this line, since I wouldn't think of it for another year.

"That's great," said Junior. "Can I use that?"

"Sure," I said. "What are his other powers?"

"Every morning he uses his X-ray vision to see whether he's developing a brain tumor."

Junior became wide-eyed as we traded premises for the character.

"He's invulnerable but easily hurt," he said.

"His mood swings are faster than a speeding bullet!"

"His sidekick is his mother."

"He's his own archenemy!"

"He's confessed to his shrink that sometimes he thinks about leaping *off* tall buildings in a single bound."

Junior's comment about suicide jolted me and I stopped smiling.

"Can you imagine?" he asked. "He'd have suicidal thoughts, but then feel even more miserable because he can't cut his wrists or overdose on pills no matter how many he swallows."

I cranked out another polite smile but didn't find his jokes about suicide amusing. I saw Junior in fifteen years, with less hair and more muscles, sobbing uncontrollably as he stood outside the hospital, talking to our mother on his cell phone. Junior would go through a long, painful emotional and spiritual convalescence after Carol's death, but at some point his "healing" would be understanding that there are experiences in life for which there is no recovery, events that disprove Nietzsche's oft-repeated bullshit that "Whatever does not kill me makes me stronger." No, some things just make us sadder. And Junior would have to live with that. I had second thoughts about burdening him with this knowledge fifteen years before he would have to deal with it. Then I reasoned that if I told him about Carol's suicide now, maybe he'd never have to deal with that specific tragedy. There would be other deaths, but they would never be as devastating as Carol's had been.

"I have to be careful," he said. "Dark Cloud could easily just become a dumb joke. It could actually be darkly ironic, possibly even moving, if it's done right."

I hadn't thought about Dark Cloud for years, but still regarded it as a great idea.

"I'd read that," I said.

Junior's grin made me wonder about the last time I was as happy as him.

"I can see the first issue: twenty-two pages without any dialogue," he said. "And in every panel Dark Cloud, in costume, sits slumped in a chair, staring at a television in a darkened room. Until on the last page, he gets up and leaves, then returns with a bag of potato chips and sits down again. It could be sensational."

I laughed. "I guess. If you like to read comic books as performance art."

"That's the idea! Then everyone will be waiting to see what happens in the second issue."

"You might want to bring it down from 'Everyone.'"

He conceded the audience for Dark Cloud might be a tad less inclusive than "Everyone."

"I'm actually thinking of taking a drawing course at Pratt," Junior revealed.

I took several drawing courses but never became convinced my abilities were good enough for the evolving hyperrealistic style of comic books. I was more Snoopy than Dark Knight. I didn't imagine that in twenty years many successful graphic novels would be drawn in varied styles ranging from detailed photorealism to blocky cartoon. It rattled me when critical and commercial success fell upon graphic novels whose drawing style I could have done—maybe even better.

"Save your money. Most successful illustrators start drawing in high school. You can't start in your twenties."

"Hmmm, you have a superhero's body," Junior said, "but you sound like Dark Cloud's archenemy, Mr. Negativity."

His flirting was a mixture of coy and heavy-handed. We really needed to discuss that and Carol. No wonder I wasn't getting laid then. I wanted to tell him: You have so many opportunities to please guys with your mouth and the first and most effective way is to shut up.

"I'm not negative." I sounded especially defensive because Taylor often accused me of the same thing.

Then it occurred to me I could use Junior's interest in me to get him alone. I was randy all the time in my twenties—and if a man I was attracted to reciprocated my interest, then I would drop my pants and everything else. Now, I didn't want to hook up with Junior. I couldn't have sex with myself—it seemed gross. But I did need to talk to him privately.

"What time do you get off?" I asked in a low voice.

Junior's eyes widened.

"I work till five thirty," he said. "Sylvia's letting me leave early because I have class at six."

I couldn't remember taking a class back then. My puzzled expression prompted an explanation.

"I'm learning Pascal."

I vaguely recalled taking a stupid computer programming class at the New School.

"Skip it. Trust me, it won't make a big difference in the long run."

"I only have four more classes."

"Some day Pascal will be as obsolete as Etruscan. The average person will never need to know how to program a computer. Study typing. That will always be useful."

I'd never learned to type properly, and half of my business was conducted online. If I could type with more than two fingers, my work-week would be shortened considerably.

Junior's face puckered. "How do you know?"

I was tempted to yell, "Because I'm you and I've already lived through all of your misdirected energy, useless tangents, and dead ends." Instead, I said, "History's repeating itself. Everyone's telling us now that we need to learn computer programming. But it could be like telling a man in 1890 that he needs to learn how to run a power plant because in the twentieth century everyone will need to know how to make electricity."

Junior's face became rigid, and I couldn't tell if he was on the verge of becoming angry or bored.

"Well, I'll take my chances."

It spoke volumes that I knew Junior better than any person on Earth and I still didn't trust that I could be completely honest with him. I felt myself becoming angry—I didn't realize how stubborn I could be—and then Sylvia came out of her office.

"John, I need to speak to you," she said, glancing forcefully at us, before returning to her lair.

"I've got to go," Junior said.

"Meet me after class?" I asked.

He thought for a second before grabbing a notepad and pen from his desk.

"Give me your address."

I wrote it down and he smiled broadly. "I'll see you around nine," he said.

As I left the gallery, I recalled that I'd had a lot of bad dates in my life, but Junior faced the most disappointing letdown of them all. The guy he was interested in was himself.

3

WALKING BACK to the Finney Room, I felt increasingly anxious and wondered whether I should have told Junior about Carol's death already. What if something happened to me before nine o'clock? Opening the door, I hoped to find Taylor seated at the computer, playing online Scrabble, killing time while he waited for me to show up. To my disappointment, he wasn't there.

I turned on the computer and opened a file named "Telephone directories." After a few clicks, I found Carol's address and telephone number in Crescent City, California. I wasn't even sure if the candlestick telephone would work. After all, who was paying the bill? But Taylor would have thought of that and taken care of it. I picked up the receiver and heard a dial tone.

Before dialing Carol's number, I tried to figure out what I should say. My first thought, shouting an unsolicited "Don't kill yourself!" would be the iciest of cold calls. Carol would think I was crazy and hang up. Then I considered that perhaps I shouldn't call. I was trying to change the future and it might backfire. What if my call first implanted the idea of suicide in her mind, making me ultimately responsible for her death? It was a valid concern because every warning is also a dare: I'd always thought that if God hadn't hung a big forbidden sign on the tree of knowledge, Adam and Eve might still be Gardening.

All these thoughts were just a way of letting me pretend that I wasn't scared. Scared that I couldn't prevent her death and afraid that my failure would fundamentally alter my outlook on life, convincing me that none of us have any control over our fate. Even if it's true, who wants to live with that oppressive belief?

Carol's phone rang five times before she answered.

"Hello." She sounded out of breath, as if she'd run up a flight of stairs.

"Carol. . . ."

"Hi, Groovy. You sound like you have a cold."

I noted that my voice must have aged, but was so powerfully moved upon hearing Carol once again that I couldn't respond right away. I became choked up. My sister had always called me Groovy. It was a little private joke between us. I'd always loved the word—groovy has always been my highest praise. I'd started saying groovy in the late '60s— trying to sound groovy—when we were kids. But after Carol's death, I played back an old message she'd left on my answering machine. When I heard "Hi, Groovy," I suddenly understood that she never used the word ironically. Carol really regarded me as her groovy older brother living in New York.

"I'm a little congested." It was close to the truth. Hearing Carol's voice put me on the verge of crying.

"I was just thinking of calling you. Mom called last night. She said the girls in Card Club were taking her to a Thigh restaurant. Yes, not a *Thai* restaurant. Thigh. She said it repeatedly: "I'm not sure if I like Thigh food." Of course, I told her no one likes 'Thigh' food . . ."

I laughed but also felt as if I might sob. Carol had always regaled me with yarns about our mother and the Card Club "girls"—friends my mother had been playing pinochle with for almost twenty years and would still be playing cards with twenty years later. It was odd but felt completely natural to be chatting with Carol again. I relished hearing her voice at a time in her life when she was happy and contented. After purchasing my first cell phone in the late '90s, I used to call Carol all the time, often sharing recent conversations I'd had with our mother. For instance, a day after our mother attended her first bris, I called Carol to tell her, "Mom said, 'It was very interesting. I didn't know the Jewish people don't believe in original sin. They believe that you're born good but that you'll eventually disappoint everyone.'"

For months after her death, when something funny or odd happened, for a split second I'd think, "I have to call Carol." Then I'd remember she was dead and my grief would be heart-wrenchingly renewed. I still had the same phone and never could bring myself to delete Carol's name from my address book, even though seeing her name was always painful.

"Uh, Carol, I need to talk to you about something."

"Is everything okay?"

Now she sounded worried. I was gay and lived in New York in 1986. She probably thought I was about to tell her I was HIV positive.

"I'm fine."

"You're sure?"

"Yes. Look, this will sound crazy, but I had a terrible dream last night. It took place fifteen years from now."

Telling her I had a bad dream was hokey, but I thought it was a plausible way to introduce the subject of her suicide without resorting to the conversation-ending declaration: "I'm a time traveler from the future . . ."

"Is this your roundabout way of telling me that you've become a telephone psychic?"

"Just listen."

"All right."

I'd snapped at her. I'd never realized before that telling a lie because the truth was unbelievable was more stressful than straightforward dishonesty.

"I received a message on my machine to call the sheriff's office. Someone there told me that you had shot yourself. In the head. You'd been taken to a hospital. I cried out and crumpled up as if someone had struck me. You were living in New Jersey and we'd spoken three times that day. I'd invited you to come to my place to have dinner that night but you said no. I'd really insisted. You'd been depressed for a year but had recently told me you were feeling better. I drove to the hospital. You were on life support but there was nothing they could do."

"You shouldn't read *The Bell Jar* before going to bed."

"It was the most horrible thing that—it was the most horrible thing that had ever happened to Mom, Kevin, Alan—or me."

"Are you crying?"

I'd hoped she hadn't noticed.

"Now you're scaring me."

"You don't understand. I was there when we took you off life support."

Is there any way to make a young healthy woman imagine her own death? It was like asking her to remember her own birth.

"John, I'm not going to kill myself. I've never thought about doing that. It was a bad dream."

"But your life could change in fifteen years. You have to promise me that you'll never kill yourself. We have to make a pact that if you ever think about doing it, you'll call and tell me. I love you and would do anything for you."

"Don't worry. It was a nightmare."

"No. You have to promise me."

I made her swear that if she ever had suicidal thoughts she would call and tell me. Even if she felt that she didn't want to burden me with her problems, she had to call me.

"Now I'm starting to feel depressed," she joked.

"You know depression runs in the women in our family. Nan had it and Mom has it and you could have it too. You should just be aware of it." An idea occurred to me. "Maybe I'll start sending you a self-help book every week."

"If you do that, then I will kill myself."

After we hung up, I felt devastated by how much I missed her. Even talking to Carol about her own death had been enjoyable. The call made me more determined to save her. I was satisfied that at least my sister would never forget our conversation. She never forgot anything, an ability that I used to admire. She could recall things that happened in our lives that I'd completely forgotten. After her death I found a photo of the two of us in our early twenties. Carol's wearing hipster sunglasses and her long hair is streaked silver on the sides à la Bride of Frankenstein. I look stoned and I'm wearing a huge gray wig that looks tossed on my head. I have no memory of that picture, but Carol would know exactly when and why we were dressed like that. It was only after Carol's death that I understood that having total recall was a curse, making it impossible to forget any of the sad moments in your life, all the while adding new injuries.

But Carol's last comment had been a joke, which made me doubt whether a phone call would have enough impact to change the course of her life. In our family, jokes were a way of expressing your feelings or avoiding your feelings or an even more confusing mixture of concealing and revealing. I needed to really convince Carol that I was telling the truth and that she was in danger. You'd think persuading someone happy that someday they're going to be miserable would be the simplest task in the world; after all, isn't every life story a comedy with an unhappy ending? Then I thought, My case would be strengthened if she met both of me: her brother from the present and the same brother from the future. I couldn't do this by myself and neither could Junior. We needed to visit her together.

I didn't need to look up my parents' telephone number. I knew it by heart. What would I say to my dad? I couldn't remember any telephone conversation between us that hadn't been perfunctory. "How are you?" "Fine." "Me too." "Bye." Now I was going to ring him up to tell him that I was his son from the future and he was going to die of alcoholism. It would seem like the cruelest prank phone call in history. It would be better to wait and do it face to face. I felt uncomfortable about putting it off, but the alternative was so preposterously disagreeable that I decided to risk it.

Then I also considered trying to prevent Taylor from becoming a Republican. Not doing anything was untenable. I'd warn Taylor if he was going to be hit by lightning, and he was about to be struck by stupid and nasty. In order to shield him from that doom, I'd need to give him a detailed explanation of the history of the United States for the next twenty years. The thought of recounting all the hypocrisy, lies, and mean-spiritedness was depressing, but I also worried it would sound boring and unbelievable. In 1986 Taylor was finishing up his PhD at MIT, his parents were divorced, and during summer vacations he still sometimes helped his mother run her dry-cleaning business in Queens. I looked up her telephone number and dialed.

Mrs. Esgard's gruff "Hello" always sounded like she wanted you to reply, "Good-bye!" I asked to speak to Taylor. "Taylor!" she shouted. At first, his mother had terrified me. I wasn't used to a mom who sprinkled scorn and praise on her children with every sentence. My personal favorite was the time at Christmas when she opened her present and said, "My son's a genius who doesn't know his mother never wears purple." Mrs. Esgard had grown to tolerate me, but I never lost the impression that she thought her brilliant son could do better than a comic book dealer.

"Taylor," she yelled once more.

"Hello?" he asked.

"Hi, Taylor, my name's John Sherkston," I blurted out. "We haven't met yet but I'm from the future and in five years we're going to meet and become boyfriends."

"Let me take this call upstairs," Taylor said. "Stay on the line; I'll just be a minute."

I waited while he went upstairs and picked up another phone. I thought for sure that he would hang up on me, but one of his strengths as a scientist was his inexhaustible curiosity. Anyone who mentioned time travel to Taylor had his attention.

"So you're from the future?" Taylor asked. "Who's the president then?"

"George W. Bush, the vice president's son."

"Really? I've never heard of him."

"Count your blessings."

"How did you get here?"

"I used a time machine that you're going to build. See? I know you've always been fascinated by time travel even though your professors think it's kind of silly."

"That's true, but I need more corroboration than that," Taylor continued, sounding unfazed by everything I had said. "Tell me about what my boyfriend will look like in the future."

"I'm tall and . . . I have thinning hair."

"They can invent a time machine, but not a cure for baldness?"

"Not yet."

"Are you a genetically altered super-soldier? With muscles practically bursting through your uniform?"

"Um, no. But I work out. I'm muscular."

"How's the sex between us? Do I get off on your freaky, pumped-up bod?"

"Um, it's good."

"Prove that we're boyfriends. Tell me what I like to do in bed."

I shared our usual sexual practices with him, but then added, "Whenever you have an orgasm, you let out a quiet moan that sounds like a cry of regret, as if you've dropped something fragile and watched it break."

"Yeah, that's good. But don't a lot of guys moan?"

It seemed that we had gotten off track. I wanted to make sure I told him what I needed to say.

"Look, that's true, but what I'm really calling about is that in fifteen years, terrorists will hijack jets and fly them into the World Trade Towers, and that event will change you." I paused for a second, concerned that telling him "You'll turn into someone I can't love" would sound trivial. It wouldn't make any sense without telling him about the entire history of the Bush–Cheney administration. Then I said it anyway.

44

There was no response from Taylor and I became nervous. "I can explain."

"Are these terrorists really muscular and sexy?"

"No! They're . . . *terrorists.*"

"But could they be muscular and really sexy?"

I was slow on the uptake and tried to answer his question logically. "I guess anyone can theoretically become muscular and sexy."

"And you came back in the time machine I built just to stop this attack by having hot sex with the muscular, sexy terrorists so they'll miss their flights?"

"No!" I said in exasperation. "I, um, came back in time . . ." I couldn't tell him why I came back in time. I had no idea why Cheney sent me. And it wouldn't make a good first impression if I mentioned talking about buying vintage comic books in order to get enough money to divorce him.

"It was because of an accident," I said, struggling to invent a story. "You went to talk to the president on your cell phone and I accidentally hit a switch." I thought my lie sounded plausible.

"Well, I like the sound of your deep voice," Taylor said. "But can we skip this crappy terrorist story and say that you're a huge, muscular, super-strong android sent from the future to fuck me? What are you wearing?"

Oh, Jesus. I'd forgotten how much he enjoyed phone sex back in the '80s and that sci-fi sexual fantasies had always turned his crank. I'd once overheard him having a serious conversation with another queer sci-fi geek about whether you could program a teleporter to scramble a man's atoms and then rearrange them so that he'd lose the love handles he beamed down with, and beam back up with broader shoulders and a bigger dick. Taylor probably thought I was part of some time travel porn scenario that some guy had cooked up. I was tempted to just go with it, but thought that it would be my luck to be caught beating off when Taylor showed up, along with a team of scientists. Somehow telling Taylor that I was having phone sex with him as a young man wouldn't make the situation any less humiliating. I decided if I was going to make a convincing argument against him becoming a Republican, I would have to attempt to explain everything.

"After this terrorist attack, the entire country naturally backed our president, but he used this support to lead our country into an unnecessary war that he had planned the whole time."

"All right, you suck at phone sex! Don't ever call me again."

"Wait!" I shouted. "I'm not calling for phone sex. You really do invent a time machine and I am your boyfriend from twenty years in the future."

Don't think I wasn't aware that anyone would have a hard time buying that.

"Well, if I can invent a time machine, can't you at least invent a story that gets me off?"

Taylor hung up. I'd failed. I felt sad that I probably wouldn't have another chance to prevent Taylor from becoming a Republican. At any minute I expected to be returned to the future. I thought, If only Al Gore had been president on 9/11, Taylor's patriotic reaction might have turned him into a conservative Democrat, tough on crime and defense, soft on senior citizens and sea otters. I could live with that, since it could also describe me.

My success rate at altering the future with cold calls seemed to be nil, but I was still in Good Samaritan mode and tried to remember other circumstances where my foreknowledge could help people. In addition to tripping up Death, I considered whether I could delay any of the other three horsemen of daily life: Disease, Divorce, and Dullness. I immediately thought of Disease and all my friends who'd died of AIDS. Why didn't I think of bringing back crates of drugs with me? I asked forgiveness from Shawn, Jorge, Will, Kevin, Bob, Kim, Mark, Marcus, Cully, and others whose names I'd forgotten.

During the twenty-year interval, other deaths had occurred in my life, but it was frustrating to grasp that I couldn't prevent most of them. They weren't accidental or intentional; they were deaths by old age or illnesses that were incurable in 1986 and would still be incurable in 2006. (It would just be cruel to call up people like my uncle Bill and say, "You're going to wake up dead in two years.") Interfering with Divorce seemed presumptuous because relationships usually began well before ending badly. Who was I to deny someone a possible life-changing fuck before his boyfriend or girlfriend turned into an asshole? I could play the spoiler for Dullness, trying to prevent dull people from doing dull things (I planned to make a living will giving my loved ones permission to pull my plug if I ever take up solving Sudoku puzzles), but the thought of preventing dullness bored me. I had to accept that graves yawn for some people because even the earth knows every minute spent with them will be an eternity.

I examined myself carefully in the cheval mirror. There was nothing I could do about my hair loss. There's something essentially demoralizing about looking in a mirror and asking, Would I fuck me? Trust me, if you're ambivalent, it will ruin your day. But I didn't want my appearance to disappoint Junior and then have him become suicidal. (This actually concerned me, since similar plot twists frequently occurred in science fiction stories.) I decided to go to Canal Jeans and buy myself a more flattering shirt and a pair of pants. It was absurd, but I was nervous about dating myself.

4

THE DOORBELL CHIMES startled me when they rang at 9:13. (The chimes were another part of the steampunk décor. Taylor's thoroughness was impressive and annoying.) When I opened the door, Junior seemed nervous. He said hello as his glance darted around me almost as if he couldn't decide where to begin undressing me with his eyes. Then he took in the Finney Room's cartoonish furniture, which embarrassed me. But Junior thought it was cool and was fascinated by the steampunk air conditioner, where cold air blew from a window-unit faux bronze bas-relief of the three heads of Cerberus.

Soon Junior was on me. He aggressively kissed me, using his roaming hands to check out my arms, back, and shoulders. I kissed him back partly out of surprise and partly out of curiosity. Over the years several guys had told me I was a good kisser, and this was the first time I had a chance to prove it. When Junior stuck his tongue in my mouth and pressed his hand against my crotch, I abruptly pulled away from him.

"Slow down."

"Okay.

Junior awkwardly backed away from me. An older man wasn't supposed to rebuff the advances of an attractive younger man; it overturned the entire natural order of gay life.

"I just want to get to know you a little better," I said, cringing at hearing a line I'd used before on other guys I didn't want to sleep with—mortified that I was now using it on myself. (It also bothered me that the cliché had never made any sense, as having sex is inarguably one way of getting to know someone better.)

Junior was quiet, and I knew exactly what he was thinking: All right. Where's this going? He was wondering if I was one of those guys who announced after he got you hard that he didn't want to have sex on the first date. I'd always thought, If you're going to give me a boner then give me a fucking break too. Why wait? Seize the gay.

"There's something I've been meaning to tell you since we met."

Junior's face stiffened, braced to hear, "I have this bunny outfit . . ."

I took a deep breath. "I'm you from twenty years in the future. You're actually standing in a time machine. And I need your help with something before I return to my time."

Junior's expression didn't change, and I was mystified that he seemed to have no reaction to my announcement. He sighed heavily before he spoke. "You know I've had guys change their minds about having sex with me after they get me back to their apartments, but this is the most fucked up lie anyone's ever told me. If you didn't want to sleep with me, why not just suggest some sex act so disgusting that I'd immediately head for the door?"

The telephone rang. Who the hell could that be? I thought. My number was not just unlisted; it had probably been nonexistent until a day ago. I picked up. I thought it might be my Taylor from the future.

"Hello?"

"Look, some guy just stopped by, asking me if I'd been contacted by someone who claimed to be from the future. Someone by the name of John Sherkston."

It was Taylor, but he wasn't from the future. It was his younger self whom I'd spoken to earlier in the day.

"What did you tell him?"

"I lied. There was something cyborg about him that I didn't like. You'd better watch your ass. This guy's a freak."

"What does he look like?"

"An old bald dude with glasses."

I assumed they'd send Taylor to rescue me, but this guy sounded like Cheney. There was no way the vice president would be trying to rescue me. Would he? Of course, it was a government project; Taylor was too valuable to send back in time. Perhaps they sent a bald bureaucrat to fetch me.

"He gave me the creeps. He has this glassy-eyed way of speaking that looks and sounds psychotic. If I was you, I wouldn't let him find me."

His advice raised a question I had.

"How did *you* find me?"

"I have a friend who works in high-tech telecommunications. He's developing this last-call return feature and he's letting me try it out. I use it on all my phone sex partners. I like to stay in touch with the good ones and keep track of the bad ones."

It didn't surprise me that Taylor could *69 callers long before the phone company offered the service. He was buddies with scientists and engineers from around the world, and they were always giving him sneak previews of their latest inventions. I recalled he had a camera phone years before anyone else. There was an awkward lull in our conversation as we both ignored that I had been placed among the bad phone sex partners.

"So are you from the future?"

"Yes."

"Awesome. Now do you remember any of this?"

"No."

"Nothing?"

"No." It took me a moment to grasp that he was asking that if our conversation had already occurred in my past, then why didn't I remember it?

"My guess is that your physical body and memories haven't changed from your old past," Taylor explained, "while your new memories—the re-altered neurons—don't physically exist yet in your brain. It will interesting to see if your new memories will instantaneously appear when you return to . . . what year are you from?"

"2006."

"And why is this dude looking for you?"

"I have no idea. They're probably afraid I'll change the past and alter the future."

"They should look on the bright side. Maybe you'll change history so every guy in the future will be a genetically altered über-stud."

I thought about how easily President Bush had authorized torturing terrorism suspects, and I considered what lethal force he would authorize in order to stop someone from possibly interfering with his future. But I wasn't about to return to my time until I enlisted Junior into becoming our sister's guardian.

"This guy described you as a bodybuilder. Is that true?"

I could see where this was leading.

"Sort of."

"Well, would you like to meet for coffee?"

"I'm sorry, but I'm in relationship." With you, I wanted to add.

"I thought I was your boyfriend," he said.

"You are," I said, thinking having sex again with the young Taylor would be hot. "But I don't have time. I'm sorry."

Taylor pressed me to meet him, but I wasn't going to be sidetracked from saving Carol by the memory of Taylor's then-crisp six-pack.

"Just one more thing. Do I really invent a time machine?"

"You do."

"Wow! That's cool. I'm sorry. I've gotta go. I'm speaking to the Physics Club at Stuyvesant High School tomorrow and have to prepare."

Stuyvesant was the premier science school in the city and Taylor was a graduate. I thanked him for calling, and he said one last thing: "Be careful."

Junior had overheard my conversation with Taylor and appeared to be understandably more confused.

"Look, I can prove that I'm you, but we have to go."

"Go? I just got here."

I found two duffel bags in the closet and opened one of the dresser drawers. Junior's eyes popped at the sight of all the cash.

"Someone's looking for us."

"Us? Who?"

"Someone from the future."

"Well, if he's from tomorrow, can't he wait till then?"

I glanced at him and smiled to acknowledge he'd made a joke, then began to fill the bags with stacks of bills and rolls of double eagles.

"How much money do you have in there?" Junior asked.

"I have no idea."

Junior shook his head and his expression became grim.

"Why does every guy I meet have to turn into a freak? Just 'cause we bear a resemblance to each other, suddenly you're me from the future? Fuck."

"I'm not a freak," I said. "I just seem weird because I'm you in twenty years."

Junior's smile returned.

"Right. Because that's the most normal sentence anyone's ever said to me."

Since we didn't have time, I didn't try to explain what I'd meant. "You know what I mean," I said.

"Not really. But I guess I should know because you're me."

I gave the sarcastic prick the finger and opened the bottom drawer. When I removed the guns, Junior looked aghast.

"What are those for?"

"We might need them."

"To have sex?"

Junior stood up and moved quickly toward the door, but he held back from opening it. He seemed to be scared of me and also intrigued, which is sometimes how I felt about myself.

"This was a bad idea," he said.

I was listening to him, but I was also trying to think of a way to signal to Taylor where I'd be going without tipping off whoever was searching for me. I needed to think of something that only Taylor would understand. Nothing came to mind.

Junior and I both abruptly stopped moving when there was a knock on the door. There was no peephole, so we couldn't see who it was. A raspy voice shouted, "Police, open up." I signaled for Junior to be quiet and then motioned for him to move toward the window. I opened the window and picked up the two bags.

"You're taking the fire escape?" Junior whispered. "It's the police. We have to answer the door."

His naïve law-abiding Boy Scout persona was cute, but I found him aggravating at that moment.

"It's not the police," I said quietly. "I told you, someone's looking for me. Now follow me."

"No! You don't try to escape when the police knock on your door." We were on the fifth floor, and I had to admit the fire escape looked rickety. Then suddenly several bullets ripped through the door, and the fire escape appeared to be much sturdier.

"Do the police shoot through doors?"

Junior shuddered and followed me as I quickly climbed out the window.

5

As soon as we reached the street, I grabbed a cab. After I signaled to the driver to pop the trunk to stow my bags, Junior's lips opened as if he was going to say something, then he made a motion to leave, but I grabbed his arm.

"Let me go!"

"You have to come with me. I'm sorry but you're involved now, and there's a chance they might come after you next."

"Who's 'they'?"

"I don't know exactly."

"You don't know exactly? What? Do you have so many killers targeting you that you can't keep track of them?"

My answer was to open the door to the cab and push him into the backseat. I sat down beside him and said to the driver, "We're going to the South Bronx, 283 Alexander Avenue." Junior's eyes bugged out. "I'll give you ten dollars extra if you hurry."

"How do you know my address?"

"Because I'm you and I lived in that shitty neighborhood."

Junior stared ahead as if he was considering whether I might be telling the truth. I kept watch out the rear window of the cab, waiting for someone to come out of the front of the building. The door opened and a portly man walked out. The figure was too dark to identify until he stepped under a streetlight. He turned toward us. He was balding and wore silver wire-rimmed eyeglasses. His crooked smile turned his head into a jack-o'-lantern that was still sitting on the porch a week after Halloween. He reached into his coat and pulled out a pistol that had a long silencer attached to the end of the barrel. "Let's go!" I shouted as Junior began to turn around to look. "Get down!" I yelled, pushing him down in the seat as the cabbie stepped on the gas. Our pursuer fired off two shots, and the few people on the street scrambled when one bullet hit a parked car and another dinged a garbage can. No one else on earth had his ghoulish grin; it looked as if he whitened his teeth with the blood of newborn infants. He'd also missed two clear shots. The lousy marksmanship alone was enough to convince me that we were being hunted by Dick Cheney.

"Drop me off at the corner of Houston," Junior said tremblingly, after we turned down Greene.

"No, I can't."

"Yes, you will! I don't know what shit you're into but my first dates usually don't end with gunfire."

The cab stopped at a red light on Houston. I gave the cab driver circuitous directions to the South Bronx in an attempt to lose Cheney, then told Junior who I thought our pursuer might be.

"I think the future vice president of the United States is trying to assassinate me."

"Tell the driver to drop you off at Bellevue."

"I know. I'm still trying to wrap my head around that one. But I'm telling you the truth."

"I'm not stupid. I've seen *Terminator*. Just because you're built like Arnold Schwarzenegger doesn't mean you're from the future."

Junior was more belligerent than I recalled. I'd never thought of my younger self as argumentative, but apparently I'd become a sharp-tongued New Yorker earlier than I thought. He peered out all the windows, trying to decide what to do.

"Let's just go to your place," I suggested. "Then in the morning, if you want me to go, I'll leave."

"Why would the vice president want to kill you?"

I glanced at the cabbie. He remained focused on his driving and appeared not to be following our conversation. I assumed either he didn't understand English well or it was commonplace for taxi passengers in New York to discuss why our nation's leaders wanted to murder them.

"He might be trying to stop me from changing history."

We took Greenwich Avenue down to Eighth Avenue and passed Uncle Charlie's, a video bar. During my first year in the city, when I didn't have many friends yet, I used to go there almost every Saturday night. The '80s was the decade when gay men decided that watching television in a bar was a novel way to meet men. Predictably, it merely replicated an evening watching television with our families: no one talked, and by the end of the night everyone seethed with resentment. I ended up hating that bar, since I always left alone.

"Why did you come back here?" Junior asked.

"I was talking to the vice president . . ."

". . . the one chasing us?"

"Yes. We'd been talking about how you could make money with a time machine, and he sent me back here."

"Why?"

"I have no idea. At first I thought it was to help me make money. I don't know what to think now."

"What did you need the money for?"

I decided to tell him the truth. I'd have to reveal something about his future in order to convince him of my story.

"I wanted to break up with my boyfriend. I wanted the money so I could move out and *not* have to move to Astoria."

"I really pray that you're not me because you sound like a total loser."

"I'm sorry to break the bad news."

"Please stop with the bullshit. You're not me! There's a resemblance but you're bald and wear glasses and you have a bump on your chin that

I don't have." He pointed to a spot on his chin to indicate the bump he was talking about.

"That grew in after I turned thirty."

"Well, if you really were me, you would've had that removed long ago."

"My dermatologist said it couldn't be removed without leaving a scar."

"Then what the hell's this?"

Junior pointed to a long purplish scar on my right wrist.

"That happened two years ago. A friend had an ice-skating party for her birthday at Rockefeller Center. It was stupid. All her friends are middle aged; we don't need to fucking ice skate. Within the first five minutes, I fell and broke my wrist. I had to have surgery."

Junior's face called me a liar.

"I grew up in Buffalo and know how to ice skate. It looks like a suicide attempt. And who's the friend?"

It was Donna Carlino, and our friendship had cooled after my accident. I'd met her at a comic book convention.

"You don't know her yet. You'll meet her in fourteen years."

"That's convenient."

This wasn't going well. I sounded like a delusional liar. It never would have occurred to me that it would be difficult to prove my identity to myself. I directed our cabbie to head up Eighth Avenue and then turn right on Forty-Second Street. We stopped moving at Fortieth Street when we became stuck in traffic. I kept looking out the rear window to see if we were being pursued and saw a dozen other yellow cabs creeping up Eighth. I wouldn't be able to tell which one was Cheney's until the first bullet hit us.

"Are we being followed?" Junior asked.

"I have no idea. He has to be stuck in traffic too."

"For someone who almost got assassinated by the vice president, you don't seem very worried."

"I don't know what else we can do."

"We could try to lose him by getting out and taking the subway."

"Good idea." I paid the driver. We got out and began to walk up Eighth Avenue to Fifty-First, then cut over and down Broadway. In Times Square in 1986, half the people walking around looked like they wanted to kill you and the other half looked like they had something to hide. Every old man, every balding man, every pudgy man, and every man wearing eyeglasses made me do a double take to make sure it wasn't Cheney. I picked up the pace to get us out of there.

It was thrilling to see Times Square restored to its proper sleaziness. I felt a sense of pride that I'd lived in the Big Apple when it was still a symbol of sin and temptation rather than rebranded for tourist families as a wholesome once-a-day fruit. It made me nostalgic to see our nation's insatiable appetite for pornography still publicly proclaimed on "Adult" theater marquees instead of furtively stashed away on our computers. *The Heinylick Maneuver* was playing at the Eros, and *Sperms of Endearment* was at the Adonis.

When the Adonis Theater was being demolished, I was riding in a taxi on Eighth Avenue and saw the word "Adonis" dangling perilously from the marquee above a pile of rubble. I longed for a camera, as the image seemed to be the perfect metaphor for being middle aged.

At Forty-Fourth, we cut over to head to Grand Central. "This will all change," I said, with a wave of my hand. "All the porn theaters will be closed or torn down and this will become Times Squaresville." I tried to not to react like some grumpy curmudgeon mooning over the good bad old days, but seeing all the changes in the city made me painfully aware that the passage of time is the demolition of each day.

Junior smiled. "Will there be protests to save the porn theaters by thespian do-gooders like Colleen Dewhurst and Tony Randall?"

"Yeah," I said. "They'll give earnest television interviews where they can get all actor-y and lament, 'If they tear down all the adult-movie theaters and strip clubs in New York then where will the porn stars of tomorrow learn their craft?'"

As we waited for the 6 train, Junior's brief spell of levity faded. "Who's my first grade teacher?" he asked.

"Miss Chalmers."

His mouth fell open.

"Fourth grade?"

"Mr. Brophy."

"Fifth grade?"

"Mrs. Bodkin."

"Name my friends in high school."

"John Silecky, Vic Soucise, David Tomaselli, Tom Papia, Bruce Burns, Matt Kozlowski, and Donny Damon."

We boarded the train, and several heads turned when he asked, "Where'd I jerk off for the first time?"

"In my bedroom when it was painted that electric blue color. I was thinking about Kirk Garcia."

"How do you know these things?"

"I told you."

"Would you believe your story if you were me?"

"No. I'd think I was nuts." I was conscious of my wallet in my back pocket and reached for it. "I have my driver's license." I pulled out the license and Junior examined it carefully.

"It expires in 2009. And what's this shiny stuff?"

Junior was referring to the holographic image of the state seal of New York.

He seemed to be considering the possibility that I might be telling the truth. There was a blob of something on my eyeglasses that had been annoying me since I'd gotten on the subway. I removed them in order to clean them with the lens cloth I always carried in my pocket. Junior looked into my eyes and his look of panic faded as his expression changed to astonishment.

"Your eyes are my eyes," he said. "Only older and . . . sadder."

I nodded.

We got off at the first stop in the Bronx at Third Avenue and 138th Street. Junior lived on a street of red-brick brownstones that looked like an Edward Hopper painting—if a Hopper streetscape were surrounded by half a dozen towering public housing projects. I found my cell phone in my jacket pocket and showed it to Junior. He was impressed by its design—it reminded him of the communicators on *Star Trek*—although I'm not sure it helped prove my story. It could be powered up, but I would need to search for another decade to find a signal. As we walked to his apartment, Junior warned, "I have a dog."

I smiled. "Ravi."

"You're good," he said as got out his keys. Junior rented the bottom floor of a brownstone. The owner was a woman he'd met on a catering job who worked at *House & Garden* magazine. There were bars on the windows and two metal gates that had to be opened before you reached the front door. I had Junior look carefully to see if anyone had tried to break in. Everything appeared to be normal, and Junior bent down to pick up his mail off the floor. We decided it was safe when we heard Ravi panting behind the door, and I imagined him wagging his tail. He was a mutt, predominantly a golden retriever, and I was eager to see him again. In twelve years he would have to be put down due to kidney failure. Taylor and I had both cried uncontrollably at the vet's.

When the bolt turned and the door opened, Ravi's tail wagged rapidly and he barked once at Junior. Then his tail stopped moving and he curiously sniffed my legs. His tail began thrashing once more, and he jumped up on me, then got down and ran over to Junior, and then ran back to me again.

Junior turned on a light. "He likes you. And he doesn't like everyone."

"He knows me."

"Oh, right." Junior opened the back door to let Ravi out in the yard. "Would you get me a beer?" he asked.

"A beer?"

I forgot that I still drank in 1986.

"It's in the fridge. Have one. Don't worry. It's light beer." He called Ravi's name once and he ran outside.

I wasn't concerned with the calories but with the alcohol. Quitting drinking had been the hardest thing I'd ever done. I could never show my face at another meeting if I became my own enabler.

"You'll have to get it yourself. I don't drink."

Junior glanced through the mail he'd grabbed. "It's just one beer," he said.

"That's how it starts! First it's one beer, then two, then you move on to three Dewar's and soda after work. Then you switch to vodka gimlets and pretty soon your days and nights are measured in cocktail hours."

Junior stared at me as if he thought I'd been drinking. "Does that mean I become an alcoholic?" he asked.

"Yes," I said. "But when you quit, you stay sober."

I wanted to reassure him that there were problems in his future that he could handle successfully.

He shook his head and opened the fridge and took out a green bottle of Rolling Rock. "Well, that news makes me need a drink," he said before twisting off the cap. "Are you sure you don't want something?"

"Just a glass of water."

Junior opened a cupboard and got out a glass while I looked around. I couldn't believe I'd lived in such a small space. It was one longish room that was almost filled by my American Empire sleigh bed. My first boyfriend in Buffalo had been an antiques dealer and he'd sold me the bed for three hundred dollars. There was also a matching Empire dresser, a cheap end table topped with a TV, a round white Formica kitchen table with four matching chairs, and a futon that looked like it had grounds for a medical malpractice lawsuit for a botched sofa-to-bed operation.

I removed my shirt and pointed to a bumpy scar-ridge on my right shoulder.

"This is where we got six stitches after we went pool-hopping with Tommy Mattea. We slipped trying to hop over a chain-link fence."

"That's pretty impressive." His eyes glanced at the scar but focused on my shoulders and chest. "How long will it take us to get those muscles?"

"Not as long as you think."

"Now I hope you are me because I want that chest."

"You're getting there," I mumbled. Junior looked me over carefully, inspecting me like a rental car customer who's checking his vehicle for nicks and dents before leaving the lot. I quickly put my shirt back on to hide the scar on my lower back.

In 2004, I'd had a malignant melanoma removed. At first, my doctor thought that the cancer had spread, but it hadn't. Taylor had been incredibly thoughtful and supportive when he heard my news. "Don't worry. We'll get through this." It had taken me a year to fully recover from the intensive chemotherapy. Supposedly I was fine, but after you turn forty, you began to suspect that you're always in remission from some cause of death. It rattled my confidence about breaking up with Taylor when I recalled with gratitude how considerate he had been through the devastating blows of my father's and Carol's deaths and my cancer.

It's frequently claimed—and we all hope it's true—that facing death will be revelatory. Insight will be a form of compensation: you'll learn the secret of life shortly before you go belly-up. But it's really a leap of faith to expect people's brains to function better than they have for their entire lives merely because they've just had the shit scared out of them.

Cheney's had four heart attacks—he's faced his own mortality so often that he could pick out the Angel of Death from a police lineup. But after four near-death experiences, the vice president has exhibited no profound philosophical insight or transformative change of heart. In fact, Cheney's renowned for his lack of compassion, remorse, or even doubt about anything.

Receiving a "you're gonna die-agnosis" hadn't actually made me a better person, although it did change me. What gradually began to infuriate me was that malignant cells multiplying was considered an illness, but when people turned malignant and lost the ability to feel empathy for others, it was considered a formula for winning elections and governing. Most of Taylor's Republican friends considered it a form of "tough love" to tell shoeless people to pull themselves up by their bootstraps. My illness instilled in me one simple goal: you should try to go through life being less selfish than a cancer cell. If you can't do that then you're evil *and* an asshole.

Junior opened a bag of tortilla chips and offered me some.

"No thanks," I said.

He washed his first chip down with a swig of beer.

"How old are you?" he asked.

"Forty-six."

He didn't flinch or gasp, which I took as a compliment. His eyes crept up to the top of my head and his smile faded.

"When will I lose the rest of my hair?"

"In your thirties."

"They don't have a cure for baldness twenty years from now?"

"No. Not yet."

"Maybe we should use your time machine to go to a drugstore a hundred years in the future. I bet the cure will be sold over the counter."

"There are worse things than going bald. I don't look so bad."

Suddenly Junior shouted, "I don't have AIDS!"

He obviously made the connection that if I was alive in 2006 then he probably wasn't HIV positive.

"No."

"I can't believe it. I've been so worried."

That was one painful memory I'd never forgotten.

"You recently went to get tested and then found out your results were inconclusive," I said. "The doctor said you had to be retested. You've been afraid to go back and pick up the results."

"It's been a fucking nightmare."

"I know."

Junior smiled and said, "Right."

I'd never regarded my youth as particularly hard or tragic, but most of my friends died of AIDS during my first ten years in New York. Every morning on the subway reading the *New York Times* felt like I was reading my own breaking obituary. I'd read another depressing story about the demise of finding a quick cure, stubbing my eyes on the word "gay," as the newspaper always wrote it then, quarantined within quotation marks as if the editors wanted to prevent the word from infecting the rest of the English language.

As Junior's relief sank in, he began pacing the apartment. "What do I do for a living? What's my boyfriend like? Do I still live in New York? Am I happy?"

It occurred to me that this was getting complicated, and both of us might be getting in over our heads.

"I'm not sure how much I should tell you. Because if I tell you about your future, your foreknowledge could alter it."

"How?"

"Let's say you have a boyfriend—and you do. Well, if I tell you who he is, you might react differently when the two of you eventually meet. You might be too initially confident and that might come off as smug to your boyfriend and the spark between you two might never be struck."

"Oh, Jesus. You won't have sex with me and now you won't tell me about my future. We need to alter the future so I don't become so overly cautious."

"You've read enough time travel stories to know that I could be right."

"How come you're not attracted to me? Am I too skinny?"

"No. I'm not attracted to you because you're me. And you have to quit thinking of yourself as a geek. From my vantage point, everyone looks good in their twenties, at least in comparison with their middle-aged selves. But please don't become conceited."

"Then how come no one's interested in me? I haven't had sex since Halloween."

It was June and I must have made a face.

"Even you're appalled."

"Being sexy isn't just about how you look, it's how you behave. You need to be confident."

"Well, I'd be more confident if I wasn't the first gay man in history to be rejected by himself."

"Do you really want to make out with yourself?"

"Yeah, why not?"

"It's weird."

"It's as close to my twins fantasy as I'll ever get."

I gave him a condescending smile.

"It's not any weirder than masturbation when you think about it," he added. "And that's universally beloved."

"You should respect my feelings," I said.

"And you should respect mine." He grabbed my right hand and placed it on his crotch. He was hard. I laughed.

"Now you're laughing at my dick? You're literally a self-hating homosexual."

"In this case that's actually a sign of good mental health."

"You know, you're the first guy I've ever brought back here."

"And in a way, you still came home alone."

"Thanks for pointing that out. That really helps my self-esteem you're trying to build up."

Asking someone to come to your apartment in the South Bronx was a deal-breaker in 1986. The general attitude among gay men was if you have to leave Manhattan to get laid, you might as well keep going and head back to Ohio or Kentucky.

I swallowed hard. "There's something we need to talk about."

The full import of what I was about to do made me pause. I was replacing one burden of mortality with another. Instead of worrying about his dying of AIDS, Junior would worry about his sister killing herself. His vigilance over her might poison their relationship, and the weight of that knowledge might even cause Junior to become depressed. But Carol's death was the worst thing that had ever happened to me and would be the worse thing to ever happen to him. Junior didn't deserve that.

"It's about Carol." I stopped to take a breath. Junior looked so innocent. "In fifteen years, she's going to kill herself."

His brown eyes clouded with pain. "No," he said, as the terror in his eyes registered that I was telling the truth. His body shuddered slightly. I felt despicable. I'd made him envision something that he never would have imagined. His face abruptly flushed with fury.

"Jesus Christ, you are the most depressing person I've ever met! First you make me feel that my life will suck, and now you're telling me my sister's life will suck even worse. "

"My life doesn't suck."

"You're bald, you're broke, and you're dumping your boyfriend. Sounds bad to me."

"That's not how I think of myself. I'm pretty happy and successful, and you will be too."

"Wanna bet?"

"I have a decent job. I have friends. I'm close to my family. I'm healthy."

I didn't mention my recent cancer scare. Telling him that would muddle my story.

"I'm forty-six and can still give guys in their twenties a boner."

Junior's cheeks became rosier.

"I also have a sense of humor and I'm adventurous. I'm actually one of the happiest guys I know."

I was telling the truth. I had experienced several devastatingly horrible events in my life: I'd endured a decade where I and every gay man in America felt like Tom Sawyer witnessing his own funeral thousands of times, and yet I still thought of my twenties as incredibly exciting and fun. I'd lived through my father's sad death by alcoholism and my sister's devastating suicide, survived cancer, and still thought of my life as happy. I didn't understand why but I still felt lucky. It wasn't denial, because I had suffered. The only thing I could think of was that my double helixes must function like mattress springs, since I seemed to be very resilient.

Junior sat down on the bed and stared at the floor. His sadness made me feel close to despair. Even with a second chance to change my life, I still didn't know what I was doing.

"I'm sorry to be telling you this. I'm worried that knowing this will fuck you up. Or fuck up your relationship with Carol. But I think you might be able to prevent her death. I couldn't go back to my time without trying to prevent it. Wouldn't you do the same thing?"

Junior nodded. "Yes."

He stood up and removed his dress shirt and hung it on a hanger in order to get one more day of wear out of it. He wore a white T-shirt underneath. His eyes met mine.

"Why did she do it?"

"It's kind of complicated, as you'd expect." I tried to think of where I should begin. I had several theories, but they'd require quite a bit of explanation. The digital clock on the floor read 1:07. "Let's talk in the morning. We shouldn't now. It's too late. I just want you to be on the lookout for her depression. You have to really let her know that you'll be there for her."

"You're leaving me to handle all of this?"

"Well, yeah. I could be yanked back to the future at any moment. I won't be here."

"You're here now. And no one's rescued you yet."

"I know. Thanks for reminding me."

"Hey, bad news goes both ways."

"You can handle this."

"Don't dump all this on me. We should both go see Carol. We'll convince her that you're me. Well, me as a chrome-dome."

"At least I'm not pencil-necked."

"I'm getting some muscles." He raised his right arm and flexed. An egg-shaped bicep popped up. Not bad for someone who'd only been working out for six months.

"You've got to help me with this. Then you can go back to breaking up with your boyfriend. And let me just add: I'm really looking forward to being single at forty-six."

"Don't tell me how to run my life."

I'd said it seriously, but we both began to laugh.

"We can fly out to California," Junior said. "I get time off during the summer."

The art gallery shut down for two weeks every summer. Sylvia still paid me, which was incredibly generous.

I tried to recall what airport security was like in 1986.

"Do they make you show ID at the airport?"

"They'll want to see your driver's license."

We were silent for a moment as we imagined trying to board a plane with a driver's license issued in 2001.

"We could drive," I suggested. "It would take about a week."

"I've never been out west."

Junior took off his undershirt and undid his belt buckle. It was shocking to see that I had no body fat then. "Do you think we'll be followed by your vice president?"

"I don't know. Hopefully he doesn't know I'm with you."

Why was Cheney trying to kill me? Was he trying to prevent me from changing the future? It made no sense. He had sent me back. Plus, the past had already been modified by my presence. Couldn't he just return me to my time without altering any more of the timeline? Then a more ominous and intriguing idea occurred to me: what does he know about what I'm going to do that I don't even know yet?

Ravi walked over to me with his ball in his mouth and dropped it in front of me.

"Can we bring Ravi?"

"Of course."

Spending more time with sweet Ravi would make me miss Bartleby a little less. He'd also make our grim mission less grim.

The two of us got ready for bed. I kept on my T-shirt to conceal my scar. Junior looked under his sink for a spare toothbrush but came up empty.

"Is it wrong that sharing my toothbrush with you kind of grosses me out?" he asked.

"I'm glad you said it because it grosses me out too."

Junior shut the bathroom door when he peed.

"You're pee-shy around me?"

"I don't know you well enough to feel comfortable."

"If that statement doesn't prove you need therapy . . ."

He came out of the bathroom in his white Calvin Klein briefs.

"How does she die?"

"You've had enough bad news for one night."

"Tell me."

"No. That's it for tonight."

He opened his mouth to reply but stopped.

"You're right."

We got into bed. The sexual tension between us had dissipated—Junior appeared to be genuinely upset—and I felt enormous tenderness toward him. I wanted to hug him but thought he'd take it the wrong way. Then I decided that was possibly the most fucked up thing I'd ever thought in my entire life.

"I'm really sorry I had to put this on you."

"It's all right."

His voice wavered and cracked like a kid going through puberty.

"No, it's not. C'mere."

I reached out and enveloped Junior in my arms and hugged him tightly. He didn't seem to know how to respond but eventually relaxed. After a minute, we self-consciously rolled away from each other.

"Good-night."

"Good-night."

I was glad Junior asked me to go with him. He sounded too young to handle my life.

6

AT NINE A.M. the ringing telephone awakened us.
"Don't answer it," I shouted when Junior threw off the blanket.
The answering machine picked up, and after Junior's outgoing message played we heard a beep. "Hi, John." There was a long pause. "It's Mom." Then there was another longer pause. "Call me."

Junior shook his head. "She always sounds like she's giving dictation."

My mother never fully became comfortable leaving a message on an answering machine or voicemail. Her messages were either extremely brief, almost as if she thought leaving an impression of your voice on an answering machine would steal your soul, or they were long monologues as if the message were the equivalent of a note in a bottle tossed in the sea and she never expected a response. Her messages had become legendary among my friends. I couldn't share with Junior about the time she'd called when our father was dying, "Ohhhh, I was hoping I would get you in person and not get this machine," she'd said. "I hate to have to leave this as a message but I don't know what else to do. Dad wasn't doing well yesterday so I took him to the emergency room at the hospital. They admitted him right away. It doesn't look good." Then she switched to her most chipper voice: "Oh, by the way, this is Mom!"

She began to leave a message until Junior picked up. "Hi, Mom. No, I got home late. A catering job." Junior wasn't being honest. Of course he couldn't mention he'd slept with himself last night. My life then was full of half-truths, things I said to protect my nice guy image, ignoring that admitting I'd stayed out late last night at a gay bar was probably less damaging to my reputation than being found out as a habitual liar. I got up to pee and then put on the teakettle to make coffee. After Junior began to drink coffee at the gallery, he had bought a French press for his apartment after his chef friend Lauren had insisted a French press made the best coffee. The purchase furthered my vision of myself as urbane. In Buffalo, coffee passively dripped into a pot while New Yorkers were pushy and leaned on their beans.

The doorbell rang and I jumped. In the South Bronx in 1986 only burglars and Jehovah's Witnesses dropped by unannounced. It had to be Cheney. Although it didn't make sense that he'd give us a heads-up for a second time. I reached for one of my Glock 22s, which I'd loaded before bed. Holding the gun didn't make me feel more secure; I'd only shot a gun once in my life, with my father when I was ten years old.

"I'll see who it is," I whispered before walking to the front of the apartment and stealthily moving the window shade aside. Taylor, the young Taylor, was standing outside. Junior approached the door, and I put up my hand warning him to stay where he was. I found it difficult not to stare at Taylor. It was five years before we would meet, and he looked close enough to the young man I fell in love with to captivate me once again. Taylor's body was hard, a quality in men that I've always found contagious. There were a few significant differences from how he looked when we'd first met. His black hair bristled, probably spiked with Tenax, the green aromatic French hair gel that I and everyone else used back then. He also sported a dyed fluorescent blue streak on the right side of his head. It's an article of faith among gay men that a new hairstyle is an outward manifestation of an inner transformation; what stigmata are for Roman Catholics, highlights are for us. To his credit, Taylor was probably the only New Wave–styled young man who could correctly explain the physical properties of his blue streak with a lecture about protons and shortened wavelengths of light. A shiny red shirt clung to his chiseled body. If you have a displayable body, you can't go wrong promoting your buffitude in snug-fitting polyester. It gains other men's interest by showing off your physique, and also encourages them to think they have a shot with you since the cheesy style reveals you're not that bright and will be easy prey.

Junior moved closer and I stiff-armed him.

"I'll take care of it," I whispered.

"Who is it?"

I didn't say anything, trying to decide whether I should tell Junior about Taylor. It seemed excessively cautious that I was trying to keep them apart because I didn't want to jeopardize their eventually meeting and falling in love—especially since I was planning to break up with Taylor. Perhaps I'd be doing all of us a favor if I introduced them now and they disliked each other immediately.

"I'm not sure I should tell you."

"Why?"

Junior dropped any pretense of obeying me and glided past me. I tried blocking him, aware of the loaded gun in my hand. I didn't offer much opposition, as I easily imagined the pistol accidentally going off with disastrous results. He easily maneuvered around me, opened the door, the first gate, and then gaped at Taylor through the second gate. He opened it and within seconds, the three us stood near the entrance to the apartment, under the stairs, uncertainly staring at each other.

"What's the big deal?" Junior asked.

I remained silent, allowing him to fill in the blank while I tried to think of what to tell him.

"Is he someone from my future?" I must have blanched, because Junior asked, "Really?" Taylor examined Junior's face as if he was trying to recall his name. I shifted nervously and Taylor glanced at the pistol in my hand.

"Are you John?" he asked me. Junior and I answered, "Yes."

Junior studied Taylor but I couldn't tell from either of their expressions whether each found the other attractive. They looked slightly bored but also expectant—the default expression of youth.

"*He's* my boyfriend?"

I don't think Junior meant his question to sound as insulting as it did.

"And *you're* him?" Taylor asked, gesturing with his hand to indicate Junior and myself. I considered lying, but nothing credible came to mind. I hate when my ability to lie fails me; it makes me feel that I'm letting people down when they can't depend on my dishonesty.

"Yes," I said.

Taylor carefully looked at each of us as if he was trying to determine whether the before and after models in the ad were actually the same person.

"I know," Junior said. "It's hard to see the resemblance."

Taylor eyed my chest and arms.

"Yeah, because he looks great."

Now Junior was insulted.

"Sorry, I didn't mean it like that."

Taylor said his name, almost as an apology, and then offered Junior his hand. Taylor looked especially handsome when he was confused; doubt softened his features, while his fear of being thought ignorant prevented his face from going completely slack.

"How'd you find us?" I asked.

"You're listed in the telephone book."

I immediately panicked, thinking that Cheney could also look up Junior's address. I stepped outside and walked up the two steps to the sidewalk. Two guys were playing a game on a table outside the bodega across the street, while another guy was sitting on the steps of a brownstone, smoking a cigar, between bites of a pear, which looked disgusting. I didn't see Cheney, but we weren't safe here. And now Taylor might be a target. Cheney knew he'd spoken to me. But Cheney couldn't kill him or else no time machine. He might lock him up though. I had no idea what to do with Taylor, except maybe take him with us. Traveling with the two of them might be unpleasant—I pictured adolescent sexual tension mixed with incessant demands that I stop the car every time we passed a hunky farmer. But I couldn't let Cheney change Taylor's past. I wanted Taylor out of my life, but I didn't want to remove him from my history. (Most of my relationships have been like life itself: even knowing the unfortunate ending isn't enough to make me want to forgo the experience.) It seemed unfair that even on the second go-round of my life I still had no control over my destiny, that the future in the past was as unknowable as the future in the present. We all live with an innate sense of foreboding, but time travel only increased my anxiety. In addition to knowing for certain that bad things would happen, I had to worry about a whole new set of possible calamities. With a sense that I was probably fucking up all our prospects, I suggested that we should go inside. I didn't like standing in front of the house with a gun in my hand. (Although part of me wanted my South Bronx neighbors to know I was packing heat.)

Once inside, Ravi sniffed Taylor for the first time, then Taylor petted him, causing Ravi to plop down on the ceramic tile floor, offering up his belly for a rubbing. The only seating in the apartment was either on the futon or the bed. Junior offered Taylor a seat on the lumpy futon while we sat on the sleigh bed, whose mahogany frame creaked heavily. "God, I forgot how much noise this bed makes," I said before leaning against the headboard, while Junior scooted over to lean against the footboard.

"Why'd you come looking for us?" I asked.

"Curiosity," Taylor said. "It's not every day someone calls me up and claims to be my time-traveling boyfriend. Then a few hours later some psycho shows up asking about my time-traveling boyfriend. And when you told me I invent this time machine, I thought I should meet you."

After hearing Taylor was responsible for my visit, Junior relaxed and asked him if he wanted some coffee.

"That would be great," Taylor said. "Just milk, please."

Junior hopped off the bed to get his coffee order. It was fascinating to observe my eagerness to please an attractive man, although it was so patently blatant that it made me a little ashamed of myself.

"There is something else," Taylor said, after taking a sip of his coffee. "You started to tell me in our phone call that we're boyfriends and then I change and become someone you can't love. It sounds like we break up. Why?"

He sounded hurt; obviously that was the real reason he sought me out.

"We haven't yet; I haven't told you."

"What did I do?"

Taylor bit his lower lip, a nervous tic I was long familiar with.

"It's complicated." I did owe him an explanation, especially after he saved us from being ambushed by Cheney.

Junior's face jerked with impatience. "Tell him. It's our lives, too."

I decided to be blunt.

"You'll become an asshole, join the Republican Party, and support the worst president and vice president in U.S. history, and if that vice president shows up here, and there's a good chance he will, he'll gun down all three of us."

Taylor looked away from me while Junior gaped in disgust. I regretted saying anything.

"That was harsh," Junior said.

"There's more to it than that. You need to know everything before it will make sense."

"Quit stalling and tell us," Junior demanded.

"You're withholding information," Taylor said. "Information we have a right to know."

They made a reasonable point; I was again playing God with them, knowing their destinies but refusing to reveal them, which is often the only way we can change our fates.

"You did some things I don't approve of, and after a while I'd had enough."

"I cheated on you? I can't believe I'd ever cheat on you."

"No, you didn't, and thanks." I tried to sound nonchalant, as Junior was observing us, and I didn't want to start flirting with Taylor and make him jealous.

"You'll support a Republican president in twenty years who's worse than Reagan," I explained.

"Worse than Reagan?" Junior asked. "How's that possible?"

"Evolution. In the future assholes will be much larger than they are today."

Junior suddenly snapped at Taylor. "You support Reagan?"

Taylor bridled at his accusation.

"I don't support him. He's ignored AIDS, which is unforgivable, although he's done some good things for the economy." This statement hardly seemed to mollify Junior—any praise of Reagan—nice hair— would have enraged me then—and I decided to hold my tongue about Reagan's so-called improvements to the economy. I didn't want to piss off Junior any more. At that moment, it was hard to believe Junior and Taylor would ever fall in love; although if they didn't become boyfriends, wouldn't I have suddenly returned to my own time?

"I don't really give a shit about politics," Taylor added. "Right now my life is all about physics. I go to the gym and think about atoms. That's pretty much my day."

Junior smiled forgivingly. He seemed to accept the need to work on your triceps as a legitimate reason to stay disengaged from participating in citizenship. Observing your own shallowness at first hand is disillusioning.

Junior rose from the bed and walked into the kitchen and opened the refrigerator. He leaned down, peered inside, and appeared to be taking inventory.

"There's got to be more to it than that," Taylor protested. "I don't support idiots."

"You became a Republican after 9/11," I said.

"What's 9/11?"

"I need coffee." I got up and poured myself a cup before explaining again about September 11, 2001. I told them how the entire world watched the towers fall on television.

"You mean that wasn't just a lousy phone sex story?" Taylor asked.

"No, it wasn't."

They had a lot of questions and were horrified by the details—people jumping from the towers, survivors with ash-covered faces walking the streets of New York. How President Bush flew around in circles for nine hours because he was afraid to return to DC. Then the revelation the following year that Bush and Cheney had been warned on August 6 about terrorists hijacking jets and had done nothing. Taylor and Junior were shocked, but not as shocked as I thought they would be. Their relative composure after hearing about watching people die on television was explained when they both mentioned watching the Challenger space shuttle explode six months earlier.

Junior closed the refrigerator and opened a cupboard and removed a yellow mixing bowl. "I'm going to make breakfast if you're hungry." His outburst of hospitality didn't surprise me. I would've tried to keep Taylor in my apartment too.

"We have bacon and eggs," I added, knowing they were a favorite of Taylor's.

"That sounds great."

While Junior cracked eggs into the bowl, I made bacon in the microwave. Taylor offered to help, but I told him to sit at the kitchen table.

"Vice President Bush is president in 2001?" Taylor asked.

"No, he wins in '88. His son George W. Bush is president in 2000."

"Who the fuck is he?"

"He's nobody right now. He's a failed oilman in Midland, Texas, but he'll become governor of Texas, then run for president."

"What's the 'W' stand for?" Taylor asked.

"Worst," I said.

"Two George Bushes become president?" Junior said. "I'm praying that you come from a parallel universe where there are four Nixons and three Hitlers."

"No, sorry. We just have one of each."

Taylor asked, "Is the second Bush better than the first?"

"No."

"Oh, Jesus." Junior poured a little milk in the bowl before scrambling the eggs. "Because the first one sucks."

"He'll seem like George Washington compared to his son. At least he didn't invade Iraq, only Kuwait . . . but that's . . . oh, never mind."

I felt it was my duty to explain the differences between the two Bushes and the Gulf War and the Iraq War.

"You know how Karl Marx said history repeats itself, first as tragedy, second as farce?" I asked. "Well, Marx had it backwards, and those two presidents are the textbook example of that phenomenon."

"There must be some differences between the two," Taylor said. He was an indefatigable fact-checker and preferred raw data to someone else's summaries.

"In the Gulf War, Saddam Hussein of Iraq invaded Kuwait and Bush senior went to war to preserve the principle that you can't attack a neighboring country just because it has abundant natural resources and a small population. Which—come to think of it—is probably why Canada was our ally in that war. The Iraq War followed the path of most wars in history: a group of leaders invent some reasons to lead a nation to war, and the nation follows to its lasting regret."

Of course Taylor pressed me for more details on the Iraq War.

"Bush Junior might have been attempting to prove to his father that he could accomplish what his father wouldn't even attempt— overthrowing Saddam Hussein. But most Americans in my time think it's beyond fucked up that Bush Junior is working out his father issues with other men's sons."

"Haven't you just described all of human history?" Taylor asked. "Men working out their father issues with other men's sons."

Junior stopped whipping the eggs and added salt and pepper. "Two Bushes and two Iraq wars? Are you making this up?"

"I wish I was."

He poured the whipped eggs into the frying pan. "Does that mean we only have Republican presidents for the next twenty years?"

"No. President Clinton serves two terms between them."

"Who the fuck is he?" Taylor asked.

"Right now, he's the governor of Arkansas."

Junior carefully turned the eggs with a spatula to keep them from browning. "Some fucking redneck, I bet."

"Actually, he's not."

"Well," Junior said, "if he's a Democrat, he must have done some good."

"He did, but people liked him because the economy boomed and we were at peace. He tried to reform health care and failed. He couldn't get gays into the military. He didn't really accomplish as much as he should have, because in his second term he was impeached due to a sex scandal."

"They impeached the president for fucking someone?" Taylor asked.

"A White House intern. Actually, he didn't fuck Monica Lewinsky. She blew him and he stuck a cigar in her vagina."

"Wow. Sounds like the White House of Ill Repute," Junior said.

"You're making this up," Taylor said. "It sounds like a sleazy Mexican porn movie."

Junior laughed. "Imagine the dialogue: 'Yeah, baby, put that cigar in my oval orifice!'"

It actually made me feel nostalgic recalling that our country once had so much leisure time that our nation's leaders and our entire media could waste a year on the president's blow jobs. I preferred having a president who would rather spill his splooge than other men's blood.

Junior and I both simultaneously reached for the bottle of ketchup on the counter.

He stared at me in astonishment. "I was just going to do that."

"See?" It was another confirmation that I was telling the truth.

Taylor's eyebrows did the puzzled dance. "We both like ketchup on our eggs," I explained.

"How did the president's sex life become public knowledge?" Junior asked as he poured himself the last of the coffee.

"Monica was forced to testify and she backed up her story with a jizz-spotted blue dress."

"She didn't clean it?" Junior winced.

"A nasty so-called friend encouraged her to save the evidence," I said. "Someday that dress will be in the Smithsonian or sold on eBay."

"What's eBay?" Junior asked. I explained to them how we could all become billionaires by starting a business devoted to online auctions.

Then Junior asked, "What's online?"

My elaborate explanation of the nature of our online world years before it happened should be cited in history books as an early instance of virtual reality.

When Junior asked Taylor to get plates and silverware, he noticed all the boxes stacked against a wall, labeled with comic book titles.

"You collect comic books?"

"Yeah." Junior's expression turned steely, braced for a belittling or dismissive remark. If you openly admit to loving comic books as an adult, then the one superpower you need is to be invulnerable to ridicule.

"So do I." They both smiled, relieved not to be the only geek in the room. Taylor and I had first met at the Comic Con in New York, when Taylor came to my booth looking for issue #114 of *Adventure Comics*.

Taylor reached out to lift the lid of a box labeled "The Incredible Hulk," but his hand froze in midair. "Is it all right if I look?"

"Um, sure. But please be very careful."

"I will."

Taylor gently removed an issue of the *Incredible Hulk*, sealed in a glassine envelope, from the carton.

My transition from comic book collector to dealer required me to cash in my painstakingly acquired collection, a series of transactions that made me feel I was selling my soul piecemeal. Parting with my hoard made me aware of a paradoxical aspect of capitalism—at least among art and antiques dealers—you sell what you love to gain what you desire: money. It would be an exaggeration to say selling my beloved collection made me nonmaterialistic, but there was a hazy approximation of a Zen-like letting go—in exchange for the full retail price—every time I sold a gem mint *X-Men* #14. The exchange was more than fair though, as it allowed me to make a living doing something I didn't hate.

Taylor riffled through the contents of the carton until Junior shouted, "Breakfast is ready!" Then Taylor returned the issue to its place and carefully closed the carton.

It was warm in the apartment and Junior suggested eating out back. I argued it might be unsafe, but Junior said, "We'll only be out there a half hour," and I acquiesced. It was disconcerting to actually hear myself being talked out of doing something sensible for a moment of pleasure.

Behind the brownstone was a small yard fringed with a strip of garden running along a chain-link fence. On one side of our building was an abandoned brownstone boarded up with plywood, and on the other side was Milton's backyard. He was the old queen who lived next door—that's how I always thought of him back then—and it was a shock to realize he was probably close to my present age. Beyond our fence was an overgrown no-man's-land of ailanthus trees and blue morning glories gone feral. Junior had planted the morning glories the previous year, and like invasive weeds, they had escaped from our yard and overrun the surrounding area, shimmying up telephone poles, braiding trees, threading a derelict shopping cart, and garlanding a deserted brownstone half a block away. We assembled our plates in the kitchen and carried them outside along with our juice glasses and coffee cups. The sun was out, but the humidity from the day before had disappeared. It was idyllic June weather, where you're tempted to turn your head to look behind you, since it seems impossible that anything could cast a shadow on such a glorious day.

"How are we driving out to California?" Junior asked.

"I thought we'd go through New York. And we have to leave today."

I explained that if Taylor found us, then Cheney could also. "We're sitting ducks."

"I can't just walk out on Sylvia." Junior slowly shook his head. "She's been really nice to me. It's not right, not to give notice."

I sympathized with Junior's distress. Sylvia was the best boss I would ever work for, and while she might be upset about the inconvenience of finding someone to fill in for Junior, I trusted she wouldn't make him feel guilt-ridden.

"Tell her the truth. Tell her that it's a family emergency. Your sister suffers from depression and you're worried she might commit suicide. She'll understand. She's not going to be angry with you."

Junior expressed his fear that he'd have no income when he returned. "I worked really hard not to worry about that." I recalled how I'd lived luxuriously on a pauper's budget, a way of life only possible in New York during the '80s. My cushion of savings was never more than two thousand dollars, but I never felt poor. I supplemented my income by working catering jobs where I'd eat filet of beef with a morel sauce and, what at that time was a new and exciting dessert, tiramisu, the same dinner I'd just served to Jackie Onassis, in sight of a Picasso, a Rothko, or a Julian Schnabel. I opened one of my suitcases of cash and gave Junior enough money to cover his rent for a year. (His rent was four hundred dollars a month. It furthered my case for being him that I knew how much he paid.)

"Can we stop in Buffalo?" he asked.

"Cheney could find out where Mom and Dad lived in 1986," I said. "We'd be targets there too."

We'd stop long enough to disillusion our father about his retirement and make him so depressed he'd start immediately drinking heavily. We were the cross-country bearers of unbearable news. Cheney really knew what he was doing. If you really want to torture someone, send him back in time just far enough to make him feel compelled to change his life.

Junior considered being bumped off in Buffalo, before expressing a more pressing concern.

"Mom's worried no one's coming home this summer to go out on the boat."

My father had bought a small outboard boat, which was kept docked in a shabby marina on the nearby Niagara River. Soon after the purchase, "the river" became more prevalent in my parents' vocabularies than it was in Huckleberry Finn's. Every summer my mother expected her children to make a pilgrimage to Buffalo to go out on the boat.

"We'll go to Buffalo," I said, "but only stay a day and one night." Somehow I'd manage to get my father alone and give him the heads-up that he'd soon drink himself to death—yeah, that sounded like a pleasant chat—and Junior wouldn't have to know about it. Then I advised Taylor that he should accompany us. "Cheney knows you know I'm from the future. He's probably afraid I'll talk you out of inventing the time machine. I don't know what he'd do to you, but I can guarantee it won't be painless."

"If I refuse to invent the time machine," Taylor said, "he can't threaten me."

"But you must invent it because I'm talking to you."

"That's true."

Taylor pondered this conundrum while Junior goo-goo eyed him, daydreaming about the sleeping arrangements on our trip.

"Who is this Cheney?" Taylor asked.

Junior spoke before I could respond.

"Supposedly the vice president of the United States."

Taylor's lips pulled back into a doubtful sneer.

"And he's traveling back in time to kill American citizens?"

"I know it sounds crazy," I said, "but no one in my time would find that hard to believe."

"You make him sound psychotic."

"He advocates torturing prisoners and locking people up for years without trials. He and Bush established a concentration camp in Cuba on Guantanamo Bay. He lied to start the war in Iraq. He's ruthless. I don't trust him and you shouldn't either; you have to come with us."

"Bumping me off would change history," said Taylor.

His welfare wasn't my only concern.

"You know where we're going and Cheney could get that out of you."

I couldn't risk Taylor inadvertently stopping us from saving Carol.

"I won't tell him."

"He tortures people to make them to talk."

"I've made plans to go out to Fire Island for the next two weeks. I'll hang out there. We'll see him coming."

"He'll track you down, because you invent the time machine."

"I still can't believe I invent a time machine." Taylor was jubilant and asked me half a dozen scientific questions that I couldn't answer. He took my ignorance in stride—he always did—and merely said, "Well, I guess I'll figure it out later."

Junior was moon-eyed with newfound admiration. "That's really cool," he said.

"I'm supposed to start in Los Alamos in two weeks," Taylor said. "I'd have to tell my mom something about leaving early."

In college, Taylor worked part of every summer at various high-profile research labs. I rolled my eyes, knowing how Taylor's mother questioned everything he did or said, except when it related to science or his scientific career. "She'll believe you," I said. "If you told her the world was flat, she'd throw out her globe."

Taylor pursed his lips but didn't dispute my statement.

"What do you do?" Junior asked.

Taylor explained he was getting his doctorate in physics.

"What's your field of interest?"

"Time travel."

"I should have guessed," Junior replied before asking him how he became interested in physics.

"You don't have to be polite," Taylor said. "Whenever anyone talks about physics, it's like a neutrino passing through your body. I could scientifically prove it happened, but it never has any impact."

"I wasn't being polite," Junior said. "I'm interested."

His declaration sounded suspiciously sexual to my ears, but Taylor didn't react and I couldn't tell if he even picked up on it. Taylor always thought talking about physics was dull, even though I explained to him my belief that people are at their most interesting when they talk about what they truly love—with the notorious exceptions of actors and Scientologists.

"So what do you think?" Junior asked Taylor. "Are we changing history?"

"Yes. But from what he—or, I guess, you—said, it sounds like the future should be changed."

"How much worse could it be?" I asked.

"A lot worse," Taylor warned. "No one alive now can predict all the changes over the next twenty years. So the adverse effects could be major or minor."

Junior piped in. "So the cum-stained dress becomes cum-stained culottes."

I looked at Taylor. "You told me that history might not significantly change even though the past might be altered. You used the example that six plus three or two plus seven both equal nine."

"I said that? When?"

"You will."

Taylor pondered the idea before asking, "Did I just get that idea from you? Or did I give it to you? Or both?"

"I have no idea," I said, thinking, Was that possible? I asked Taylor and he grinned.

"I think for the first time in history we just pinned down the position of an electron," he responded.

When we finished eating, I suggested going back inside. I didn't like us sitting outdoors. For all I knew, Cheney could be watching us by satellite, although I wondered if the optical technology was that far advanced in 1986.

The dishes were left in the sink for washing later, and Junior and Taylor sat on the bed. I ended up on the futon, which smelled doggy and slightly moldy.

"Tell us about the future," Junior said. "What's the biggest change we'll see in twenty years?"

His question made me smirk, since I was looking directly at a gay porn video, *The Pizza Boy: He Delivers*, sitting on top of Junior's VCR. "I can't. It could influence the future of your orgasms."

"Just tell us," Taylor said.

"We'll all have multiple personalities in twenty years."

They stared at me as if I'd just spoken in Mandarin.

"Everyone will have a name, a screen name, and a secret screen name."

Personal computers were still expensive and uncommon in 1986, and I explained how everyone would own one or even two computers in twenty years, and then I had to elaborate on the pervasive world of the Internet and the concept of being online. I said that someone named Joe Blow might have a public screen name such as JBlow237@aol.com that he used for business and his family and friends, but in addition, he might have a secret screen name for going online for sex: JoeBlowme@yahoo.com. Then I regaled them with stories about the dawning of the age of online hookups, cybersex, porn websites, and webcams, making it sound like computers were just sex toys with keyboards.

"What's your secret screen name?" Junior asked.

"If I told you, it wouldn't be secret." I wasn't sure if I wanted them to know every detail of my life; but I went on to explain to them the irony of the idea of "privacy" in the Internet age. "You see, in my time, millions of strangers will be able to read online about my most intimate sexual fantasies, but I maintain a delusional sense of privacy by not discussing them with the people who know me best."

"Bossygaymanwhowantshisownwayoneverything," Junior suggested. "All one word."

"Too long and too revealing. You sell your physical attributes and conceal your emotional characteristics. 'Hotneurotic' is not a good screen name."

"Middleagedstud?" Taylor offered.

"Too dowdy. You're trying to come up with a sexy name that will intrigue other hot guys. 'Middle-aged' is only a turn-on if your screen name is 'Geezer488.' Secret screen names take one kinky aspect of a person or a sexual fetish and make it emblematic of his entire identity,"

I explained. Then I recalled my own screen name history. "Unless you're looking to hook up right away—then you might go for something vulgar like 'FuckmeASAP.' You see, Americans are lazy and hate to type, so every abbreviation and shortcut will flourish. The word 'for'— F-O-R—will always be written with the number 4. And T-O will always be the number 2."

"Prince does that in his song titles," Taylor said.

I admitted that I'd forgotten about that but pressed on with my history of cybersex: "If you type something funny in an instant message, you'd never write, 'laugh out loud,' you'd type LOL and everyone will understand." I had to pause to explain instant messaging and gave a few other examples of online abbreviations, the slacker's Esperanto. I didn't discuss emoticons. They made the future sound more pitifully childish than I was willing to admit. "For example," I said, "if Ravi was a gay man and had a secret screen name, he would be 'Asscurious398' or 'BigWoof996.'"

Junior looked down at Ravi and petted his head. "Hello, Asscurious398!"

"Your world sounds kind of exciting *and* depressing," Taylor said.

"It will be," I admitted. "But that's the other big change. In twenty years everyone will be on antidepressants. America's about to become a pharmacological wonderland where there's a pill for every mood."

Ravi came over and rested his head on my knee. I reached down to pet him.

"It's strange," I said. "Most people will claim their pills work and that they're individually happier, but no one will claim that humanity is collectively happier."

"Am I on 'em?" Taylor asked.

"Yep," I said.

"Do they help?"

"Yeah, they do." He seemed relieved. Like just about everyone I knew, Taylor was prone to depression. They say depression runs in families, making it sound as if some folks' DNA is tied in a hangman's noose. The women in my family suffered from depression, as did Taylor's older brother. From anecdotal evidence, it sounds like depression has always been part of humanity's genetic heritage; we all have two eyes, two legs, and two moods: dissatisfied and unhappy.

"Am I on them?" Junior asked.

"No. The depression gene seems to have skipped us."

"It's ironic that science is proving one of mankind's oldest superstitions," said Taylor. "Some people are born damned."

"Can you guys be ready to leave this afternoon?" I asked. I had to change the subject, as talking about depression seemed to be engendering it.

Junior and Taylor seemed surprisingly fine with leaving for Buffalo that day. Taylor could get a refund on his plane ticket to Albuquerque, and admitted his mother would believe him if he told her a prestigious assistantship spot had opened up in Los Alamos at the last minute. I told him to go home and pack, emphasizing that he shouldn't tell either of his parents the truth of his whereabouts for the next two weeks. We arranged for Taylor to meet us at Sylvia's gallery at four o'clock, since I still had to go into Manhattan to buy a car. I'd never paid cash for a car before and wanted to give myself plenty of time in case there was a problem. However, I assumed the sale would go smoothly, as there had to be plenty of shady types in the city who went shopping with a suitcase of C-notes.

After Taylor went home to pack, Junior called Carol to ask if he could visit her with a friend.

"He's a comic book dealer," I overheard. "No, not that kind of friend. Yes, he's one of the gays." I forgot that Carol and I always referred to "the gays" after our mother once used the term. "He asked me to accompany him on a cross-country buying trip. It's good experience and won't cost me anything. Yeah, he's paying for everything." Money was a good selling point with Carol. She didn't like the idea of spending yours when someone else could and should pay. "I'll finally get to see your house." They talked for a few more minutes about when she should expect us, then said their good-byes and hung up.

I started washing the dishes and Junior dried.

"Why don't we get a convertible?" he asked.

"I don't want the sun beating down on me."

"We'll be out west. It would be fun to drive with the top down."

I held out my arm. "This is why." I ordered him to hold out his arm for comparison. "Do you see those spots? Do you see those fine wrinkles? Notice how my skin's slightly crepier compared to yours? It's called sun damage."

"I'll wear sun block."

I remembered something I wasn't sure I remembered correctly, one of those memories that looks real but could be a mirage.

"I think I read something about how sun blocks don't actually work now."

"You think you read? You're starting to sound like a bad psychic; if you're going to predict the future, don't start your sentences with 'I think.' You lose all credibility."

I had to restrain myself from telling him about my skin cancer. "I'm sorry if I don't have instant recall of everything I've ever read. But I do remember reading something about sun blocks. We're not buying a convertible."

Junior looked grudgingly accepting of my intransigence.

"So . . . no convertible?"

"No."

Junior shrugged off his disappointment and suggested we buy an environmentally conscious Honda Civic. "It burns less fuel and will help stop global warming." I was taken aback that he was aware of climate change. I recalled being concerned about the disappearing ozone layer, but couldn't recall or perhaps didn't want to remember being concerned about global warming. "How do you know about that?"

"There was a story about it in the *Times* last year."

Had there really been over twenty years of inaction? It angered me that global warming had been acknowledged as a front-page threat to our planet in 1985 and yet our country had done absolutely nothing to stop it. It made me disgusted with myself and everyone else.

"What's wrong?" Junior asked.

"I'd forgotten how long we've been talking about global warming."

"Well, they must be trying to stop it in your time."

"No. Our president doesn't believe in science. None of the Republicans do. And the Democrats have been afraid to do anything. They didn't want to stop people from driving their beloved gas-guzzling SUVs."

"No one's doing anything?"

I shook my head and felt ashamed. "Not really. SUV should stand for Selfish Uncaring Vehicle."

"What about that guy from Tennessee?" Junior asked. "He held congressional hearings about climate change."

"Gore?"

"Yeah."

I explained that for the next two decades Gore would be the only political leader to talk about global warming and would often be ridiculed for it.

"Gore ran for president in 2000 against Bush and won the popular vote, but Bush stole the election."

Junior stared blankly, and I questioned whether I could explain the Florida recount accurately.

"The election ended up in the Florida Supreme Court, which voted for a recount. Then Bush took the case to the Federal Supreme Court and they voted against a recount. I still think Gore might have won had they gone forward, but at this point it's a case for conspiracy theorists."

"Dad must have loved that."

Our father loved a good conspiracy theory, but he was dead by 2000. I stammered for a second. "Oh, yeah. He does." Then I added, "We shouldn't talk any more politics." I didn't want him to know the entire history of the United States for the next twenty years. I was afraid that he would become bitterly cynical.

"I don't get it," Junior said. "I thought our country would become more progressive. There's been a backlash against Reagan's anti-environmental policies. I joined the Nature Conservancy and the

Wilderness Society, and so have thousands of other people. The environment shouldn't be partisan; we all live on the same planet."

"Not really. We live on Gaia while the Republicans live on Liar."

Junior's eyes became piercing. "You're still a member, I hope."

I remained silent as I tried to think of a valid reason as to why I'd let my memberships lapse. It would've been easier to present him with a flapping ivory-billed woodpecker. Sloth and intermittent spasms of frugality weren't an acceptable excuse for my apathy. Junior's face turned bright red.

"Jesus Christ, in your time is everyone in America a fucking moron just jerking off to porn on his computer?"

"Yes."

It was a relief to admit it.

7

LATER THAT DAY, around four o'clock, I drove our brand-new red Camaro onto the Westside Highway. Junior told us how Sylvia had revealed that her father had committed suicide. She had urged Junior to do everything he could to help his sister. Sylvia reassured him that she knew he wasn't quitting, but taking a leave of absence, and even insisted on paying him for the entire week.

"Well, I'm not surprised," I said. "I remember her fondly."

"You remember her?"

I could sense Junior's body going rigid in the passenger seat.

"You make it sound like she's dead."

"I didn't say that." He didn't need to know that Sylvia died of an aneurysm in the late '90s.

"You don't have to. I can hear it in your voice."

A Bronski Beat tape was playing. I'd tried to buy a Camaro with a CD player, but the dealer only had one Camaro, with a tape player, in stock. It turned out to be fine. Junior still owned a lot of tapes. He had brought along a stack for the trip, music from the '80s, reminding me that pop songs are my most efficient means of emotional recall.

Whenever the first chords of a cherished song such as "Smalltown Boy" started, it guaranteed three minutes of nostalgia that lived in a perpetual now.

"Are Mom and Dad still alive?"

"Yes!"

"You're lying. I know it."

Junior switched tapes, appropriately enough to Dead or Alive's "You Spin Me Round." That song roused a toe-tapping, head-bobbing Pavlovian response, memories of me dancing on Sunday nights at the Palladium on 14th Street. I was glad Junior couldn't read my mind, because while I was engaged in a serious conversation with him, in my head I was carefree.

"Is it Dad? The men in our family always die first."

"No! It's no one."

"You're a walking obituary page. I don't want or need to know about everyone who's died."

"Then stop asking," I said. He was right. I needed to be more careful. Over the course of a normal life, deaths are often random and appear unannounced. Junior didn't deserve to have a lifetime of head-stones dumped into his lap.

In the rearview mirror I could see Taylor playing with Ravi. I was glad we brought Ravi with us; otherwise, we would be driving a Honda Civic. Once I mentioned that Ravi would make a napping target in the backseat for Cheney's bullets, and that a Camaro had more horsepower than a Civic, Junior dropped his concern for the environment as quickly as a redneck would chuck an empty out the window of his pickup. It made me feel guilty manipulating Junior, but I also felt a sense of accomplishment, which was pathetic. Not knowing how to press your own buttons would be as lame as not knowing how to masturbate. In order to win Junior's acceptance of my gas-guzzler, I vowed we would cross the country planting ponderosa pines and living off roadkill. Junior yeah-yeahed me before making me pony up some real cash for the Nature Conservancy and Wilderness Society.

In a few hours we were upstate and started passing cast-iron blue-and-yellow historic markers along the route that were impossible to read from a moving car. Instead, we had fun imagining what they commemorated. "Former site of the Schumann farm," said Junior, "the first family in Oswego to think the winter's too fucking long."

"Site of the Battle of Herkimer Falls," Taylor announced, "where for six months in 1812, Heidi Schiffmacher refused to have conjugal relations with her husband, Otto, until he agreed to move somewhere warmer."

"On this site in 1786," I declared, "the Mohawk Inn was built where travelers and local settlers unsuccessfully tried to drink until they forgot where they lived."

Upstate New York proved that you will jinx a place if you name your towns after cities like Carthage and Troy that peaked thousands of years ago and have since fallen into ruins. We passed dozens of ailing small towns with going-out-of-business districts, roadside farm stands selling fresh-picked misery, and greasy spoons where you wanted to tip the waitress a one-way bus ticket. The few prosperous upstate towns seemed to fall into three categories: prison towns where the inmates were bitterly resented because most of them had a chance of parole while all of the town's inhabitants were lifers; mediocre SUNY college towns where the gym is always larger than the library; and towns that desperately capitalized on a singular claim to fame: Cooperstown had baseball, Corning had glass, Ithaca had Cornell, and Seneca Falls honored its feminist heritage with a Ladies' Night at the Stumble Inn.

The sun set around nine, and the boys fell asleep after we stopped for dinner at a diner. The darkness delayed the onset of my mixed emotions about visiting western New York. My family had lived along both sides of the Niagara River since the Revolutionary War, when my loyalist Canadian ancestors had fought in Butler's Rangers with the British and Iroquois against the Americans. My mixed heritage of being a Canadian Patriot and an American Traitor seemed to reflect how I felt about where I grew up. I truly loved Buffalo and western New

York, visited at least once a year, and would always feel they were intrinsic to my identity. I was proud of Buffalo's lack of pretension, where civic pride in being the birthplace of Buffalo wings exceeded its also being the home of Louis Sullivan's architectural masterpiece, his Guaranty Building. But whenever I've read or heard the expression "You Can't Go Home Again," my gut response has always been "Thank God!"

After passing Rochester and approaching Batavia, where my father worked every day at the state police headquarters, Junior and Taylor woke up.

"How close are we?" Taylor asked.

"About an hour," Junior and I answered simultaneously.

I thought it was too late to meet my parents for the first time, and suggested we stay at a motel near the Amherst campus of UB. The boys were as tired as I was and agreed. It would have to be all motels this trip, since we were traveling with Ravi. We weren't sure if the Amherst Stardust Motel took pets and had already decided to sneak him in.

The front desk clerk told us there was a conference at the university and they had only one room available, with two double beds. I took it since we were exhausted. I didn't comprehend how awkward our sleeping arrangements would be until we were in our room and I saw the two beds. There were a few flirty glances directed at me from them as we undressed, although I did notice Junior and Taylor focused more on each other once they were down to their briefs. Junior wouldn't suggest sleeping with Taylor because he didn't want to hurt my feelings, and I knew from experience that Taylor preferred someone else to take charge of all matters relating to sex. He was one of those works-all-the-time, mentally preoccupied guys who gave the impression that having an orgasm was always intensely satisfying, as it was one less thing to think about.

"Why don't you two share a bed," I suggested. "I'm bigger than either of you." They appeared to politely consider my suggestion, pretending that the idea had never occurred to them.

"You should get your own bed," said Taylor. "You did all the driving." Junior added, "I'll share with Taylor."

I'm not sure if anything happened between them, since I passed out immediately. But I did notice at breakfast the next morning, the two of them were bleary-eyed and groggy. They could barely manage to order poached eggs and dry wheat toast, although when I ordered sausage and French toast, Junior's eyes momentarily perked up with disapproval. I'd forgotten that I didn't become a morning person until my early thirties. Accordingly, I began to think about the age difference between us.

"Did you tell Mom about Taylor and me?" I asked after the waitress refilled our coffees.

"No."

"Why not?"

"You know Mom. She'll assume we're boyfriends."

My mother then wasn't the mother who would later prefer to celebrate Christmas Eve at my house with twelve gay men rather than spend it with my straight brothers and their families. "They're boring!" she claimed. When I first came out, my mother temporarily adopted a strategy of opposing my homosexuality by using the simple method of deciding it was not homophobic to dislike all homosexuals if you found specific things to dislike about each one of them. After meeting one of my boyfriends, she'd comment with a semblance of geniality, "Does he do anything else besides lifeguarding?" or "His shirts are too tight." She tempted me to respond, "Well, I like my boyfriends' bodies to be as thinly veiled as your contempt." Admittedly, I dated some truly dumb hunks in my early twenties, but I had no doubt that if I'd introduced my mother to someone homely but sweet, she would have complained that I could do better.

"I think she'll like me," I said, concerned that my own mother wouldn't like me. My fear exposed the unspoken shame of all families: if you didn't know the people you were related to, would you befriend them? In the days when families hunted and gathered, this wouldn't be a question worth pondering, but once butchering a mammoth stopped being a household chore, we began to suspect families are chain gangs held together by manacles of DNA.

"She'll think you're some strange old gay guy," Junior said. "We'll remind her of Gary and Roxanne."

Gary and Roxanne were a married couple who moved in across the street from my parents. He was twenty years older than his wife, and the difference in their ages kept my mother's neck firm and flexible from all her disapproving head-shaking every time their names came up.

Junior suddenly blurted out, "What if she figures out you're me?"

"She didn't figure out you were gay. How's she going to figure out I'm her son from twenty years in the future? Time travel isn't something she thinks about. She hates science fiction."

Junior smiled. "That's true. She calls every science fiction show *Spook Alley.*"

My mother had always let me watch whatever science fiction television series I was currently infatuated with, but she was too pragmatic to enjoy fantasy; if she gazed into Alice's Looking-Glass, she'd notice streaks and immediately wonder if she'd get stuck cleaning it.

"Well, Dad won't have a problem with me," I said.

"Even if he did, he wouldn't say anything."

One of the most comforting things about our father was that he never pried into his own feelings, and, out of a sense of fairness, he extended the same courtesy to everyone else.

"Do you want to just drop me off?" Junior asked.

"What am I? A pariah?"

"More like a grandpa-riah," we both said simultaneously. It was astonishing to see that we did occasionally think exactly alike and also gratifying to see that my mind still worked as quickly as Junior's did.

Junior looked ashamed of his own embarrassment, and his head tilted downward as if avoiding eye contact with me rendered him invisible. I considered not meeting our parents to please Junior, but it would make me miserable and I needed to see my father once more. Junior could hardly accuse me of being selfish for wanting to see my parents.

"I want to see them again."

"Again? Who died?"

"No one," I lied. "It's just an expression. I meant I'd like to see them young again."

"I know you're lying," Junior declared before turning his head away to stare out the window. I felt awful. No one should know when their parents are going to die; if you love your parents, and I did, it would only make you needlessly sad, and if you loathed them, it would only make you frustratingly impatient. I'd already burdened Junior with the suicide of our sister; adding our father's death would make me insufferable.

Junior rubbed his forehead slowly. "What am I going to tell her?"

He appeared to be ashamed of me being twenty years older than him. Normally, aging occurs gradually, and yet here I was, him, instantly middle aged. It had to be as disturbing as going through puberty in a day would be.

"I don't know." Then an idea occurred to me. A lie that involved money entering Junior's wallet would probably placate our mother. I'd worked for some major oddballs over the years, but she never made derogatory comments about any of them—even the guy who looked and sounded like a carny who hired me in high school to sell souvenirs at Buffalo Sabres hockey games. Her goodwill could be bought; she'd glad-hand anyone who signed her kids' paychecks.

"Tell her what you told Carol. I'm a comic book dealer who asked you to accompany him on a cross-country buying trip. I'm paying you and you're gaining experience."

Junior nodded. "That might work."

"What are we going to call you?" Taylor asked. "It might be weird if you're both named John *and* look like you're related."

"I hadn't thought about that," I said. Neither had Junior. We discussed possible names and settled on Kurt, as a tribute to Kurt Vonnegut. All of us loved his early science fiction stories.

I felt uneasy as we turned onto Palmer Avenue. At my parents' house, I always became a Janus-like figure, simultaneously glad to be there and anxious to leave.

My parents still lived in the same house I grew up in, a Dutch Colonial revival with a gambrel roof that they'd purchased from my grandparents, a house that my mother would still be living in almost sixty years later, in 2006! This isn't uncommon in Buffalo, where once people acquire a living room, they often end up dying there. We lived in Kenmore, an older suburb of Buffalo. When I was young, elm trees formed a canopy over the street, and driving to our house was like passing through a tunnel. But in the late '60s all the trees died from Dutch elm disease and were replaced by other species that still looked spindly more than thirty years later.

We pulled up to the back door, where my parents had recently installed a cement driveway next to the house, which served as a patio during the summer and off-street parking for my mother's car during the winter. A gas grill, a teak umbrella table with matching chairs, and several colorful windsocks mounted on poles were carefully arranged next to a whimsically painted wooden sign that said, "Your smile is all the sunshine I need!" The paint on the sign was weathered, giving the message a plaintive air when my mother left it sitting out all winter. In the flowerbeds surrounding the house, she planted ceramic geese, wearing floppy yellow hats and blue kerchiefs about their necks, and a ceramic squirrel, frog, and turtle. In her assessment of people, my mother was often brutal and shrewd, but she liked to think of herself as sentimental, making the saccharine décor of her yard as misleading as a witch's gingerbread house. She was kneeling on the ground, leaning over a flowerbed, wielding a three-pronged gardening tool, swinging it viciously, bringing up green-stemmed weeds with each blow.

My mother stood up and turned in our direction when she heard the car doors open. Her smile at seeing Junior was instantaneous. She was fifty-three—only seven years older than I was—and she was still slim, with her hair dyed a frosty golden shade that I thought of as "Hard Blonde." Ravi jumped out of the backseat and immediately squatted on the lawn to urinate.

There was a hurried round of introductions, handshaking, and a kiss on the cheek from Junior. "You didn't tell me you were bringing the dog," she said before crouching down to pet him. Ravi immediately rolled on his side, encouraging her to rub his stomach. "Frisky will be fine with him for one day," she added.

I'd forgotten about my mother's crazy, antisocial cat but knew Ravi ignored cats and Frisky hated and avoided everyone—except for my mother—so I didn't foresee any pet problems. Taylor politely complimented her garden, and she smiled. "I love flowers, but killing bugs and pulling weeds in my garden is more fun than growing things. It's awful. If I go out and kill things for an hour, I feel like a million bucks!"

"Jeffrey Dahmer probably said the same thing," I joked, but no one laughed and everyone looked vaguely confused. Of course, the famed cannibal/serial killer was probably still premeditating in 1986. Fortunately, everyone decided to step around my remark as if nothing had been said.

My mother had questions, and Junior explained he was accompanying me on a comic book buying expedition, pointedly mentioning that he was getting paid, before adding that Taylor was a friend of his who was getting a free ride out to New Mexico. It sounded reasonable, and our mother smiled acceptingly and then invited us into the house for coffee.

"How far west are you going?"

"California. We're going to see Carol."

She seemed surprised we were traveling that far but didn't ask any more questions. I was sure she had some, but she would wait to get Junior alone before asking them. We entered the back hall and climbed the four steps to the kitchen that our father had remodeled in the early 1970s. The bottom halves of the walls were covered with blue paneling imprinted with a wood-grain pattern, a faux finish tall tale that was about as believable as a gigantic blue ox named Babe. On the refrigerator hung long out-of-date family photos, cartoons cut out from the *Buffalo News*, held up with Buffalo Bills and Sabres magnets, and my mother's combination shopping and to-do lists that read like a cryptic outline for a murder mystery, written in her old-fashioned good penmanship cursive: "Be tough," "Throw out books," "Worrying doesn't help," "Sponge candy," and "Knife sharpening."

On a wall hung a recent purchase of my mother's, a clock that marked the hours with portraits of different species of birds instead of numerals. On the hour, the call of each species cried out. It was already a quarter past whip-poor-will. There was also a motivational plaque featuring a photo of dewy-eyed baby bunnies on heavily shellacked redwood printed with a gold-tone calligraphic message: "Today— Anything Is Possible!" I always found the message more ominous than comforting, but my mother liked it, and so I resisted pointing out to her the message's ambiguity. (Like a farmer making foie gras, my mother thought a heart needed to be force-fed in order to enlarge it.) We sat down at the kitchen table as my mother pulled a package of unbleached coffee filters out of a cupboard. Junior commended her for buying them. "You're helping the environment."

She pursed her lips while scooping coffee into the filter. "I don't know if I like these. The brown coffee filters look exactly like the white ones, used. How do we know that's not what we're getting?"

Junior and I smiled, and seeing that it was all right to smile, so did Taylor. She then smiled tentatively, indicating that she hadn't tried to be funny but knew she had been. "It wouldn't surprise me."

Junior opened a cookie jar to check the contents. "You've been listening to Dad too much."

"I don't listen to him!" she said, swatting the air to brush away that idea.

A small calico cat crept up the back stairs, saw strangers and Ravi in the kitchen, hissed fiercely, and then retreated back down the steps into the basement.

"Is she afraid of the dog?" Taylor asked.

"No. Frisky's not afraid. She hates everyone! She only likes me."

My mother sounded thoroughly delighted about nurturing her cat's xenophobia.

Junior asked where our father was, and her reply was, "He's out."

Growing up, I knew more about Santa Claus's workday than my father's. When my father left the house to work for the state police, none of us could exactly say what he did all day, and on his days off, we couldn't have told you how he spent his time either. In some ways his leaving the house was like letting the cat out—he went somewhere, but no one in our family was especially curious about what he did or where he went. (There ought to be a special word for mysteries that interest absolutely no one. I suggest *ennuigma*.) From his occasional remarks, I assumed my father visited car mechanic friends at their body shops, got a haircut, or ran errands. When his parents were still alive, he visited them frequently—they'd lived ten blocks away—but since their deaths, I wasn't sure how he filled his time. As an adult, I knew my father's job title, First Sergeant, and his rank, second in command of Troop A, which encompassed the eight westernmost counties in New York State. I also knew he no longer went out on patrol, and had a desk job at the state police headquarters in Batavia. I pictured him ordering badges and bullets, but after that I blanked. For years I was under the mistaken impression that we were very different men until I grasped that I probably showed the same lack of interest in his life as he did in mine.

He walked through the door a few minutes later. He was the same age as my mother, fifty-three, and his formerly jet-black hair was now salt and pepper. He looked like a cop from central casting, six feet tall, burly and broad-shouldered, mug-shot handsome, and he always kept his smile holstered, used only as a means of last resort. In his gray state trooper uniform, he appeared intimidating, and when he raised his deep voice, he never had to reprimand his children more than once. He grinned warmly and welcomed Junior enthusiastically, but there wasn't even a feigned attempt at physical contact between father and son. This was years before hugging became customary between men. He shook my hand and Taylor's and repeated our names while my mother informed him that my older brother Kevin had called from Syracuse. "He couldn't get the day off to come home and go out on the boat."

"You can't really get much time off when you start a new job," said my father as he walked down the hallway that led to the bathroom and removed his police pistol from the linen closet. Throughout my childhood, he always stashed his loaded gun in the linen closet among the towels, and it amused me to recall that he had routinely done something that would be considered recklessly negligent and probably illegal later. He unloaded it on the kitchen table in preparation for cleaning it.

There was a lull in the conversation, and Junior asked how Kevin liked his new job. He'd recently become a paramedic.

"He's doing great," my father said. "He knows his stuff inside and out, although he might have to work on his people skills." He smiled. "On a recent ambulance run, he asked, 'So your wife has asthma but you didn't call us until after she smoked a carton of cigarettes?' Her husband said, 'You don't have to be sarcastic.'"

All of us laughed. "Having a sarcastic paramedic showing up at your door might make you think twice about dialing 911," Junior said.

"Yeah," said my father. "Kevin will help stop your old pain, but if you're stupid, he'll give ya a new one."

My father genially asked Junior about what he was doing and where he was headed. After telling him that we were traveling to California, my father suggested stopping in Roswell, New Mexico.

"What's there?" Taylor asked innocently.

"It all goes back to Roswell," my father declared, polishing his revolver while explaining that the government had been engaged in a massive cover-up. "The local newspaper headlined that the government found a flying saucer. Then the Feds went in and covered it up. In 1947 Roswell only had a population of 22,000. Back then, everyone knew everyone else. The editor wouldn't get that story wrong."

Taylor glanced at Junior but kept a bemused smile on his face, signaling to him that he didn't need to be rescued from our father's lecture; a neutral expression would have been a cry for help. Junior and I were no longer embarrassed by our father's habit of casually discussing the conspiracy theories he subscribed to: the Roswell UFO cover-up, the Kennedy assassination, the faked Apollo Moon Landing, and others. Our dad was odd but remained enthusiastic about life—both terrestrial and extraterrestrial—and since he distrusted everyone equally, his chipper paranoia almost felt like an expression of brotherhood. Our father could afford to relax. He was onto all the schemes; it was the poor dummies who don't know what's what who should be terrified.

"Newspapers get things wrong all the time," Taylor argued as our father's lecture stirred the rationalist in him.

"Honey, will you cut the lawn on our grassy knoll today?" my mother suggested sweetly. She looked at Junior and quickly rolled her eyes.

"I saw that," my father observed without raising his head. My mother had decided long ago that figuring out the trajectory points of bullets fired from a Dallas schoolbook depository was a harmless hobby, but there were times when she wished my father took no interest in anything, like her best friend Marge's husband, Dennis.

"So you're interested in the Kennedy assassination?" asked Taylor.

"'Interested' isn't the word," Junior said.

Our father was an expert on the Kennedy assassination and had achieved a modest renown among the "Assassinistas," as we derisively called them, for writing the article "Was Zapruder the Shooter?" for *The Depository*—the quarterly journal of the Kennedy Assassination Association—laying out the case that Abraham Zapruder had actually shot the president. My father wasted no time in advancing his theory to us.

"He's the last person you'd ever suspect. You put a gun in a home movie camera. There's a big bang but no one looks at the guy holding the camera. Then afterwards, he comes forward with the only film of the assassination and no one thinks of connecting the dots."

Taylor put down his empty coffee mug. "How do I know you didn't do it? You own a gun."

"Hey, that's fair," he agreed, nodding his head. "The only way you can solve any crime is to follow all the leads. I've collected guns since I was a kid. I own fifty-eight rifles and pistols—everything from a vintage Henry rifle to a Kalashnikov—but I'm not a gun nut. Gun nuts worry that the government will take away their weapons, while I'm convinced the government's trying to circumvent our right to bear arms by inventing a force field that will make bullets useless."

My father was nominally a member of the NRA and the Republican Party but routinely disagreed with them. He was convinced moles had infiltrated both organizations and most of what they put out was disinformation.

Junior suggested showing Taylor the Albright-Knox Art Gallery and then meeting my parents on Grand Island for a late afternoon boat trip. He wanted to show off Buffalo to Taylor, but I was worried about Cheney.

"We should keep to our schedule," I warned.

"It only takes an hour or so," my mother said.

She was right. Visiting the museum would throw us off for an hour, and I didn't want to leave. Time travel was allowing me to experience a bizarre but delightful sense of homecoming. I wanted to spend more time with my parents when they had both been happy.

Our father said he had to buy a valve of some sort for the boat's engine, and I invited our mother to come to the gallery with us. Junior's smile wobbled, indicating he wished I hadn't. I'd forgotten that I became closer to my mother after the deaths of my father and sister. I considered her to be a friend and good company, but Junior had only moved out of her house two years before and still had rope burns from her apron strings. My mother was a member of the Albright, and as we drove down Elmwood Avenue, she offered us her opinion of the current Georgia O'Keefe retrospective that was on display.

"She married this guy in New York. Then she went to Santa Fe and got creative. She has all those paintings. One looks just like the other. Hills in one after another after another."

"Mock her," Junior said.

My mother faced him. "I just did," she said.

8

THE ALBRIGHT-KNOX has always been my measure of a great art museum. It has a superb collection of art, mostly European and American paintings and sculptures, mostly from the nineteenth and twentieth centuries, several acknowledged masterpieces (even New Yorkers are impressed), and it can be viewed in two hours or less, tops. It's housed in a Greek revival building built during the Pan-American Exposition in 1901, joined with a severe but complementary Modernist black glass box addition built in 1962.

Junior and Taylor were eager to see the O'Keefe retrospective. That made sense; it was 1986 and New York was in the heyday of its love of Santa Fe, a short-lived fling. The two mindsets are incompatible; hanging a cow skull on the wall of your apartment in Manhattan only triggers the impossible-to-extinguish fear that dead bones attract rats and roaches. Within a few years, my—and everyone else's—Hopi silver bolo ties and hand-forged wrought-iron demitasse spoons ended up in storage units.

"I'm going to look around while you check out Georgia," my mother declared as she encouraged us to see what we wanted versus doing what we felt obligated to do—not abandoning her. Junior and

Taylor encouraged her to come with us, but she shook her head. "All those flowers and skulls." She scrunched up her nose. "It's like she's trying to cheer me up about dying." She flapped her hands as if she was fanning us up the staircase to the exhibit. "You go. I'll be fine." The remarkable thing is that she did want us to do what we wanted; her selflessness was tied to her often-professed credo: "If my kids are happy, I'm happy." Still, spending time with her children made her happy, and I announced that I'd stay with her and told Junior and Taylor to go ahead. My mother gently patted her hair in anticipation of spending time with a friend of her son. As the boys ascended the staircase, we walked down a corridor to one of the main galleries and stopped in front of one of my favorite paintings—a wonderful self-portrait of the young Degas, looking haughty and yet also vulnerable. "Would it kill him to smile?" my mother asked as we gazed at his likeness. "He's only twenty. I'll bet he had bad teeth." Suddenly, I imagined my mother recording an audio tour for the Albright. My mother liked art, but she had no reverence for the artistic, and her response to every painting was what every modern artist claimed to want, a fresh and unpremeditated viewing. "If I could steal one painting, it would be this one," I said in front of Giacomo Balla's futurist masterpiece, *Dynamism of a Dog on a Leash*. The painting is a foot-level view of a dachshund being walked, and the motion of the dog's moving paws, the moving leash, and his mistress's moving boots are painted in repeated sequences, suggesting action in a way that alluded to the relatively recent invention of motion pictures. Balla's painting must have seemed radical at the time, but it also must have always been seen as incredibly charming.

My mother grinned. "This is one of my favorites too. I look at it as a life lesson: Always Busy, Going Nowhere."

In front of Frida Kahlo's *Self-Portrait with Monkey*, my mother shook her head. "This one upsets me. The monkey's eyebrows are less noticeable than hers."

As we moved on to Arshile Gorky's *The Liver Is the Cock's Comb*, my mother ignored his masterwork and smiled at a guard who smiled back at her. When we were out of earshot, she said, "It's not artists who suffer for art but museum guards. Look at the one standing over there."

I gazed at the man she indicated. His face looked as if he'd been stifling a yawn for an eight-hour shift.

"Imagine spending forty years staring at these walls," she said. "I'm surprised he hasn't burned the place down."

I laughed and she did also. "You're right!" I said. "A truly sensitive person could never enjoy an art museum. The plight of the guards would be too upsetting."

"It's better than assembling windshield wipers."

She was referring to my Uncle Joe's job, but didn't feel the need to explain herself.

"Let's get a coffee," she said, jerking her thumb toward the museum cafe.

"Sure."

I felt nervous conversing with her, having to pretend she was someone I was meeting for the first time. It's not like I hadn't lied to my mother before, but the novelty was that I was pretending not to be her son instead of pretending I wasn't straight, sober, or interested in what she had to say. I briefly fantasized that perhaps my mother would be revealed as completely different from the woman I knew, but felt I knew her too well for that to happen.

"What made you join the museum?"

"It's peaceful and quiet. Except when they do that video art. I don't like art that talks. I come here to get away from people talking. I don't want to have to tell art to shut up."

We were seated at a table, and the hostess handed a menu to each of us.

"I'm not up on art like you guys, but I like it. Even the stuff that's wacky. And boy, do we need art in Buffalo. When you see your breath for six months a year, you can't forget life is short and winters are long."

I couldn't remember if my father ever came to the art museum, and I asked her if he did.

"I brought him here once. He hated it. He kept saying, 'I could do that!' About those . . . paintings . . ." She couldn't remember the term and gestured broadly, splashing the air with her hands.

"Abstract Expressionists?"

She nodded. "That's it. Well, I told him if you can do that, then do it! The kids could use the money. That shut him up, until we left, then he told me he never wanted to go there again." My mother shrugged. "You can't change people." This observation was another one of her signature philosophical beliefs. It sounded like an expression of hard-bitten cynicism but was actually a proclamation of her tolerance and acceptance of the myriad likes and dislikes of her family and friends. Whether it was my refusal to eat raw onions and celery, or my attraction toward men, or my father's love of working on cars and his animosity toward de Kooning and Pollock, she accepted her gay, vegetable-bigot son and her autophile, philistine husband. She shrugged. "You make your own fun!" This was her other bedrock principle on how to live. I'd heard her say it many times and knew she meant that you shouldn't be afraid to entertain yourself by reading a book, or pursuing a hobby or interest that others might not share. I'd made my sister laugh when I told her I regarded it as being supportive of masturbation and solitary drinking.

I was naturally curious to hear what my mother really thought about me and also wanted to enjoy the irresistible opportunity to shamelessly talk about myself under the guise of expressing an interest in someone else.

"You must be proud of John for moving to New York and doing well."

"I am." Her smile seemed constrained.

"You don't think he's doing well?"

"I just want him to get ahead," she said.

"He is. He's close to starting his own business."

"I thought he wanted to draw comic books, not sell them. I don't want him to get hurt."

Her concern was touching and I tried to reassure her that he was making the right decision.

"He's afraid he's not talented enough," I explained.

"Well, did he try? He might be happier as a failed artist than working as uh . . . almost anything. Men who hate their jobs hate their lives. Then we learn to hate them because they're either dull or mean. You should do what you want because you can't predict how your life will turn out. No matter how smart you are. And he's smart. All my kids are smart. I'm not." There was a pause, and I was about to tell her that she was smarter than I was—not as book smart maybe—but she was more emotionally intelligent: a better judge of character and better at dealing with adversity. "But I'm not stupid, either." She smiled and took a sip of her coffee. "Can you really make a living selling comic books?" she asked.

"You won't get rich, but you can do all right."

She pushed her lips around, as she was trying to prevent them from frowning.

"You should see people's faces when I tell them he wants to draw comic books. 'Comic books?' They say it almost as if he's simple." Her face dimpled with resignation. "And I haven't even told them he's . . . I expect plenty of smirks about that."

She would learn to pronounce the word "gay," eventually telling friends, neighbors, and relatives, proving that while you can't change people, people do change. My mother would change for the better.

"It took guts for John to move to New York," I said. "He has lots of friends. People really like and respect him."

I wanted my mother to be proud of me, but my praise only seemed to darken her mood.

"No offense to you, but selling comic books? It's barely a step up from being a newspaper boy, and he did that at fourteen."

I was hurt. She made it sound as if loving something as an adult that you had loved as a child was a form of pedophilia.

"I make a decent living doing something I love."

My mother appeared to regret her last comment.

"I'm sorry. I was rude. If he's happy . . ."

I didn't respond immediately. I was angry. My mother had never told me she thought my job was juvenile to the point of being shameful. It felt as if she'd been lying to me for twenty years. I couldn't remember if we had ever talked about it—but if we had I'd probably snapped, "I've made up my mind" and dismissed her advice.

She asked, "Would you hand me the melk?" pronouncing the word "milk" with her strong Buffalo accent.

"Are you in, uh, a relationship?" she asked. Relationship was a new term for my mother, and she was still getting used to saying the word.

I sighed. "I am."

"You don't sound too happy about it."

I confessed that I was going to break up with him.

"I'm sorry to hear that."

"Thanks."

"Is it all right to ask what's wrong?"

I explained that there were several things but mostly it was because he became a conservative Republican.

"Do you argue about anything else other than politics?"

"No. Not really."

"Sounds perfect to me."

"We disagree about the president."

"He'll be gone in two years. At least that fight will end. Some fights last forever."

I didn't want to discuss my breakup with Taylor. I didn't want to give her any more reasons to think I was a loser. The waiter brought us our order, a plate of restaurant-produced "homemade" cookies. The chocolate chips looked artfully placed by the curator of cookies.

"I didn't like John's last boyfriend," she admitted. "He always wore these ridiculously pointy-toed dress shoes. You can't trust a man who wants his feet to be the center of attention; it makes you suspect him of trying to distract you from closely observing his lying face."

She was talking about Matteo. I knew she didn't care for him, but had never heard her express her distaste so directly. She was right about him. He was a liar who once tried to tell me a hickey on his neck had been caused by walking into a stop sign.

I flagged down the waiter to ask for our bill. I wanted to get out of there and insisted on paying, which I knew would endear me to my mother since we both liked having someone else pick up the check. She strolled alongside me as I scanned the galleries looking for Junior and Taylor. I found them standing in front of Andy Warhol's *100 Cans* but didn't say anything and just stared off into space.

"Are you all right?" Junior asked.

"It's nothing."

"What's wrong?"

I didn't want to him to lose confidence when he was just starting out on his new career and also have him become angry and resentful about our mother.

"Nothing."

Junior's face snarled. "Just tell me."

I snapped back, "Mom thinks we're losers for loving comic books!"

Junior looked toward our mother, who'd stopped to examine a new acquisition. "Not so loud," he said.

He asked me what she said and I told him. Then he asked me, "Has she ever said anything to you?"

"No."

"Then she clearly never told you because she knows it would hurt your feelings. She never wanted to ruin our dream."

He was right. She never undermined our confidence even though she disapproved of our career choice. I had many friends whose parents crushed their dreams before they had a chance to fail. She walked up beside me. I had to stop thinking of her as Mom, because I felt I'd accidentally say it at some point.

"Did you enjoy the museum?" she asked Taylor. "Sometimes I don't like the art, but I love seeing the people."

Taylor praised the museum as I'd expected. I was usually the one who suggested seeing an art exhibit, but he usually enjoyed them, often noticing things only a scientist would see. In Oslo he had been fascinated by the theory that the red sky in Edvard Munch's *The Scream* was inspired by the explosion of Krakatoa in 1883. He spent a weekend researching volcanic meteorology when we returned home. I'd made Taylor laugh when I told him, "Leave it to a scientist to find a way to talk about the weather through great art."

The weather in Buffalo had changed since we entered the museum. Dark clouds had rolled in off the lake and the wind had picked up. It had the feel of a thunderstorm: Mother Nature breathing down your neck. On the drive home, we discussed whether we would go out on the boat. My mother announced that she didn't care one way or the other; she was just glad to have Junior home.

We pulled up to the house and found my father playing lawn darts in the backyard with a friend whose back was to us. He was balding with gray hair and was dressed in a red short-sleeved shirt, chinos, and cowboy boots. He easily tossed his dart, which cleanly arced through the air and landed within the plastic hoop on the ground. Then I noticed a black satchel sitting on the ground. The man turned around, and Cheney chuckled triumphantly. I panicked and considered letting my mother out and stepping on the gas. But what if he did something to them? He appeared to be unarmed, not counting the lawn dart in his hand. I wasn't going back to my time until after Junior and I spoke to Carol, but I did want to know what the fuck he wanted with my parents.

"You'll never beat me," bragged Cheney. "Every time I toss, I just imagine a liberal in the hoop—then bull's-eye!"

My father grinned politely as he picked up his bottle of Genny Cream Ale and took a swig, and then Cheney did the same. It was inconceivable that my father was chummy with Dick Cheney. Somehow it would have been less disconcerting to see him playing lawn darts with Genghis Khan.

"Who the hell is that?" my mother whispered. She intensely disliked anyone infringing on time spent with her family. She tolerated her children bringing home visitors, because she thought entertaining their friends encouraged her children to visit. But her husband wasn't going anywhere and she wasn't obligated to entertain *his* friends.

"It's *him*," Taylor said emphatically. "The guy who came to see me."

"Humpty Dumpty over there is Dick Cheney?" Junior asked. "He looks like he should be chasing us in a golf cart."

"He's more dragon's egg than Humpty Dumpty," I warned. "Don't underestimate him. He's one of the most cunning and vicious politicians in American history."

My mother had been listening. "You know him?"

I nodded. "We know him from New York."

"Why is he here?" she asked.

"I'm not sure," I said. I wasn't exactly sure what to tell her. Branding him as a war criminal would be hard to convey in the thirty seconds we had before we'd be standing next to him.

"Do you like him?" she asked.

"No."

"Why not?"

"He's not nice," I said. My comment sounded like faint disparagement, but I knew that whenever my mother used that phrase, it was always damning.

"Politicians," my mother snarled. "Sometimes I think we need freedom *from* speeches."

Junior and Taylor looked to me for some guidance as we walked into the backyard.

"Let's just see what he has to say," I said, visibly patting my backpack for Junior and Taylor's sake. I had one of my loaded Glocks inside.

"He better not ask him to go out on the boat," my mother warned.

"There wouldn't be room for all of us," Junior observed.

My mother cheered up. "You're right!"

I looked over at Taylor and widened my eyes to signal that we'd have to improvise, as we walked to where the vice president and my father were standing. I overheard my father asking, "Why is a congressman from Wyoming looking me up in Buffalo?"

"Well, I'm working. Next year's the fortieth anniversary of the Roswell crash and I'm trying to get Congress to open a full-scale re-investigation. And I heard you're pretty knowledgeable."

Until that moment I never would have believed my father was susceptible to flattery, but his face glowed like a UFO. Then his smile vanished as his innate skepticism returned. (A person could be both a true believer and a knee-jerk skeptic, as my father proved repeatedly.)

"How do I know you're not just trying to use me for a new disin-formation campaign?"

"You don't know," Cheney said. "And I don't know if I'm being lied to by my contacts in the administration. They could be using me. But isn't that one of the greatest things about being an American? We're free to believe our government is lying to us and will never reveal the truth about anything."

My father nodded in agreement. Cheney proved once again that the most easily gulled patsies in America are white men who don't trust anyone.

"So what do you think?" my father asked. "Was it an alien spacecraft? Were alien bodies recovered? Have you been briefed on the crash?"

"Well, if I'd been briefed, I'm sure it was probably classified and I'd not be allowed to talk about it."

My father's face crash landed. Cheney's lips jumped, but it would be an exaggeration to say he smiled.

"I can tell you this. In July 1947, there were newspaper reports of a flying saucer crashing in Roswell, New Mexico, and in November 1947, the most important invention of the twentieth century, the transistor, the first semiconductor, was 'invented.' You do the math."

"I knew it!" my father said as he glanced at Cheney's empty beer bottle. "We need to get you a refill." Then my father remembered his manners. "This is my son, John, and his friends Taylor and Kurt and my wife, Sue." At the sound of her name, my mother offered a put-on grin that looked as if she had found the missing half of Cheney's smile. "This is Dick Cheney. He's a congressman from Wyoming."

"*The* congressman from Wyoming," Cheney corrected. "We only have one."

Taylor stepped forward and shook Cheney's hand. The vice president looked him in the eye. "Glad to meet someone here who's registered Republican." Taylor's jaw dropped as Junior and I burned with outrage. Cheney stood there with the same stingy smile, leaving his face half-cocked for nasty. Taylor had always claimed that he was registered as an independent, and now Cheney had forced him out of the voting booth.

"You are?" I asked.

Taylor's cheeks flushed. "I signed up on an impulse in '84. But I registered as an independent last year."

"Independent of a brain," I sneered.

Junior stepped forward awkwardly to shake Cheney's hand. After the vice president said his own name, he jerked a thumb to the car we'd pulled up in. "I was glad you weren't driving today after that DUI accident your friend Cliff had." Cheney grimace-grinned, which made it appear that he found happiness excruciatingly painful. I'd never told my parents that I'd been a passenger in a car accident in college. It was during a visit to see my friend Cliff Briando at SUNY Brockport for a weekend of nonstop beer drinking and bong hits. No one was hurt when Cliff's car hit a tree, but he had insisted we leave before the cops came. Our concerned mother now immediately asked Junior about it, pressing him for an explanation. He had to fess up.

"Don't be too hard on the boy," Cheney advised. "It's not a good thing, but it shouldn't hurt his career plans. Nobody expects someone who sells *Batman* for a living to be perfect." Cheney leisurely picked at the label on his beer bottle with a thumbnail. "Look, I had a DUI when I was young and it never damaged my prospects. And I work with someone whose wife went through a stop sign and plowed into a car, killing her high school sweetheart. She doesn't talk about it, naturally, but she chain-smokes and suffers from bouts of depression."

Cheney glanced at me. He clearly was signaling we were the only ones here who knew that the someone he worked with was the president of the United States.

"Well," I said, "some people have car accidents while other people have hunting accidents and shoot their friends in the face."

He ignored my comment about his infamous hunting accident and suddenly turned toward my mother. "I'm sure you know about depression. You've been down, haven't you?"

My mother's face recoiled. She rarely talked with her family about her period of deep depression twenty years earlier, and she never discussed it with strangers. "Yes, but I came back!" She hurtled the phrase at him. He had definitely pissed her off. Cheney's use of the phrase "you've been down" struck me as odd and menacing; it was the exact phrase my mother used when she discussed her depression. Evidently, the vice president had background checks done on all of us and seemed to know everything about our histories.

I stepped forward and shook his hand. He didn't say anything for a moment, and then clearly grinned. "Nice to see you again, PigBitch479."

My mother's blue eyes flashed. "What did you just say?" she asked Cheney.

"It's just a little joke we have," he said genially.

"Well, it's not very nice," my mother responded.

I'm sure my face turned red. I'd only used that secret screen name once, one afternoon after Taylor and I had a fight in the morning. I'd found a large check he'd written to the Republican National Committee. He went off to work on his time machine, and during the afternoon my anger became horniness and I decided to have cybersex. The screen name I created had actually been a goofy homage to Taylor and myself since I was the slob or pig in our relationship and he was the bitch. Everyone standing around Cheney and me had a did-he-say-what-I-think-he-said look of social stupefaction. I had to hand it to Cheney; he took a sip of beer, clearly enjoying that he wasn't about to explain anything.

"Nice to meet you, 'Bin Laden Determined to Strike—August 6, 2001,'" I replied.

I thought that CIA warning should be shouted at him and Bush every day for the rest of their lives. I was disappointed that Cheney's expression didn't change. His ice-blue eyes continued to deny the existence of global warming.

"Does anyone want a beer?" my father asked to ease the tension. "I'm just going to run to the store."

"I feel bad drinking in front of an alcoholic," Cheney said with a nod toward me. "Summers must be hard. I work with a dry drunk and he gets mean every summer like clockwork. His staff and my staff just wish he'd have one Jim Beam and quit bustin' our chops."

His comparing me to George W. Bush infuriated me. My mother and father looked at me with newfound suspicion. Their son was associating with someone who'd overcome his addiction to alcohol; this seemed forbidding to them. In our family, sobriety was the great unknown.

"Oh, don't torture yourself," I said. "I'd rather have you drowning your sorrows with beer than waterboarding me."

The right side of his mouth twitched for an instant.

"You're a bodybuilder; surely you've heard 'no pain, no gain.' The same goes in politics and warfare."

The sun went behind a cloud, which seemed to signal that even it was afraid of him. Everyone was still watching us, but my mother picked up my father's empty beer bottle off a table. She looked at me, then at the vice president.

"If you stay out here drinking, you'll be hit by lightning."

It was a warning to us, but it sounded like she was cursing Cheney. My father turned toward Junior. "Dick worked as chief of staff for President Ford. And Ford was a member of the Warren Commission."

"I hate to disappoint you," Cheney said, "but Ford was convinced by the lone gunman theory."

"What do you think?"

"Just because you have a lone gunman doesn't mean there aren't a lot of hands pulling the trigger."

My father nodded in agreement. "Have you heard this story going around about this time machine? Supposedly the government's been working on one for twenty years."

"That's all we need. Liberal jackasses trying to change history."

"I know, it sounded a little nuts to me. But you never know."

"And you never will." Cheney stopped smiling, which actually seemed to make him happier. His cheeks became rosier and his posture relaxed; it was like watching a thorn blossom.

"I'll be right back," my father said. "I'm going to just run to the store."

He walked over to his large convertible, and as soon as he pulled away my mother turned on Cheney.

"All right, get out," she said. He appeared unsure if she was serious or not. "I mean it. Leave."

"Mom," Junior said tentatively, which only irritated her further. He wasn't trying to stop her, but just making sure she didn't endanger herself or us.

"We don't know him and he's calling our guests . . . names." She turned to Cheney. "Get the hell off our property or I'm calling the police."

"I need to talk to these gentlemen in private," Cheney announced, using his hands to indicate the three of us. "My daughter Mary really likes Wonder Woman and I thought they could help fill some gaps in her collection."

My mother appeared conflicted; she knew Junior could make some money, but she also disliked Cheney.

"Your son has to make all the sales he can or he's going to end up broke at forty."

That was it. She could express doubts about her children's choices, but strangers couldn't. "And what do *your* kids do for work?" she snapped.

"They work for me," he replied.

"Figures. Too stupid to go out and do it on their own. Probably no one else would hire them."

I'd never seen Cheney angry up close before, but when his face turned purple I understood why he'd had four heart attacks.

"My son doesn't need your money now or then." Mom's blue eyes drilled Junior. "Do you need to talk to him?"

"No," he responded. "I don't even know him."

"That's enough for me," she said. "Get the hell off my property."

Cheney picked up the satchel that was sitting behind a lawn chair. It was too small to hold a rifle but large enough for a pistol. If he made any motion to open it, I'd pull out my Glock.

Cheney didn't appear to be leaving. He stood grimace-grinning at us until my mother shouted, "Did you hear me? Get the fuck out of here." Her voice quavered briefly. "I can't believe you made me use the F word in front of company." Cheney took his right hand and pressed a button on the watch he wore on his left arm. Obviously, he had refused to wear a bracelet. Cheney vanished and our mother spun toward me, her blue eyes flashing. "What the hell is going on?"

9

COMING OUT TO YOUR MOM as yourself from twenty years in the future is a lot more difficult than coming out to her as gay. For one thing, my mother didn't demand proof that I was gay: she took my word for it; but she accepted my identity as Junior-in-twenty only after Junior and Taylor vouched for me, and after I took a ballpoint pen and inked up my and Junior's right thumbs and showed her that our prints matched. She thought we were kidding at first but then came around to seeming to believe us. Predictably, both of my coming out stories received the same response.

"What are we going to tell your father?"

We'd moved inside the house and were sitting in the large, sunny living room, drinking iced tea, while Ravi dozed in a patch of sunlight on the carpet. I was tempted to remind my mother she had said the exact same thing a year earlier when Junior came out to her. And my reaction was still the same. He'd handle the news better than she would. He already believed in flying saucers and ancient Greek supercomputers; his son traveling to the past in a time machine wasn't much more of a stretch.

She couldn't take her eyes off my scalp. Her disappointment in my hair loss made me feel like a careless child. She noticed that I noticed her staring. "I'm sorry. It's going to take me a while to get used to it." She gestured vaguely in the direction of her hair.

Her next question was "Who was that?" I gave her a brief description and short history of Dick Cheney. I assumed she would find my story impossible to believe, but she had a less idealistic view of human nature than I did. She seemed to think a homicidal vice president was more probable than little green men.

"What's not to believe?" she said. "I know for a fact that he's an asshole, and now you tell me he's the vice president." She smiled and shook her head. "Oh, I shouldn't talk like that." She habitually apologized for her cursing, and my sister and I always dreamed that one day she'd say, "Fuck! I can't believe I swore again!"

I didn't tell her that Taylor would someday be the boyfriend with whom I would eventually want to break up. She would understandably become confused about whether she should love him now or hate him later. Her loyalty was always with me—she never sided with any of my exes—and her knowing that Taylor wasn't permanently affixed to our family would make her begrudge him every time she sent him a check for his birthday, cooked him dinner, or offered him a second glass of wine.

Our safety was her next concern. She wanted to know what we were doing and basically implied that the best way to ensure our well-being would be for me to immediately return to my own time. I couldn't do that. Junior and I looked at each other. I didn't want to tell her about Carol's suicide, but then thought, since we'd all eventually feel responsible for her death, maybe the best plan of action would be to make everyone feel responsible for keeping her alive. My mother observed Junior and me glancing at each other.

"What now?" she asked. It was a phrase that she used throughout her life as an acknowledgment of pending bad news while also an expression of her impatience to deal with it.

At that moment I was disoriented about whose life I was leading: mine from the old present or mine from the new present? When my sister killed herself, I'd called my brother Kevin that night, and he had volunteered to drive in from Syracuse the next morning to tell my mother so she wouldn't be alone when she heard the news. I lived in New York City and would undergo my own trial of driving to the hospital in New Jersey and seeing Carol's body on a respirator with raw gunshot wounds poorly bandaged on both sides of her head. The next morning I would have to demand that the doctors take her off the respirator. But even during my ordeal, I knew Kevin had the more heart-breaking experience awaiting him, telling a mother about the death of her child. For a parent, contemplating the death of your child is taboo, unspeakable, and unthinkable; and before allowing that primordial fear, that saber-toothed black cat to cross your mind, you stop and think of something else, anything else. Even the most rational parents believe that thought is an ill omen. I felt distraught. Through a quirk of time travel, my brother's horrible duty was now mine.

"Fifteen years from now Carol will fall into a severe depression," I began haltingly, adding, "like you did" not to hurt or blame her, but to suggest the magnitude of the crisis. My mother had struggled for years with severe depression, hospitalizations, electroshock therapy, and for a time she even wore a wig. She felt that she couldn't take care of her hair, let alone care for four children and a husband. She did understand the comparison, because her skepticism changed into rapt concern. "And she'll kill herself," I added.

I didn't know how she'd react when I said those brutal words—with disbelief, tears, or even anger directed toward me. She looked bewildered; then her blue eyes shadowed and her expression became lifeless. She turned toward Junior. "Do you believe him?" He nodded and replied in a low voice, "I do."

"Not my Carol," she muttered softly. She teared up before asking, "How did this happen?"

I tried to clarify her question. "How did she do it?"

"No. I don't want to know that! What led her to this?"

It would take a coroner with the insight of Shakespeare or Chekhov to write out the actual cause of death of a suicide. Everyone connected to the victim feels guilty. Each survivor searches his memory, questions his actions and inactions, wonders if doing one thing differently could have made a difference. Shrinks tell survivors they aren't responsible for someone's suicide. While that makes sense intellectually, it's hard to believe emotionally because life demonstrates daily how our actions cause feelings that rule our lives. You can start your day in a bad mood after spilling coffee on a clean shirt, or begin the day feeling elated after discovering that you do have enough milk for one more bowl of cereal. We've all heard stories that illustrate the role happenstance plays in our survival, how someone missed taking the plane that crashed when he got stuck in traffic. After a suicide, every survivor measures everything he did or said with the same incidental life or death consequences. If only we'd done this or that, he or she might have lived.

I described to my mother how Carol's husband, Ed, would be in a car accident, how he'd have several back operations, how he'd go on disability in his early thirties, then become addicted to painkillers. And then how Carol would slip into a deep depression, feeling she had no way out. I held back on some things. Carol's failed marriage played a large part in her death, and if my mother felt that my brother-in-law was endangering her daughter's life in the slightest way, she'd turn against him now, immediately and irrevocably, creating a new set of problems.

"Didn't we help her?" my mother asked. "Did you? Did Kevin, Alan, and Dad? Did I?" She became agitated and seemed poised to board the next plane to California. I reassured her we didn't see it coming. "Her last year was bad," I explained. "She had been depressed for months, but she finally said that she was starting to feel better. On the day she died she called me three times. Asking me about little things. I thought it was strange but not worrisome. I asked her to come to my house for dinner that night. I really insisted, but she said, 'No.'"

My mother softened when she heard this and looked at Junior. "She loves her John."

I explained how when things got bad, I called Carol every day, asked her to move in with me—I almost said "us," before I realized I would need to explain that Taylor would become my boyfriend. "I repeatedly told Carol how much I loved her," I said, tearing up. It was a reversal of roles. I'd always been the one who called Carol asking for her help. She helped me buy my first car, rent my first apartment, and hire my first plumber and electrician. On some level it was difficult to imagine her feeling helpless.

"I only figured out later that if you're the one who everyone in your family goes to for help, then whom do you turn to when you need help?"

"What can we do?" my mother asked.

Without sounding like I was blaming her for my sister's death, I tried to think of a way to gently suggest to my mother that she could help Carol by not being so critical of her. I explained that we would all feel complicit with her death and that we had to be aware of what we said, because criticism could hurt her. My mother seemed to understand, but I had my doubts. My mother was sweet with her sons but much tougher on her daughter, just as her own mother favored her brother over her. My sister was also equally tough on my mother and never forgot a slight or insult. Carol once angrily mentioned to me, when she was in her late thirties, how my mother had not brought her a bouquet of flowers when she came backstage after the junior class show. In fucking high school. I was tempted to tell her that she and my mother should celebrate the twentieth reunion of her grudge, but I didn't, since she was already furious.

I shied away from confronting my family's craziness. I was brought up to believe unconditional love is a complete surrender of all your moral, ethical, and aesthetic standards. It means never discussing open secrets, overlooking failings, ignoring lapses of judgment, disregarding irrational dislikes and outright prejudices, consenting to disastrous choices about love and hairstyles, and bestowing blanket tolerance for addictions ranging from alcohol to Xanax. (If, God forbid, someone in our family needed a guide dog, it would also have to be trained to look the other way.)

I frequently received back-to-back phone calls from my sister and mother, each bemoaning the other one's nastiness. It was frustrating trying to mediate a short truce between them before another battle started. Often there were times when negotiations were impossible, as they'd stopped speaking to each other. It always upset me and I would always try to persuade one of them to relent, but I also appreciated that by not communicating they were prevented from saying anything hurtful. It irritated me that they wasted their precious hostility on each other instead of directing it against deserving strangers like I did.

I looked at my mother and tried to believe that she would watch her tongue for the next fifteen years without my having to address her troubling relationship with her daughter. She loved Carol. I had no doubt about that. I believed my mother could change her ways in order to save her daughter's life. My fantasy ended when I thought, We have to hope for the best. In our family hoping for the best was a notion that children gave up before they stopped believing in the Tooth Fairy. You need to take action and can't just sit around hoping.

"You two will fight a lot over the next fifteen years and you'll need to be careful about what you say to Carol. It hurts her and she never forgets anything."

Junior frowned slightly before my mother let me have it. Her temperament was essentially easygoing, but questioning my mother's conduct with her children brought out the mama bear in her. I've noticed how naturalists never mention that mama bears protect their reputations more aggressively than they defend their cubs.

"Don't you come from the future blaming me for her death! She's the one who likes to fight. I don't."

I didn't point out that she seemed to be enjoying the dispute she was having with me.

"Mom, I'm not blaming you. I just don't want to leave any bases uncovered. We don't know what might help her so we have to try everything. We all just have to be more aware of Carol's problems."

"Don't call me 'Mom.' I just met you! She starts the fights."

I looked angrily toward Junior, waiting for him to back me up. It's not like he couldn't; my sister and mother had been battling since Carol was in high school.

"Mom, you both say mean things," Junior said.

"Don't team up with him! How do we even know he's telling the truth?"

Junior rubbed his chin before answering her. It was strange to witness a habitual gesture that I recognized but had never seen before.

"Because only someone from our family would know how screwed up your relationship with Carol can be." We both knew his statement could infuriate my mother, and I admired Junior's diplomatic use of "screwed up" instead of "fucked up" and "can be" instead of "is." "And if he's me— and he is—then he knows that will piss you off and only something as big as Carol's death would make me kick over that can of worms."

My mother considered this and calmed down, but couldn't resist adding, "If we're screwed up, it's her fault."

Junior walked over to where my mother was seated on the couch and sat down next to her. I sat in a rocking chair, comforted by the back-and-forth oscillation, which mirrored my own indecisiveness. Taylor was seated in my father's orange velour recliner, his face fixed in an expression of polite horror. I couldn't imagine Taylor wanting to date Junior. The normal course of dating is that you meet the family and witness how fucked up they are only *after* you've fallen in love. This free sample of family would make me think twice about buying the product.

"That's the problem," Junior said. "At this point we can't figure out whose fault it is. We don't know who cast the first stone, because you're both surrounded by rock piles. We just need one of you to stop it."

Junior's eloquence surprised me. I was proud of him and, I guess, of myself.

"Well, if I have to change, then what about you and your brothers?"

Junior looked at me, signaling with his eyes that it was my turn to answer her. It was kind of nice having a tag-team partner to assist me in an argument with my mother, and I wondered if identical twins felt a mutual advantage also. "Yes," I said. "There's . . . that . . . I . . ." I glanced toward Junior and changed pronouns. "We all need to do things differently. I made at least one decision that I deeply regret." I explained that I should have flown out to California when my sister suddenly dropped out of rehab for her addiction to painkillers. I was on the other side of the country, driving to a stupid comic book convention, and we had talked for hours on my cell phone as she reassured me that she knew what she was doing. (First, I had to explain to my mother how everyone would have cell phones in twenty years—including her—then I explained that that month I went over my allotted minutes and my next cell phone bill was six hundred dollars.) Carol had claimed the rehab center wasn't what she'd expected; it was dirty and depressing and she could find a better rehab program closer to home. I wasn't there to verify her story, and yet she had always seemed sensible and I sort of believed her, although I also suspected she was lying. I asked her if she was just backing out of rehab and she answered no. And then I asked her if she was lying to me, which in retrospect seems like the dumbest question ever. My sister had a long, freely confessed history of deception. I don't think she ever had a job where she didn't end up committing some form of white-collar crime in order to get back at her stupid, malicious, and frequently sexually harassing male bosses.

It had never occurred to me that she would kill herself. Violent suicide was the one vice that didn't appear to run in our family; we preferred more sedentary forms of self-destruction. Many of my relatives spent decades reclining in front of their televisions, looking as if they were rehearsing for being laid out in a box. In our family, food, alcohol, and tobacco were the Three Graces of suicide; their irresistible appeal was that they allowed you to enjoy life while you ended it.

When my sister needed help, I didn't understand that in order to save someone's fucked-up life, there are no shortcuts, and you can't throw someone a life preserver from the comfort of a deck chair. I begged Carol to stay in the city where the rehab center was located and told her I'd join her there in two days. She said yes, then the following afternoon she called to inform me that she'd flown home. At the time, it was easier to accept her promise that she would go into rehab near her house than it was for me to drop everything and fly to her and insist that she stay in rehab. It was a monumental miscalculation, and while I didn't pull the trigger on the gun that killed her, I convicted myself of being a coconspirator. Her death created unappeasable guilt, because whatever I could have done seemed in retrospect so small a price to pay in comparison to my loss.

"It doesn't matter that I didn't know she was suicidal," I said in summation. "I still wish I had a second chance."

Junior, Taylor, and my mother were understandably subdued after my confession. My mother broke the silence. "It's not something you could know. If we went around thinking everyone might be planning on killing themselves, we'd be more nuts than them."

Junior and I laughed at her logic, which was irrefutable, making my mother smile.

"I'm right," she declared. "Aren't I?"

"You're right," Taylor said. He could have never known beforehand—even her children wouldn't have known for sure—but his affirmation didn't strike my mother as supportive, it struck her as interfering. She glared at him. "Tell me why you're here again?"

Taylor glanced at Junior and me, asking for permission to speak. I nodded, realizing the future was already present. My mother had lost a daughter, she might as well gain a son-in-law.

"I'll become John's boyfriend and invent a time machine."

My mother took this in, then glanced at his hair. "Will you still have that blue streak?"

Everyone laughed, and I assured her he wouldn't.

"Good," my mother said before she smiled warmly at Taylor.

I saw a bowl filled with sponge candy sitting on the coffee table and remembered something else I needed to tell my mother.

"Carol's going to gain a lot of weight over the next fifteen years and you're going to say things about it that will hurt her."

"She's going to get fat too?" my mother asked. She sounded as if that were reason enough to kill yourself.

"That kind of comment doesn't help," Junior said.

Her reaction convinced me that saving Carol's life was going to be tougher than I thought. There were so many uncontrollable variables, even with foreknowledge to guide you. There was one reason to be optimistic, though: clearly I was disrupting the past, irrevocably fucking up my life and possibly Taylor's and my mother's and even my sister's in order to save my sister. We weren't assured of success, but at least we wouldn't regret not having tried to do something.

My mother sighed. Her expression was grim but stoical. "Well, thanks for dropping by; the next fifteen years sound like fun."

"Don't worry about the next fifteen," I responded. "If we save Carol, the rest of our lives will be much happier."

She considered what I'd said and her mood brightened. "You're right. Helping Carol's the important thing." I was always impressed with how, no matter how riled up my mother became, she could always step outside of herself and focus on someone else's plight. She had worn slippers in a psychiatric hospital, and the experience seemed to give her a universal ability to walk in anyone else's shoes. When I had called home immediately after my brother had told my mother the news of Carol's death, I heard her uncontrollable wailing in the background, and my brother told her I was on the phone. When she sobbed, "Oh, John . . . ," I said, "I'm sorry, Mom," but couldn't continue, as I began to violently bawl in the lobby of the hospital. My mother abruptly stopped crying and said to my brother, "Oh, John loved Carol." She would cry again over the next weeks and months, but in an extraordinary display of compassion, she would concern herself with comforting her sons with their grief rather than addressing her own pain. She smiled at Taylor. "You look like someone just hit you."

"It's a lot to take in," he said. "One minute you're telling the vice president to get the F out, the next, we're hearing something unbearably sad."

His comment wasn't a criticism of our family, but my mother bristled at the suggestion of imperfection.

"At least we're not dull."

"I still can't believe you gave him the boot," Taylor observed.

She smiled proudly. "I'm festy."

Junior and I glanced at each other. Our mother mispronounced words frequently, and her neologisms usually became prized additions to our family's vocabulary.

"'Festy'? Mom, it's *feisty*," Junior corrected her.

"Oh, shut up. Or I'll tell you to get the F out." Her choice of wording suddenly seemed questionable and her expression became solemn. "I'd better not say that anymore."

We heard my father's car door slam, and my mother looked out the window. She insisted we couldn't tell my father about Cheney's disappearance or Carol's suicide. "He doesn't need to know. It will only upset him." We rarely questioned my mother's policy of keeping certain information from my father. It sounded dubious that she maintained that a tough cop who'd been in brawls, hostage standoffs, and prison riots would crumple under the blow of an indiscreet revelation. But her view of his character was ultimately proven right. He was fragile and couldn't handle his retirement. As my father walked in the back door carrying a twelve-pack of beer, it seemed unthinkable to tell Junior and my mother, "Oh, hey, I forgot to mention Dad's going to drink himself to death." They'd rightfully want to kill me and then have to deal with three deaths in the family.

My father asked, "What happened to Congressman Cheney?" There was a split second of indecision before Junior explained that he received an urgent phone call about some UFO sightings over Niagara Falls. "He said that he would be in touch."

"It's too bad; I was going to invite him to stay for dinner."

My mother harrumphed. "Then you'd have to cook it. I wouldn't feed that bastard." My mother hated cursing, but she used "bastard" frequently and without apology.

My father appeared to be slightly surprised but didn't say anything. We all moved into the kitchen, and my mother opened the refrigerator and removed several large packages of hamburger. The first rumble of thunder caused everyone to stop and listen.

"It's gonna pour," my father said as he put the beers in the fridge. "I don't think we'll get out on the river tonight."

Everyone, except my father, pretended to be crestfallen, but we were happy to stay home. My mother bustled around the kitchen, clapping together hamburgers for the grill while Junior and Taylor sat in the living room, flipping channels as they flirted with each other. In some ways, their mutual attraction was as predictable as a high school science experiment, proof that if you mix two known ingredients, the same chemical reaction would result.

As we sat down at the dining room table, my father asked, "After dinner, do you guys want to go to Dom's for a beer?" Dom's Tap Room was a bar on Military Road. Buffalo's neighborhoods were filled with first-named joints called Mickey's, Stan's, or Dom's, always established on the ground floors of grimy, two-story asbestos-shingled houses. These bars always had an apartment above them, suggesting to me that Mickey was a considerate alcoholic who felt guilty about all the time he spent out drinking with his buddies when he should be at home drinking with his family. Then Mickey had a brainstorm and suggested to his wife that they convert the ground floor of their house into a gin mill where he could drink at home *with his buddies*.

I winced inwardly when Junior eagerly accepted our father's invitation. He didn't know our father would die from alcoholism. As we passed a plate of hamburgers, a platter of corn on the cob, and bowls of potato and green salads around the table, I had no appetite and felt scared. I'd decided to broach the subject of his impending alcoholism with my father. It had the feel of a Last Supper where I was going to tell the host his body was going to turn into Scotch and soda. My father might say I was insane and ask me to leave. It would be just our luck that the only conspiracy theory he'd refuse to believe would be that a lone drinker was going to assassinate him. Junior and my mother would be hearing the news for the first time and would surely become furious and turn on me. But it had to be done, because we were leaving the next day. I'd never discussed my father's life with him before, and it felt presumptuous that now I was going to talk with him about his death. It also seemed unfair that I was preparing to out my father as an alcoholic before he became one; it felt unconscionably premature, as if he'd rushed me into discovering my sexual orientation at age eight by pointing out exactly why I enjoyed watching Mr. Universe taking off his shirt on that episode of *The Beverly Hillbillies*. I hated my life right then but thought maybe I could save my father's life.

The meal began on a slightly awkward note as Junior and I refused the potato salad—it contained big chunks of celery and little bits of onion—our duo of don't eats. My mother seemed to forget who I was because she asked me, "Would you like some potato salad?"

"No thanks," I said.

"You don't like potato salad?" my mother asked. Junior and I looked at each other.

"No," I replied. "I'm not big on celery."

"Really?" my father said. "John doesn't like celery either." He was amused by our seemingly coincidental dislikes, but our mother became so rattled that she almost blew my cover and spilled some white wine on the tablecloth.

"People like different things," she said with put-on good cheer as she blotted the stain.

Near the end of the meal, when our plates were splattered with ketchup and smeared with mayonnaise, I cleared my throat. I picked up my glass of water and gulped down half of it. My hand shook as I set it down.

"Tom," I said, addressing my father. "You know that time machine you heard about. It actually does exist. I'm your son John from the future. I traveled here in a time machine, and I have to warn you that six years after you retire from the state police, you'll drink yourself to death."

My father listened attentively, but his blank expression made it appear that if he looked in a mirror he wouldn't be able to tell what he was thinking either.

"Oh, Jesus," Taylor said, staring at me with disbelief.

My mother shouted at me, "What is wrong with you?" while Junior spat out, "You liar!"

My father turned toward Junior and my mother. "You knew about this?"

"No," they shouted in unison.

"Is this why a congressman from Wyoming suddenly showed up in our backyard?"

"Well, sort of," Junior said. My mother became angrier and hissed at him. "This is all your fault! Look at the asshole you'll become."

"It's not my fault. I barely know him. He lied to me." Junior turned on me. "You said they wouldn't die."

"I didn't want to bum you out."

"Shouldn't I be the one who's bummed out?" my father asked.

No one answered him, but our silence was a reply.

"Do you believe him?" my father asked, looking around the table.

Junior and my mother nodded and in turn mumbled, "Yes."

My father was startled by my mother's corroboration. He might have doubted the veracity of Junior, but my mother's acceptance of my story was significant. She was routinely agnostic about everything from God to her correct weight on the bathroom scale. If she bought her time-traveling son then it had to be true.

My father studied Junior and me closely. "You do look alike, but I just thought all gay guys looked alike."

"I thought the same thing," my mother admitted.

Junior looked at me then turned his head away in disgust. "Thanks for letting me know that I'll become a lying weasel in twenty years."

"What was I supposed to do? Let Dad drink himself to death? Would you rather I hadn't said anything?"

"Yes!" my mother and Junior answered jointly.

"I don't know if I'd like that," my father said dryly before he turned toward Taylor. "What's your part in all this?"

"I invent the time machine and become John's . . ." He seemed to be weighing whether he felt comfortable saying boyfriend to my father. "His . . . um, partner."

"Do us all a favor, will you? Don't invent it," my mother said. "And while you're at it, take my advice and don't become John's partner. You don't want any part of this family."

Taylor crumpled up his napkin, and Junior sprang to his defense: "It's better to know about a problem beforehand so we can talk about and deal with it."

It had to be a better strategy than our old method, I thought, where we wouldn't even discuss our problems during our problems. My father reached for his bottle of beer and my mother barked, "Tom!"

"What?"

"We have enough problems in this family without you drinking yourself to death. Is everyone in this family nuts?"

"I have a few beers every now and then. I'm not an alcoholic."

"Not now you aren't. But I can't trust any of you." She poked a thumb toward Junior. "He wasn't gay last year!"

My father appeared to think she had a good argument. In fact, we all did. My mother looked at Junior and shook her head. "I knew you shouldn't have told Dad."

Junior poured himself a glass of wine, as he realized she was blaming his coming out for our father's alcoholism. "That's crazy," he said. "He won't start drinking because he found out I'm gay."

"How do you know?" she asked. "One follows the other."

My father pushed away his plate. "What's crazy is that my son from the future came in a time machine to tell me I'll end up drinking myself to death."

"I know it's hard to believe," I said.

"Hard to believe?" my father said. "This pushes disbelief into new territory."

"You haven't answered me," my mother said to Junior.

"Sue," my father said, "if that was going to cause me to become alcoholic, I'd be drunk now."

"He's handled it better than you have," Junior said, trying to sound impartial and not accusatory.

My mother turned on him. "So his drinking's my fault? You're blaming me for Carol's suicide and now this."

She hadn't meant to reveal Carol's death, and understood that she blew it when my father dropped his fork on his plate.

"What about Carol?" he asked.

"I'll tell you later," she said. "It's something else that's all my fault."

My father ended our conversation about his suicide and demanded an explanation of Carol's suicide. After hearing me out, he had many questions and asked how he could help. I answered, "By being alive and sober when she needs your help." My response seemed to shake him. He put down his beer.

"Neither of them's your fault," I said to our mother. "No one said that."

"You said I'll say hurtful things to Carol and she'll kill herself. Now you're saying after he retires, when it's just the two of us, he'll kill himself."

My father looked at my mother. "It's just the two of us now."

She glared at him as if he was deliberately trying to be stupid. "Not full time. You still have a job."

"You can't always pinpoint what causes what in your life," I said.

"Yes, you can," my mother responded bitterly. "At eleven a.m. this morning you showed up at my door and my life went to shit."

"I'm sorry," I said. "But I didn't want to feel I could've done something and didn't."

"You've done something, all right," my mother said. "You've made me feel I have nothing to look forward to except a two-for-one sale on caskets." Her eyes narrowed as she thought of something. "Unless we need to buy three. Am I dead in twenty years?"

"No, you're still alive."

"I was hoping I wouldn't be so I won't know you."

"We'll actually be very close."

She scowled. "I can't wait for that."

I turned to my father. "I wouldn't have said anything if I didn't think it was important."

"I hope not," he replied.

"You haven't told me what you think," I said to my father. I was tempted to add, "About anything important to you. Ever."

His body tensed and I could tell he was furious, but he tried to conceal his anger with a smile.

"What do you want me to say? Thanks for the heads-up that I'm going to screw up my life." His use of "screw up" reminded me that I never heard my father use the F word. His self-restraint was old-fashioned in a way that I admired, although I had a momentary flash of resentment. From my point of view, abstaining from saying "fuck" in front of his children for his entire life had to take more willpower than quitting drinking.

"I'm trying to help," I said.

"Well, you can't help. It's like telling me I'm going to have a heart attack. I can be on the lookout for it, but until I'm clutching my chest there's not much I can do."

"You could quit drinking before it becomes a problem."

"I could, but I'm not sure I want to on your say-so." He stood up from his seat. "Thanks to you, now every beer I have will have an especially bitter aftertaste."

I thought, This is great. Now he'll die resenting me.

"Your death really made me unhappy," I said. "It made us all unhappy."

"Well, thanks for sharing that unhappiness," he said before leaving the table. He went into the living room and sat in his chair and turned on the TV.

"Unhappiness years before it happens," my mother added as she stood up and began to clear plates. When Junior and Taylor tried to help she snapped, "Leave 'em."

I felt like a monster. It was a curse to be a fortune-teller, able to reveal people's destinies, especially the people you love. I recalled that my mother had always been disdainful about people who check their horoscopes. She'd once said, "No one ever reads, 'Tomorrow you'll be diagnosed with Lou Gehrig's disease!'" And all this pain might be unpreventable if my father's alcoholism was some unfixable genetic Make-Mine-a-Double-Helix doom. But my primary fear was that my father wasn't particularly interested in saving his own life, because the subject didn't interest him. He'd always demonstrated a wide-ranging lack of curiosity. My father wasn't really interested in too many things besides his job as a state trooper, conspiracy theories, cars and his boat, football and hockey, and his family. And he checked in on his family like he checked the weather; if we were 98.6 degrees and wind was gusting from our lungs, that was all he needed to know.

After my father's death, I became convinced the number one killer among men is boredom. Most men stay attached to their lives by their jobs, families, and sex, but my father was a few years away from retirement, his children had moved far away, and while I refused to speculate on my parents' sex lives, I couldn't imagine they were still going at it like they did when they met in high school. It almost seemed some men leave their lives as if they're walking out of a dull movie.

My mother returned to the dining room and picked up the platter that had held the corn. Our eyes met, but she turned her head away angrily. It occurred to me that I hadn't warned her about her early signs of macular degeneration and that she should start taking vitamin supplements to preserve her eyesight now. Fortunately, I gathered that it might not be the best time to bring this up. I tried to talk privately with my father later that night, but he stopped me with "I get it. I'm dead and so's Carol. We're done talking for tonight." His tone of voice was adamant, and while I considered pressing on, I didn't. In my heart I agreed with him. As I was getting ready for bed, I overheard from the kitchen my mother saying to Junior, "You better not end up like him."

"I won't," he promised.

10

OUR GOOD-BYES THE NEXT MORNING were awkward. My mother rose to the occasion and hugged and kissed all three of us after privately warning us to be on the lookout for Cheney.

"He seems more mean than smart," she said. "I've spent my life avoiding men like him and you should too."

Our father came outside while we were loading up the car and asked me how Camaros drove. It meant either he was no longer angry or had decided to pretend that he was no longer angry. With my father's emotions, that was about as specific as you could get. When it was time to leave, I knew I might never see him again, and even though I felt like an imposter son, I said, "I love you." Then he said, "I love you, too." I could have burst into tears. Of course, I didn't. I was standing in front of my father and my crying would have embarrassed both of us.

Leaving Buffalo, we drove past the closed, desolate Bethlehem Steel plant that runs for miles along Lake Erie, the cold smokestacks reminding me of columns remaining standing after a temple has fallen into ruins. Taylor asked how many people once worked there. "I think thirty thousand in its heyday." I expressed my wish that the steel plant would magically disappear, giving us the shoreline back. In the rearview mirror, Junior sulked, staring out the window while Ravi slept next to him.

"In my time, they're talking about building wind turbines there," I added. "It sounds like it's going to happen."

"Wouldn't that be great?" Taylor said. "Buffalo's bad weather finally turns out to be an asset."

"I think Buffalo will have a renaissance in the twenty-first century," I said, surprising myself. I apologized again to Junior for not being as forthcoming as I should have been.

"Well, is that everything? Anyone else dying that I should know about?"

I tried to think if I needed to warn him about his skin cancer. Would it help if he was aware of it and sought treatment sooner? I'd never realized that so many awful things happened in my life. I guess I'd never really noticed. Life usually doles out horrible events in increments, allowing us time to slowly digest pain like an anaconda after a capybara meal. And in between there are a lot of good and great moments. Here I was giving Junior overnight delivery of his life's low points without any of the highlights; no one deserved to have all of the worst events in his life revealed like guests at a surprise party.

"Now what?" Junior said when I didn't respond immediately.

Even though he was a pain in the ass right at that moment, he deserved to have his youthful sense of immortality last throughout his twenties and thirties. He'd deal with his cancer when it arrived. I wasn't going to tell him about it.

Taylor sighed. "You're like Santa Claus handing out lumps of coal."

"More like Santa Claus handing out urns of ashes," Junior corrected.

Their mutual rapport answered one question. I'd slept in the back bedroom by myself while Taylor and Junior shared the middle bedroom. I'd suspected they were going to have sex; all night they both had the expectant air of cats brushing up against their bowls. They must have hooked up, since they were behaving like a couple, each backing up the other.

"I'm sorry I didn't tell you everything," I said. "But I was afraid you'd become depressed if you heard everything at once."

"Well, it worked."

I felt the blood rushing into my face as we turned onto the exit for the Thruway.

"What the fuck would you do in my place? Let Carol and Dad die because it might hurt your tender feelings? Grow up."

A snide grin appeared on Junior's puss.

"I don't want to. I've seen the result."

Someone who shares your skin knows how to get under it.

"Why don't you go fuck yourself?" I said.

There was a moment of silence before Taylor began to laugh.

"You guys could actually make that happen," he said. "And it would be a first."

"If he wasn't such a prude," Junior said. "But now you couldn't pay me to do it."

I started to laugh. "Well, I have more bad news for you. You're not that great at flirting. You're somehow coy and desperate at the same time. Not an attractive combination. If you'd just be direct and say, 'I'm interested—let's do it,' that would get you laid more than what you're doing now."

"Really?" Junior said. "Because I just got laid."

Taylor turned his head to address both of us. "Because of me. I took the initiative, and to be honest I wasn't sure if you were really interested until we did it."

I guess you never outgrow your immaturity. I gloated that Taylor backed me up. Junior's sulking seemed to intensify and I didn't want to drive cross-county with that bundle of gloom in the backseat.

"You didn't answer my question," I said.

Junior didn't say anything, and I could see him in the rearview mirror trying to think of a response.

"All right. You had to tell me."

I admitted that my news was an abyss of a downer, but told him I actually felt optimistic. I thought we could prevent their deaths. It seemed an obvious distinction to me, but Junior didn't really get what I was saying. I struggled to explain what I meant, until I dropped the subject. I suddenly understood that my definition of optimism would be devastating to him. Being upbeat at forty-six was entirely different from looking on the bright side at twenty-six. At my age, being an optimist meant you were a hard-ass and would try to be happy and could be happy, even though you knew that horrible, truly devastating events would occur in your life. At Junior's age, his dreams of happiness still possessed the win-the-lottery illusion that you could have it all without losing any of it.

"I've been trying to figure out why Cheney visited us without doing anything," Taylor said. "It doesn't make sense. He must know something we don't know."

"And if he can reappear and disappear with that bracelet," Junior added, "he could just show up in the backseat here."

It made no sense, but I looked in the rearview mirror to reassure myself that Ravi was still hogging most of the backseat.

"Maybe he thinks we're going to fuck up his future," Junior said. "Somehow prevent the Bush presidency."

"I don't see how that could happen," I said. "We're going to drop off Taylor in Los Alamos then go see Carol. I think Cheney's here to make sure we don't fuck up the future in general."

I sped up. It wasn't clear how much time we had before he showed up again, and we probably had three days of driving ahead of us.

"Why don't we do that?" Taylor said excitedly. "Why don't we stop Bush from becoming president?"

"Because we don't have time," I said. "Let's save Carol first, then if we have time we'll save the country."

"Okay," Taylor said. "Explain something. You had to tell John about his sister and father. But why'd you have to tell me that you'll break up with me because I become a Republican?"

"You wouldn't want to know that?" Junior asked. "That's like warning you that you'll get cancer." I winced when I heard his analogy, but

Junior's comment reminded me that my political beliefs hadn't changed in twenty years. Then I wondered if that was a good thing, and quickly decided they *had* changed. I loathed the Republicans even more.

"Isn't it silly to break up with me over my political beliefs?"

"Not really," I said. "What if your boyfriend turned Nazi or Communist? Would you be saying, 'I know he exterminates people but he loves to cuddle'?"

"That's an unfair comparison," Taylor said. "There's a big difference between the Nazis and the Republicans."

"You're right," I replied. "The Nazis are better dressers."

"The Republicans believe in laissez-faire extermination," Junior said, "giving Americans the freedom to suffer and die."

Taylor put on his sunglasses. Retro black Ray-Bans were in vogue then.

"Not everything Reagan's done is bad."

"Tell me one good thing he's done," Junior said.

"He's cut taxes."

"Mostly for the richest people in the country."

"It'll trickle down."

"You'll end up in the gutter before you enjoy the benefits of trickle-down economics," I said.

"He's tough with the Russians."

I caught Junior's eyes in the rearview mirror. "John, in a few years, you'll go to Russia and every Russian you'll meet will tell you that no one believes in communism. You'll leave convinced that communism won't be around in twenty years, but you'd never guess it will be gone in five years."

They were astonished as I explained the end of communism, the liberation of Eastern Europe, and the eventual dissolution of the Soviet Union. I explained to them that it happened so quickly and, for the most part, bloodlessly that for a brief moment it inspired the whole world to feel cautiously hopeful that every event in history didn't always have to end with a chorus of eulogies.

"So not everything gets worse over the next twenty years?" Taylor asked.

"No, some things get better."

Junior sighed. "Great. The whole world improves while our family tanks."

I hated to see him looking dejected.

"It's not all bad. You're actually going to be very happy. You'll fall in love, achieve some success."

"I know, I just have to get over my father drinking himself to death and my sister putting a bullet in her head. Other than that, everything will be dandy!"

There was an understandable pause in our conversation after his outburst. Then Taylor cleared his throat.

"So Reagan's legacy won't be all bad," Taylor said. "He's helping end communism."

His reverence for empirical reasoning never seemed to include political science.

"This is why I want to break up with you!" I shouted. "Reagan didn't end communism. Gorbachev and the Russian people ended communism."

Junior commented, "You sound kind of nuts."

"You sound obsessed," added Taylor.

"Don't think I haven't thought the same thing," I replied, "but I've been hearing this same bullshit for twenty-six years. You've only had six years of it."

"Aren't the Democrats just as bad as the Republicans?" Taylor asked.

"No! The Democrats have their share of crooks, but at least their crooks are willing to hand out some money to the poor while taking a bribe. There's something intrinsically evil about the Republicans' indifference to suffering; it's okay to torture foreigners and give tax breaks to billionaires and to have millions of Americans without health insurance, because we can't afford universal health care, but we can afford a trillion-dollar Iraq War that profits a bunch of crony-owned corporations. Then they won't shut up about how the gays are immoral, and meanwhile every one of them is cheating on his wife."

I could see quite a bit of my mother's temper in myself, but I didn't mind. I never wanted Isabella to think that I was apathetic about her future.

"If you're the sane opposition, then no wonder I become a Republican."

"We've been driven insane," I muttered, before saying to Taylor, "Yeah, and thanks for lying about being a Republican for twenty years!"

"I didn't lie," he said. "I was registered for one year."

We would be soon driving over Cattaraugus Creek, and I was tempted to stop at the soon-to-be-discovered old growth forest of Zoar Valley, but we didn't make a detour. Dick Cheney loomed in my thoughts. I'd just seen a bald middle-aged man driving a Winnebago, and I mistook him for Cheney and almost veered off the road.

"Why don't you try to prevent me from becoming a Republican?" Taylor asked.

"How would I do that? Give you a lobotomy?"

"No," Junior said. "That would make him a Republican. How about a heart transplant?"

"Republicans reject having hearts."

"I'm serious," Taylor said. "How would you prevent that?"

"You've always leaned conservative."

Taylor smiled. "Except in bed."

"Well, most gay Republicans aren't conservative in bed," I said. "Speak softly and carry a big stick has a double meaning for them."

"I don't like either party right now. I criticize both of them. What changes me?"

I had an answer but didn't see exactly how we could prevent that from happening.

"Well, it was 9/11. Before that you called yourself an independent, but after that you became a Republican."

"Well, can we prevent 9/11?" Taylor asked.

After a brief discussion about how we would need to eradicate a clandestine group of Islamic terrorists based in remote countries like

Sudan and Afghanistan, we concluded that mission might be a bit too ambitious for the three of us.

"We should stick to trying to change the histories of two people rather than trying to change the history of an entire planet," I suggested.

"Unfortunately," Taylor said, "sometimes one person changes the history of the planet."

"I've always thought if only Gore had won the election, then maybe you would have become a conservative Democrat."

"Well, could we stop Bush from becoming president?" Taylor asked.

"What?" I asked. "We'll go to Midland, Texas, and what? Ruin his political career before it gets started? Get him drunk and fucked up on coke and then videotape him having sex with a hooker? Is that the plan?"

"If you think that would do it," Junior replied.

"Yeah, why not?" Taylor said. "Cheney must be afraid that you'd do just that."

These two were serious. Like we could stop Bush from happening. I couldn't tell whether I'd become cynical or if they were ridiculously idealistic.

"We don't have time to do that. We need to save Carol before Cheney finds and kills us or yanks me back to my time."

"That's fucking bullshit," Junior shouted. "You go around saying the president sucks and all these other people are doing bad things, but you're too fucking lazy or scared to try to make a difference. We're the only people who can do this. You fucking say-one-thing-do-nothing fuck!"

It was disconcerting that he was saying exactly what Cheney had said to me: Get off your ass and do something. And my mother had said we deserved freedom from speeches. Just talking about problems without doing anything about them is the most annoying and debilitating form of apathy.

Taylor asked softly, "Was I that shitty a boyfriend that you won't even try to save our relationship?" He paused and then added, "Maybe you're right and we should break up. I want a boyfriend who would try to keep us together."

They both stared at me.

"Of course, we have problems. All couples do, but the one that shut us down was our political differences."

"It's not fair to let Taylor become Republican. He's too cute for that." Junior blushed a little and I felt a twinge of jealousy. But for the first time in my life, I couldn't decide whom exactly I was jealous of: me, myself, or Taylor.

Junior added, "You'd stop him from stepping on a landmine, so why not try to prevent him from stepping in bullshit."

"We have to stop Bush Two from happening," Taylor urged.

"I know it sounds selfish, but I care more about saving Carol than I do about saving the country from Bush. I messed things up last time. I didn't force Carol to stay in rehab. I don't want to fuck up again. I'm going to finish this. Do you understand?"

"That was a decision that you made in the middle of a crisis," Junior said. "Carol's not in the middle of a crisis now. And whatever happens to you, I'll still be here. We can do both."

Our recent petty sparring made me lose sight of the fact that Junior loved Carol as much as I did. Whatever happened, he wasn't going to fuck up again. I didn't see how we could prevent Bush and Cheney from becoming our president and vice president, but I began to feel we had to try.

"I wouldn't even know where to find George W. Bush in Midland," I said.

"You said he's a nobody now so maybe his phone number's listed," Taylor suggested.

I hadn't considered that possibility, as I thought it would have to be unlisted since his father was the vice president and they shared the same name. For a moment, I savored being in a time when most Americans had never heard of him.

"I bet he's well known in that town," Taylor said. "We can track him down."

Taylor seemed to genuinely want to change not only our nation's future, but also his and my future. It was unexpectedly heartening and made me feel hopeful about both keeping us together and saving Carol. We began to pass through miles of beautiful farmland along Lake

Erie, where the verdant trees and fields pulsed with life like in Charles Burchfield's watercolors. It brought back memories of the lush summers of my childhood, an annual season of renewed hope, when dark winter gives way to light and life. I felt emboldened.

"We can only spend a day or two at the most if we try this," I said. "I won't spend any more time than that."

"Why is everyone else's happiness more important than yours?" Junior asked.

It was an unexpected question, and I had to consider my answer before replying.

"Because my heart gets broken, but it doesn't stop beating."

We drove past a billboard for the Chautauqua Institute, illustrated with a photo of a smiling father, mother, and son and daughter, and I decided to tell Junior something else about his future.

"John, not everything is negative. You're going to become a father. Everything about it will be wonderful."

Junior's joy was such a shock that for an instant it seemed indistinguishable from pain.

"Really?" he said. "For *real*?"

I smiled at his predictable response and said, "Yes, for real."

"Should I start calling you 'Daddy'?" Taylor asked.

In 1986 it had never occurred to me that I'd ever be a father, and no matter how much I denigrated myself, it would always make me feel proud that two of the smartest women I knew wanted part of me to live on. It also made me understand better the irresistible appeal of heterosexuality: any time a woman accepts a man's sperm, it can always be construed as a pat on the back of his penis.

"Is it a boy or a girl?" Junior asked.

I decided against telling him. I was elated when I first heard my daughter was born, and I already felt like I'd ruined part of the surprise. He and Taylor kept pestering me. "Look. I'm not telling you. Quit asking."

They stopped asking, and the next time I looked in the rearview mirror, Junior was smiling.

11

EVERY AMERICAN SHOULD DRIVE cross-country at least once, just to see all the amazing places you wouldn't want to live. You'll be able to rule out most of the U.S. east of the Mississippi, because you won't care for most of the people, while out west, the clincher will be the decided absence of them. There are sights to see. Passing through Ohio's Amish country, the billboards touting Amish restaurants and Amish-made furniture made me marvel that in America even a culture that shuns materialism has been effectively turned into a brand name. You'll learn the skylines of Cleveland, Columbus, and Indianapolis are as hard to distinguish as the cows you've passed, and ramshackle farmhouses will scarecrow any fancies you have of moving to the country.

As we passed through Columbus, Taylor suggested we should stop and visit its historical society.

"It's home to my favorite work of American art: a prehistoric Hopewell culture twelve-inch mica open hand."

"What's the Hopewell culture?" Junior asked.

"The Mound builders," I said. I knew the answer so it must have been something I learned from Taylor. It made me wistful that if we broke up that would never happen again.

"It's a national treasure," Taylor claimed. "It's this beautiful, almost modern-looking open palm, cut from a single sheet of mica, an emblematic symbol of our common humanity. Mica's incredibly fragile, and it survived unbroken for fifteen hundred years. Very few people know about it, but it's amazing."

I trusted his judgment. For a scientist, Taylor wasn't all nuts and bolts, and had an artist's imagination. It was the reason why he could invent a time machine.

I know I sound like the worst sort of snob, but New Yorkers are egalitarian snobs—at cocktail parties we're equally impressed by meeting what the *Times* has declared is "America's best zither player" as we are meeting this year's winner of the PEN-Beckett Award for a first novel where not much happens. In some ways New Yorkers are all Mad King Ludvigs who recognize other royal families—protocol requires Londoners and Parisians to be treated as equals—only we ludicrously maintain our sense of grandeur as we give must-be-obeyed Chinese take-out orders from tiny studio or one-bedroom palaces while sneering at commoners in Terre Haute hovelling in their four-bedroom, three-bath Tuscan Chateaus. Any sane New Yorker can have a great weekend in any part of the United States, but our minds inevitably turn to questions about what the hell people do there the other 362 days of the year.

We took four-hour turns behind the wheel since it would take two long fourteen-hour days of driving to get to Midland. I was a nervous wreck about Cheney showing up again—this time with an army backing him up. At every stop, I mistook every plump, balding, gray-haired man wearing wire-rimmed glasses for the vice president. I'd never realized there are millions of these guys. We almost ran screaming out of a truck stop in Ohio when Taylor thought Cheney was getting a cherry slurpee. Then in the men's room at a Burger King in Indiana, I almost had a heart attack when Cheney's dead ringer used the urinal next to mine.

It was my first cross-country road trip, and I soon gathered that driving across America is like the worst aspects of aging; you forget more of the journey than you remember, and feel crankier, fatter, and more exhausted than you did when you started. For their first shifts, Junior and Taylor bickered about what music to listen to, each of them sharing similarly eclectic tastes but arguing for their different mix tapes. When Junior drove, he ran a program of complementary progression, each song offering a variation on a theme. Doleful but danceable love songs by the Eurythmics were followed by doleful but danceable love songs by the Smiths, which led to doleful but danceable love songs by the Pet Shop Boys. Taylor's taste was different. He liked every song to whipsaw your emotions and loved hearing the romantic-depressive Psychedelic Furs tune "Love My Way," followed by Nina Simone's joyous-furious "Mississippi Goddam," followed by Petula Clark's giddily upbeat "Downtown."

If you're fortunate, throughout your life your lovers will infect you with incurable newfound passions. Until I met Taylor I'd always half-listened to music while driving or having sex but had never really heard a song with the same focus I brought to reading a book or watching a movie. It was unfair that I'd branded him the fuddy-duddy, forgetting that he made me understand that Judy Garland wasn't just a camp icon, *Dusty in Memphis* is the greatest music album by a woman ever, and you're never too old to enjoy Icelandic rock bands.

After Junior played the Eurythmics' song "Here Comes the Rain Again" with its catchy, imploring refrain, "Talk to me like lovers do!" the vagueness of Annie Lennox's request made me suggest a few conversational subjects that lovers never tire of discussing: "Do I have to do everything?!" "Why don't you ever listen to me?" "I'm not in the mood." I thought my jest might induce Junior and Taylor to offer their own variations on the amusing theme of how lovers' sweet nothings inevitably become salty and tangible, forgetting that neither of them had ever lived with a boyfriend, and also overlooking that my commentary might not sound as light-hearted as I supposed. They sat there looking like the worst aspects of gay life: self-loathing and a boyfriend who's pissed.

"Is that supposed to be a joke about our relationship?" Taylor asked.

"Do you realize every thing you say sounds bitter?" Junior sighed. "It's really unattractive."

I checked to see whether there were any cars tailing us, then angrily veered sharply to the right, driving the car onto the shoulder of the road with a sudden crunch of gravel before hearing the disturbing sound of glass breaking. Junior and Taylor were wide-eyed when the car stopped moving.

"I was trying to be silly," I shouted. "I'm not going to drive cross-country with you two doppelganging up on me. Do you understand?"

They stared at me as if I were turning into a werewolf. I couldn't tell whether it was fear of me at that moment or they were afraid of the prospect of spending their futures with this screaming lunatic. After pulling onto the road again, I calmed down and noticed the car was listing toward the driver's side.

"Did we drive over something?" I asked.

"I think we have a flat," Taylor responded.

We pulled over again and discovered that I'd driven directly over two beer bottles. The right rear tire was deflated. Junior and I had no idea how to fix a flat, but of course Taylor did. We discovered there was a spare in the trunk but no jack or wrenches. Junior and Taylor stared dumbly at me as if this were another failing that I should have rectified. We were in the middle of a forest in Indiana, near the Illinois border, and the last town had been miles back. I now redirected my anger toward myself. I was still a loser who couldn't accomplish a goal. Cheney would find us and Carol would die.

"And we have no fucking cell phone service!"

I felt transported back to the isolation of the pretelegraph era and went off on a rant: "Everyone will complain about how intrusive cell phones are—you'll live to see a world where people loudly negotiate divorce settlements on the street or vividly describe colonoscopies in an airplane before take off; but I can assure you—in the twenty-first century, the inhabitants of the earth will stand united for one shared value: they'd rather lose a kidney than give up their cells."

Junior and Taylor gaped at me and I calmed down. I volunteered to walk to get help, and then Junior smiled. "Do you remember the time in P-town when Gavin and I hitchhiked to Boston and I told him to take off his shirt?" he asked. Gavin Dudek had been our first boyfriend. We were college students in Buffalo. During the summer, Gavin worked as a lifeguard at a country club and his hard body and soft lips had me priapic for the year we dated. For the first time for either of us, we went to Provincetown for a vacation. We had no money and ate at cheap restaurants and stayed at the Fore and Aft, a one-star gay guesthouse owned by a gracious old queen who tried to fluff up the dowdy furnishings by assuming an air of five-star grandeur. He took leering pity on two cute twenty-year-olds and gave us a private honeymoon suite for a rate we could afford. We soon figured out something that travel guides never mention: having fantastic sex multiple times each day is an inexpensive way to entertain yourself. I'd forgotten how my gay version of Claudette Colbert flashing a shapely gam to land a ride in *It Happened One Night* had worked. Gavin had reluctantly removed his T-shirt and stuck out his thumb, and his buff torso literally stopped traffic. The next car to pass pulled over, and a middle-aged gay guy offered to give us a lift to Logan to catch our plane.

"Why don't we see if we can flag someone down?" Junior suggested.

"That worked in P-town. This is Indiana. I don't know if many of the gays are driving this route."

Junior quickly wrote out "HELP! FLAT TIRE" on a sheet of a notebook paper, ripped it out, and held it up to the oncoming traffic. I started walking ahead and hadn't gotten far when I heard voices shouting my name and a car horn honking. I turned around and saw a black pickup had pulled over. By the time I walked back, a blonde-haired young woman named Jen, who said she grew up on a dairy farm five miles away, was telling Junior about her plans to produce and sell organic ice cream—as Taylor raised the car with her jack.

"Would you hand me the wrench?" Taylor asked me.

When I did, a lug nut slipped from his hand and fell to the ground.

"Fuck! Can't anything go fucking right? Jesus Christ, I'm going to fucking kill myself."

Taylor readily pardoned our dog when he pissed in the kitchen or pooped in the hallway, but couldn't forgive himself when he dropped a multivitamin. His rage against himself mystified and saddened me. I couldn't understand why he regarded his every human failing as unpardonable when I found it easy to give a blanket amnesty to all my shortcomings. Unfortunately, every New Yorker is an armchair Freud, and I tried to find psychological explanations for Taylor's behavior. Was the cause his difficult childhood? Or was it his parents' nasty divorce? He'd told me they were verbally abusive. (We did chuckle after Taylor shared that his mother had once called him a little cocksucker when he was eight years old.) His parents were now elderly and frail, beset by infirmities, reaffirming my belief that growing old is sufficient punishment for most of life's transgressions.

Junior had watched Taylor's outburst without comment. I felt like telling him that something else he had to look forward to was Taylor's temper, but I knew that would just come off as sounding mean.

Within a half hour we were on our way, and Jen's good deed seemed to have lifted all our spirits.

Suddenly it was a gorgeous day: the corn was green, the sky was blue, and our hearts were rosebuds. At the Illinois border the welcome sign made us feel that Governor James R. Thompson had personally invited us to the Land of Lincoln, and if we needed guest accommodations for the night, we could stay at his mansion in Springfield. Junior opened the extra-large bag of peanut M&Ms he'd bought at our last stop and offered us handfuls. For the next half hour, we drove in a comfortable silence (interrupted by the occasional crackle of candy-coated peanuts), happily subdued by the hypnotic blissfulness of a car ride, which offers misleading visible reassurance that you're following a path that others have traveled, conveying the comforting illusion that, for once in your life, you have truly left your past behind and know where you're headed.

A billboard announcing a Father's Day sale at a lawn mower dealer appeared to prompt Junior to speak. "Do you honestly think you helped Dad?"

"I have no idea. He never reveals how he feels about anything."

"He seemed pretty shaken up," Taylor said.

"I think it was more about Carol," Junior said. "He's close to her."

"He's always dropped everything to help her," I said. "Maybe he'll put down the Scotch to help keep her alive."

It seemed a slim hope, but I didn't argue against it. I was trying not to believe most hopes are imaginary friends. I admitted that ever since we passed through Pennsylvania, I'd been trying to think of an effective plan of how to prevent George W. Bush from becoming president. The problem I came up against was the same one I'd had in trying to prevent my father from becoming an alcoholic: I didn't know what made either of them tick.

"The problem with straight men," Junior proclaimed, "is that when you try to figure what motivates their lives, the one or two things they do reveal seem so trivial or insubstantial that you assume they either have to be stupid or nuts."

I remembered when I used to naively believe that my gayness conveyed some special artistic sensitivity that was lacking in heterosexual men. My youthful conviction was that my boner pointed to truth and beauty, while their dicks only pointed toward vaginas. This was before I met gay men who seriously collected Barbie dolls or supported a political party that despised them.

Junior looked my way. "Gay men tend to be more forthcoming about what motivates their lives."

I tried not to vomit. He sounded like every morning he stood up and put his hand over his heart before reciting the pledge of allegiance to the Rainbow flag.

"You're in no position to sneer at straight men when you sell comic books for a living."

Junior smiled. "I never really thought of that."

"All men get a bum deal," Taylor mused from the backseat. He and Junior had changed places the last time we stopped to let Ravi pee. "Men are always accused of repressing their emotions, but since they're only permitted to reveal the presentable feelings, they shut them all down rather than play favorites."

"Dad shows his emotions at Sabres' games," Junior said. "He's always shouting at the refs or players."

"Sports allow men to have an emotional life without having to take any responsibility for it," I said. "If your team fails, it's never your fault: you were always there for them."

"Can't you say the same thing about art?" Junior asked. "If a book, painting, or play stinks, it's never your fault: you can always blame the artist."

"I think we've just explained the emotional lives of 99 percent of the men in America," Taylor commented.

"President Bush is into baseball," I said. "He was part owner of the Texas Rangers before he became president. We should keep that in mind."

"In what way?" Junior helped himself to another handful of M&Ms.

"I don't know," I said. "This is your idea. If we're going to do this, I'm going to need some help planning."

Junior passed the bag to Taylor. "That could help when we're talking to him. Straight men believe all the world is a baseball field, while gay men think all the world is a stage. Use lots of baseball metaphors to win his trust."

Junior made an interesting point, but he was wrong. "Taylor and I recently attended a six-month Ingmar Bergman film retrospective," I said. "We saw a new-to-me film every Sunday morning at eleven. Bergman's indisputably straight and he used theater as a metaphor for life just as much as Shakespeare did."

"So I'm wrong about that too."

I felt embarrassed but had been compelled to correct him. It's easy to point out your flaws and mistakes when you don't have to take any responsibility for remedying them.

"I'm sorry," I said. "Everything you say I take personally."

"Well, it isn't personal," he said. "Get over yourself." Junior smiled before he lowered the volume on the tape player. "What else do we know about Bush?"

I explained that he undoubtedly had some complicated father issues. In one of his first interviews, when he was asked if he asked his father for advice, he replied that he only sought guidance from our heavenly father. "Which I thought was insulting to both dads."

It occurred to me that George W's life was a parody of his father's.

"His father was a war hero pilot during World War II, while W. became a draft-dodging pilot in the Texas National Guard during Vietnam. In the '50s, his father went to Midland and became a millionaire in the oil business, while in the '70s, W. moved to Midland and failed in the oil business."

"Does the father fuck around?" Taylor asked. I knew from his question that Taylor was thinking about sex; he always found a way to bring up the subject whenever he was horny.

"There've been stories. I read or heard something about him having an affair with this long-time employee." I felt my lack of exact information was a huge detriment to our planning and was frustrated that we couldn't get information quickly in 1986. "Fuck, I wish we could stop and just Google 'infidelity' and 'George H. W. Bush.'"

A brief digression ensued, as I explained Internet search engines to them.

"The son's probably as horny as his dad," Taylor said. "The apple doesn't fall too far from the tree and the seed doesn't shoot too far from the cock."

"Why don't you needlepoint that one on a sampler?" I suggested. When Taylor moved on to dirty talk, it meant he would definitely have an orgasm sometime today.

Junior turned toward me. "What kind of women does the young Bush like?"

"His wife Laura's a librarian and the one woman in his cabinet—his current Secretary of State Condoleezza Rice—is a spinster of some sort." They made a few derisive comments about her unusual first name, until I explained she was African American, and then they stopped because they didn't want to sound racist.

"She and Bush are extremely close. I'm not saying he'd like to fuck her, but he seems to enjoy giving the impression she'd like to fuck him. I'm sure that's a sexist interpretation of their relationship, but I'm not imagining it. The even stranger thing is there's a good chance she could be a lesbian, and you would still think that."

"You didn't really answer my question," Junior said.

"Yeah, because I don't want to think about what gives him a hard-on. I'd say he likes women who are smarter than him, which gives us a wide net."

"A brainy hooker," Taylor said. "In Midland Texas. Finding her won't be easy."

"One weird thing," I added. "Bush's wife, Laura, was in a car accident when she was seventeen and killed a seventeen-year-old jock who was a friend and might have been her high school sweetheart."

Taylor took an audibly large breath. "So when we meet Bush, we shouldn't say, 'Hey, when you're president why don't you just give your wife the keys to the presidential limo and let her go after our nation's enemies?'"

Junior snickered, but I didn't. I wasn't twenty-six. Her accident wasn't funny after you've experienced your own horrible personal tragedies. Even though I thought she was her husband's political accomplice, I felt sympathy for her. Laura Bush was our nation's First Lady Macbeth. I seriously wondered if late at night she wandered the halls of the White House, unable to sleep because the ghosts of thousands of young soldiers haunted her, soldiers slaughtered by her husband in his personal Iraq War, young men and women who were the same age as the boy she killed.

"There's sibling rivalry between him and his brother Jeb," I said. "Jeb's younger and is supposedly considered to be the smart one in the family based apparently on his ability to speak Spanish. His mother thinks he's a genius because he can tell the maid, 'Consuelo, the *platos* in the sink are very *sucios* and need to be *lavados* right away!' There are some fucked-up mother issues in that family. I actually met a woman in New York who used to dress Barbara Bush during the '80s, and she remembers Barbara used to make fun of her ne'er-do-well son George. If his mother was making fun of him to strangers, you can bet she mocked him to his face. Oh, and young Bush is also an alcoholic, and he once reportedly liked to do coke."

"When did he quit drinking?"

"I'm not sure. Sometime in the '80s."

I couldn't recall exactly. I'd never expected to need to know this much about his life.

Junior had a suggestion. "If he's still a boozer, let's buy him drinks and he'll be our friend for life."

It takes a drunk to know one, I thought to myself.

"Is he a horndog?"

"I don't think so."

"He doesn't cheat on his wife?"

"No, he found Jesus. I remember reading he was a member of a men's Bible study group in Midland."

"Are you kidding?" Taylor said. "The reason straight men join Bible groups is because they need Jesus to stop thinking about pussy."

"Or to stop secretly thinking about cock," Junior suggested. "Is he a closet case?"

"No. I'm sure of that. It would make our life a lot easier if he was. His policies are completely homophobic, but he comes off as one of those straight guys who has no problem with the gays because he's so confident of his own heterosexuality." Bush's leering smile came to mind. "He's kind of a smirker. I'm willing to bet he's the kind of guy who loves to talk dirty but doesn't have the balls to do anything about it."

Another thought immediately challenged my assertion.

"He's also extremely cocky. He loves to win and continues to believe he won even when he clearly didn't. He lost the popular vote in 2000 by half a million votes and still took it as a mandate. Then he claimed victory in the Iraq War in 2003 with a ridiculous 'Mission Accomplished' speech, even though we're still fighting there in 2006." Our task seemed impossible. "Logic doesn't seem to work with him. He really is a mental case."

"So we've got to find a brainy, spinster whore in Midland, Texas," Junior said. "How big is that city?"

"I don't know." I wasn't sure if it was a big town or a midsized city like Buffalo. If Midland were a big city we'd have to find him, find out where he hung out, and connect with him, all in one day and night. That was all the time I was willing to spare. Saving Carol was more important to me than trying to save my life with Taylor.

"We're fucked," I said. "There's no way this will work. All I know for sure about Bush right now is that he lives in Midland, his oil company is Spectrum 7, and he's a member of a men's Bible study group. That's nothing."

Junior and Taylor encouraged me to be optimistic, but this time they did it gently and without animosity. I regarded my deep reservations as being realistic.

"He's never going to sleep with a local whore in the city where his family lives."

I imagined the next highway exit would be for the town of Drudgery and after that would be a sign telling us we were ten miles away from Nothingtodo.

"We've got to think of a plan."

There wasn't any response from either of them, leading me to believe they were pondering different scenarios. We drove a few miles further, passing an antiques mall. I was surprised when Junior didn't ask to stop, suggesting we could be passing boxes of comic books that had been stored in a farmhouse attic since World War II. Junior leaned backward to address Taylor.

"How long have you been working out?"

Oh, Jesus. I couldn't believe Junior was using that ancient show of interest. In fact, "Oh, Zeus" would have been more appropriate because that line was already old when Socrates used it on a wrestler named Apollodoros in 410 BC.

"Since high school."

"Do you work your forearms?"

"Not really. They've always been like this."

Taylor raised his right arm, twisted it, to give Junior a little show of his corded bowling pin.

"You're lucky; they're really thick. I wish I had those veins."

"You have better biceps."

I felt like telling them to get a room as they continued to compliment each other's physiques. Junior had clearly been thinking about Taylor's forearms since we stopped in Indianapolis. I'd watched his eyes bulge as Taylor pulled back the aluminum tab on his can of pop.

"Look, this was your idea to stop Bush, and now you two are putting all your energy into verbally groping each other. We don't know where he lives or works. We don't even know what church he belongs to. We have no plan. I'm not going to be able to do this myself."

"All right!" Junior shouted. "We have tonight and tomorrow to think of something, and we will. Quit being . . ."

Junior stopped himself from saying I was negative, which I appreciated.

"We can find out his Bible study group," Taylor said. "He's not Roman Catholic, I'm guessing."

"No," I replied. "And I'm pretty sure he's not Baptist. The Bushes are real WASPs. He's either Episcopal, Presbyterian, or Methodist."

"That can't be hard to narrow down."

"In Texas?" I said. "There's probably two people to every church."

"Look," Junior said. "You just call every church and say George. W. Bush suggested I join their men's Bible study group. His father's a name in Texas. People will know him. It'll take time but it can be done."

That actually seemed to make sense and to be feasible. We still didn't have a plan, but somehow knowing we could track him down without Google was calming.

Taylor asked Junior for another handful of M&Ms.

"That's something else you can look forward to," I said. "In twenty years, they'll have chocolate-covered, candy-coated *almond* M&Ms. Very adult, almost sophisticated." Taylor exclaimed, "No! That's impossible! I can't believe we'll live to see that! I thought maybe interstellar warp-drive but not almond M&Ms!" Junior and I laughed. "The future sounds fantastic! Almonds covered in chocolate with a candy coating!"

We stopped for the night near St. Louis. I'd wanted to show them Cahokia Mounds State Park in Illinois, the sparsely visited site of the largest Pre-Columbian city in North America. It definitely was a place that Junior and Taylor would enjoy, but it was dark when we crossed into Missouri, and we wouldn't have time to visit the next morning. Instead, I drove them by Louis Sullivan's Wainwright Building in downtown St. Louis, which I happily pointed out wasn't nearly as beautiful as his Guaranty Building in Buffalo.

We were going to sneak Ravi into our motel again and kept him in the car as we checked in at an Econo Lodge outside of St. Charles, Missouri. The desk clerks at cheap motels always depressed me; the pudgy young men and drab middle-aged women always gave the impression they knew it was a lousy job, but they couldn't afford to quit. It kept them supplied with free matchbook-sized bars of soap. It had to be frustrating continually checking in people who were going to have sex when you weren't getting any.

"How many rooms would you like?" asked a dour, plump woman.

Before I could respond, Junior blurted out, "Two."

He and Taylor looked slightly embarrassed, and they bowed their heads as the desk clerk gave us our room keys. I wasn't surprised that they hooked up. Years of watching nature documentaries had made me think of my penis as a shark; it required periods of rest but never really slept; when provoked, it always lunged forward. Taylor was provocation.

I was at a loss for words. "Um, okay." It took a moment to register how I felt; sometimes my nervous system's outdated wiring can't handle the voltage required for newfangled emotions. As we climbed the red-carpeted stairs to the second floor, I knew if I suggested a threesome they'd go for it, but all I really wanted to do was just go to bed. Then it occurred to me why I was cold and bothered: I was envious that after driving for fourteen hours, they still had the will and energy to have sex at two a.m.—even when we would have to get up by seven if we were going to reach Midland by tomorrow night.

I was jealous that Junior and Taylor were twenty-six.

12

THE NEXT MORNING I sniffed and noticed again the stale stink in my room that disgusted me when I'd first opened the door the night before. I'd been too tired to go back to the front desk and ask for a different room. It smelled as if a ghost with smoker's breath haunted the motel. Ravi shook his head vigorously, rattling the tags on his collar, his signal that he needed to go out. Rose-colored dew on the car wind-shields glistened in the dawn light as we strolled around the edge of the parking lot. Ravi was male but looked straight ahead when he squatted to urinate. It made him appear pee-shy, and I always respectfully looked the other way as he piddled. Junior and Taylor's room was next to mine—their curtains were still drawn—and thankfully whatever they'd done together in bed hadn't been noisy, even though I could imagine exactly what they did.

I called their room to make sure they were up. Forty-five minutes later, they were at my door, damp-haired from their showers. I was relieved they were groggy and monosyllabic, tamping down any roosterish urges to crow that they got laid last night.

At 7:30 we checked out of our rooms with the new desk clerk, a middle-aged woman wearing pink cat's-eye glasses and a large pink barrette in her gray hair. She was exceptionally friendly, making me grateful that someone so competent and pleasant had chosen such a dismal job, while I ignored the fleeting existential question as to why I would have been so unfriendly and unhelpful in the same position. Responding to our inquiry, she directed us to the nearest McDonald's by drawing a little map on the back of a brochure for the Lewis and Clark attractions in St. Charles. "You have some long-distance charges," she mentioned before adding our room bills together.

Junior and Taylor had a thirty-six-dollar phone bill. It had to be a mistake. I looked at them, expecting them to verify that none of us had made any exorbitantly overpriced long-distance phone calls at two a.m. I'd forgotten how cell phones had eliminated that standard hotel rip-off.

Junior shrugged as a prelude to an explanation. "We called Santa Fe. We need to stop somewhere at ten and call Michael."

Michael had recently moved to Santa Fe after a burst of dissatisfaction with New York. The following summer I'd visit him for the Harmonic Convergence. It would be my first trip to the Rocky Mountain West. For two days in August, we camped out on a hillside in La Cienega, south of Santa Fe, chanting ohms and sweltering in Indian sweat lodges, believing that we were witnessing the dawning of a New Age. To our lasting disappointment, the New Age turned out to be our thirties.

"Why'd you call him?"

"He's going to help us stop Bush."

"You've told him about me?"

"Yes."

"And he believed you?"

"Not at first. He asked a lot of questions. A lot. But when I told him I really believed you were from the future that was enough. I told him I—we—really needed his help."

If Michael called me up and asked for anything, no matter how strange, I would help him. There wasn't any question about that. I'd never forget how, when Carol killed herself, Michael flew to New York to stay with me that first weekend.

"He didn't express any doubts?"

"A few. But not after I explained about Cheney."

Michael always had his woo-woo side. He had read Shirley MacLaine's autobiography *Out on a Limb* and had convinced me to read it. (I enjoyed it because we all want to believe that someone on Earth has been contacted by extraterrestrials.) Then, to our astonishment, he met and befriended her in Santa Fe. So I guess his best friend calling up to announce that "myself from twenty years in the future is visiting and he says we have to stop this asshole from becoming president" fell in the same category as UFOs at Roswell or moving to India to study with a guru for six months. Michael was exceptional: if he had told me this same story, I would have believed him. But I wouldn't have believed it of anyone else.

I asked Junior and Taylor how Michael was going to help us and was told to wait and see. This irked me. I wasn't going to be treated condescendingly by them. We continued to argue while loading up the car. Junior must still have been under the influence of last night's testosterone, since he insisted on driving the first shift. I readily accepted his offer, as my right calf ached from gas pedaling the day before.

"You didn't even know who Bush was until two days ago," I said.

"We have it under control, Grandpa," Junior retorted as he pulled into the McDonald's.

As the drive-through window clerk handed us our bag of breakfast, Taylor added, "We need to buy a video camera today. Either on the way or in Midland." They both refused to explain exactly what their plan was until they talked to Michael. "I think we've got it worked out," Taylor said. "Let's not jinx it." In contradiction of his championing of scientific reasoning, Taylor embraced a handful of superstitions: he knocked on wood, avoided walking under ladders, and after spilling salt, he always threw a pinch over his left shoulder. I found his irrationality endearing; it seemed cute that a man who could diagram the molecular structure of sodium chloride could believe spooks lurked between the electrons. But it annoyed me that the two of them were grandstanding to each other.

"I might be able to improve your plan."

Junior shook his head. "You'll tell us why it won't work."

"Okay. Have it your way." I never realized what a dick I could be. I was naive and thought that observing myself from the other side of my face would give me some objectivity, but our squabbling made it harder to preserve any optimism about human nature; the whole idea of good will among men nose-dives when you can't even get along with yourself. Then I relented. The whole idea of trying to stop George W. from becoming president was a long shot. Maybe they did have a plan to stop him. I hoped they did because I didn't. We ate our breakfast in silence and then drove for the next two hours listening to Joni Mitchell songs. Her musical exactitude about her sad feelings made me feel better that I never really tried to deeply examine mine. (It made me wonder again if my interest in art wasn't just another means of avoidance, where I can enjoy other people's close encounters with profundity, leaving my own life unexamined.) We stopped at Lebanon, Missouri, to use a pay phone to call Michael and to give Ravi a bathroom break. Junior put the call on his credit card and wouldn't let me reimburse him. It lessened my animosity toward him that he wasn't a cheapskate, but it also increased my anxiety. I would run up some major credit card debt in the next few years and felt compelled to mention this to him. As I should have predicted, he said, "Death and now debt. You are the grimmest reaper of them all."

I eavesdropped on his phone call, trying to pick up something of their plan. I overheard him saying, "We can pay for all your expenses. Yeah, the gas and hotel. Yeah, we can cover that too. It won't be a problem. So we'll meet you in Midland tomorrow. We're going to stay at the Midland Yucca motel. There's only one. I know. It's cheap but that's part of the plan. Thank you for doing this. I know. Who ever thought we'd be unmaking history?" When he hung up, I pretended to be reading the headline of the *Lebanon Daily Record*, "Silo Fire Extinguished Quickly," in a newspaper vending box.

"Michael will meet us in Midland. And he's bringing Elena."

"Why is Elena coming?" I asked.

"She's offered to fuck Bush," he said.

"That's a terrible idea," I said. Elena Orloff was one of the parents of my daughter. She was a stand-up comic who lived in Santa Fe in 1986 and she wouldn't meet her partner, Sonia Derby-Katz, the birth mother of our child, for another twelve years. When Michael moved to Santa Fe, I put him in touch with her. Elena and I had been close friends since college in Buffalo when we took a writing course together. I was trying to write science fiction stories, while she wrote first-person comic essays about her African American mother and Russian-born father. We were at odds with the other five writers in the class, who, at nineteen, were trying to emulate Raymond Carver, the most revered writer of that era. Each week, the other students handed in minimalist tales about financial hardship, alcoholism, or other forms of working-class despair, tinged with odd moments of dark humor, even though they all came from upper-middle-class backgrounds where their knowledge of financial struggle was limited to working up the nerve to ask Dad for money to spend their junior year abroad. Elena and I bonded on the day she called their fiction "blue-blood collar" and then realized we were the only students in the class who paid for our tuition and books with money earned from part-time jobs.

On my first visit to Santa Fe, Elena would tell me she wanted to move to New York to pursue stand-up comedy, and six months later we became roommates. We lived together until I moved in with Taylor. Then when her career began to take off, and after she had met Sonia, Elena would move back to Santa Fe to start a family.

"Then how the fuck are we going to get Bush in bed with someone?" Junior asked. "Are we going to hire a Midland whore and let her in on your history? Elena knows the score, and she'll do it if she's still convinced after meeting you."

I was horrified that someone I loved was going to sleep with Bush. What made it more disgusting was that I thought she would actually appeal to him. She had a rack that all straight men and even the gays always commented on. Elena was very attractive in a short-haired pixie tomboy way. She was also a nerdy bookworm who read everything. I hadn't thought of her as a possible lure for Bush, as the thought of asking someone you love to fuck him is repulsively unnatural. But I also had no doubt that if Elena's future self were given the chance to get rid of him by putting out, she'd do it in an instant. In 2006 she loathed him more than I did, and my disdain was immeasurable.

"You told them everything?"

"Yes. They know you're from the future and that we have to stop this guy from becoming president."

"Does Elena really know what we're asking her to do?"

"Yes. Michael told her. She hasn't promised anything yet. She wants to meet you first, before she commits. But she said she can't stand Reagan, and if she can stop a president who's worse than him, then it's her patriotic duty to fuck him."

I was moved that my friends were doing these things on Junior's endorsement. At times, I felt like a failure, but I overlooked that one of my greatest accomplishments was that I had many close friends. I knew I was a good friend in return but didn't feel this feat needed to be mentioned to Junior, as I'd always known that. While we drove, I wondered aloud whether simple adultery was enough to prevent Bush from becoming president. "It always surprises all the pundits, but Americans can forgive almost any personal failing if a politician does his job well. If Clinton could have run for a third term, I have no doubt he would have been reelected. Even though he used the cootch of a twenty-two-year-old White House intern as a humidor. That's a pretty high bar of kinkiness to reach to make Bush unelectable."

"So do we try to find some hidden kink he has?" Taylor asked.

"His wife's a librarian, so maybe he has a librarian fetish," I suggested.

Junior began to impersonate a librarian dominatrix. "Oh, you've been a naughty, naughty boy. Your book's overdue and now you'll have to pay a big fine."

"I think anyone would find that either laughable or dull."

"Or we have him do some sexual act that's so disgusting . . ." I didn't allow Taylor to finish the thought.

"No! This involves Elena. She's going to be the mother of our . . . child." (I had almost said daughter.) I'm not going to ruin her reputation. Even if it means allowing him to become president."

"But you'll allow her to fuck him?" Taylor asked. "And us to videotape it?"

It sounded sleazy, and I was uncomfortable thinking about how we'd explain this to our daughter when she was older. What would I say when this videotape became public knowledge or, even worse, achieved immortality when it received five million hits on some Internet site? Could I really say, "Well, your mother slept with him to prevent him from becoming president, which prevented the war in Iraq. She saved the lives of twenty-five hundred Americans and a hundred thousand Iraqis by having intercourse with him and allowing us to videotape it. Your mother's not a slut; she's actually a national hero." I was idealistic and imagined Isabella as a sophisticated adult. She would be raised not to think that every act of consensual sex was immoral. She would understand that her mother had served a higher purpose by getting down and dirty with the failed older son of then Vice President Bush. If we did our jobs right, George Junior would remain as obscure as his brothers Neil and Marvin or his sister Dorothy. It occurred to me that I would have to tell Elena about our daughter. I couldn't let her fuck Bush without telling her the full story of whom it might affect. Judging from my own example, it was impossible for anyone to time travel without repeatedly changing history.

Taylor opened a bag of nacho cheese–flavored tortilla chips, which filled the car with their aroma. Junior made a pee-eew gesture, flapping his hand in front of his face. "Those are like a white-trash room freshener."

Taylor ignored his comment as he popped a chip in his mouth. "With our luck, he'll be kink-free."

"The one sure thing that would disqualify him for the presidency now is if we could make it look like he's gay," Junior said.

"But he's not," I said, "and he's never going to do something with a guy."

"Maybe we only need to make it look like he's gay."

"He doesn't actually have to be doing anything gay," Taylor suggested. "If a guy's videotaped in a room with another guy's hard cock, it's like Chekhov's comment about putting a loaded gun on stage; the audience expects it to go off sometime."

"That might just work," I said, trying to decide which one of us could get a hard-on in the presence of George W. Bush. Naturally, I thought Taylor should have to bear that burden, due to his future Republican affiliation.

We were formally welcomed to the Bible Belt by a billboard for a sporting goods shop. The caption beneath the illustration of a fisherman casting a line read: "You bring the loaves and we'll take care of the fishes!" Taylor had changed places with Junior in Joplin and drove west for the next five hours. Somewhere near Tulsa, it became apparent that there's a strong impetus to be saved if you live in the Bible Belt. Who wouldn't clamor to die and go to heaven if it guaranteed you'd never have to live in Oklahoma again?

When we crossed into Texas, I took over the driving. We still had five and a half hours to go if we were going to make it to Midland that night. Texas claims to be a western state, but it's the West of the South, which is not the same as the Southwest. I was hopelessly biased against Texas since it had inflicted two Bush presidents on us. I thought of the state as wide-open spaces filled with narrow-minded people. As the landscape became almost entirely grassland, it was hard to shake the feeling all the trees were gone because they'd all been cut down for cross-burnings on front lawns. I'd visited Texas's big cities and knew the state wasn't all boondocks. It's possible to get a dose of sophisticated culture at the Menil Collection and Rothko Chapel in Houston, or the Kimbell Art Museum in Fort Worth. Without a doubt, the gays in Texas are some of the nicest, wittiest, most enjoyable people I've ever met. But they're a few drops of smart in an ocean of stupid. And people always claim Austin is exceptional. It's not like the rest of Texas, and that's true and depressing. When Texans boast that one city in their state is progressive, it always sounds like hillbillies bragging that someone in their family still has teeth. To your average New Yorker, no one in the state was smart enough to figure out how to avoid living in Texas.

The three of us had resumed conversing again in Oklahoma, where we noticed the further south and west we traveled, service slowed to a mosey even at fast-food restaurants. The employees lackadaisically drawled your order back to you at the drive-through window—in some parts of Texas your dubba-cheeseburger could be ordered with everything but an "L." To their credit, the employees were always friendly and at the drive-through window asked, "Will that be y'all?" as if chatting through a plastic clown's head was a downright neighborly way to get to know someone.

By the time we got to Midland, it was after midnight. We found the motel Junior had booked for two nights. The Midland Yucca was a cheap, one-story motel built in the '50s on what had then been the outskirts of town. It consisted of two "wings," and Junior had specifically asked for rooms in the back. You could park your car in front of your door and come and go without being observed. I had to give Junior and Taylor credit. If we could convince Bush to commit adultery, he'd probably want a little privacy; it was clever of them to think of that. And they'd even found a place that took pets.

All we had to go on was my memory, which had already been revealed to be forgetful or completely wrong. We had two leads: Bush attended a men's Bible study group in Midland, and the name of his oil company was Spectrum 7. I hoped that would be enough.

We were all exhausted from two days of driving and slept in late. We woke up around 9:30 and had breakfast at a diner. At breakfast Junior revealed he'd discovered George and Laura Bush were members of First United Methodist. He'd woken up at 8:30 and made phone calls to the major Protestant churches in town. He'd pretended that he was looking for the men's Bible study group recommended by his friend George W.

Bush. On his third call, he spoke to a woman who confirmed the Bushes were members and that the men's Bible study group met that evening at six. Junior added, "She said, 'We had to move it to Tuesday nights. Trying to get men to show up for Bible study on the same night as Monday Night Football would take a miracle of the Lord. And that might even be beyond his power.'"

I wondered about Junior eagerly getting up early to call churches. Then it hit me. He liked Taylor and didn't want me to break up with him. In some ways I found his solicitude sweet, and in other ways I found it meddlesome. Junior was deliberately trying to change my future. At first I resented that he didn't know anything about my in-the-future-present circumstances, and yet he was making decisions for me. But then I realized I'd been doing that my entire life. It was part of the human condition; we make decisions about our futures, completely ignorant about what our futures might be. To blame yourself for your bad decisions, which we all do, is like telling a blind man to watch where he's going when he bumps into you.

After breakfast, Taylor announced that we needed to go shopping. We were going to be doing errands for several hours and couldn't leave Ravi in the car in the Texas sun. I asked the desk clerk if it was okay to leave him in the room. The sweet red-haired woman offered to watch him while we were out. She made me reevaluate my Texas-bigotry, as I had to admit that in the South, friendly people who were willing to stop what they're doing and help you did seem to pop up more frequently than they did in New York.

We went to a mall to buy a video camera and then to a nearby auto parts store to buy a spare tire and jack for our car. "We should buy some cocaine," I said, wondering how the fuck we would find a drug dealer in Midland. I doubted the elderly women who worked at the Visitor's Bureau would have a recommendation. "Michael's taking care of that," Junior said. "He works with some guy who's a cokehead and he's always asking Michael if he wants to do a line." Hearing someone called a cokehead sounded almost as archaic as hearing someone being referred to as a laudanum addict. I'd never considered that recreational drugs had their eras; cocaine was the drug du jour of the '80s, while in twenty years it would be crystal meth.

By one in the afternoon, we'd finished our errands and had nothing to do until Michael and Elena arrived at five. I suggested checking out one of the local attractions and then maybe going back to the motel for a nap. After a short discussion, we decided to visit the Permian Basin Petroleum Museum. It would be the first visit to a petroleum museum for all of us. The museum's mission statement was "We will share the petroleum and energy story and its impact on our lives," and halfway through the Petroleum Hall of Fame exhibition I felt like saying, "Please don't." The three of us imagined other museums following the path blazed by the Permian Basin Petroleum Museum, telling the previously untold stories of other regionally based industries: the Life Insurance Museum of Hartford, Connecticut, or the Microwave Oven Museum of Amana, Iowa. The Petroleum Museum strenuously tried to make a dull subject interesting, but its failure was evident in their "Kid's Section," where the clue for 3-down in the children's crossword puzzle was "the solvent used in nail-polish remover." In the parking lot of the museum, as we walked back to our car, I questioned why George Bush had moved back to Midland to become successful when moving away from there was indisputably an accomplishment.

Over lunch at a Dairy Queen, Taylor finally revealed how they planned to meet and win over George W. Bush. "You two will pretend to be father and son at the Bible study group, and your relationship will mirror his relationship with his father. At the men's study group, you'll be introduced as new members and asked to tell why you joined." Taylor nodded his head to indicate Junior, and continued. "John will tell a personal history that will be close enough to Bush's life story to intrigue him. No one's interested in a stranger's problems unless they reflect our problems. Then we're all ears. Then when the meeting's over, you'll all leave together and George will discover that he has a flat tire, courtesy of me. I'll be your other son and meet you outside after the meeting. You should cuss me out a little for missing it. We'll offer to help George fix his tire and he'll be grateful. Then we'll offer to take him to dinner, get him drunk, and then get him high on some blow. Then while he's getting fucked up, he'll meet Elena and then hopefully spring a boner. We'll get him back to the hotel and Michael will be hiding in the closet. Once they start having sex, Michael will pop out with the camera and film a close-up. Hopefully, that will be enough to keep Bush from becoming president."

It sounded like a sensible plan if you were crazy enough to think you and four friends could change the history of the world. It was uplifting that Taylor was trying to prevent himself from becoming a Republican, but I also knew he was intellectually curious and wanted to know whether it was possible to change your destiny.

Junior woke me from my nap at a quarter to five. He told me that his and Taylor's nap had been interrupted by a phone call from Michael around four. Michael and Elena had gotten a late start, due to a nasty fight Elena had with her then girlfriend. For some reason the girlfriend didn't like the idea of Elena being videotaped fucking some stranger in Texas, even if it would prevent this guy from becoming president in fourteen years. Michael thought they wouldn't get to Midland before six or seven. That would still work but made me nervous. Our plan, like most plans, would only work if everything went smoothly.

We arrived at the First United Methodist Church around a quarter after five. Our plan was to get there early to see Bush arrive and learn which car needed to receive a flat tire. We parked in front of the church, sitting slouched down in our seats waiting for him to show up. The meeting started at 6:00, and by 5:45 I thought perhaps George had other plans. But a minute later, a hard-used blue sedan pulled up and parked on the street in a space that was reserved for church staff. A youthful, handsome, kind-of-sexy man opened the car door and hurried to the church entrance. At first, I wasn't sure it was George. It took me a moment to recognize him. The adjective "sexy" had never come near my head before when I thought about him. George walked briskly, wearing khakis and a blue dress shirt with the sleeves rolled up. Taylor whispered that George's business must be doing poorly. His car was practically a junker. I was still stunned that Bush had once been objectively attractive, although he still didn't do it for me and that would never change. There are some people who undermine the whole notion that sexual orientation is innate. If Bush and Cheney were the last men on Earth, I would choose not to be gay.

Junior palmed the handle of the car door. "Just follow my lead," he ordered before getting out. I followed him inside the church where a handwritten sign, with the words "Men's Bible Study" and a downward-pointing arrow, indicated a set of stairs leading to the Don and Millie Stabler Family Fellowship Room in the church's basement.

There were about twenty-five men attending the meeting. All of them were white, and most of them looked to be in their midthirties to early forties. Set in the drop-ceiling were rectangular, clear plastic panels, covering fluorescent lights, which shone an unflattering, greenish hue on the fellowship room, making everyone look sinned-against.

Shortly after six, the moderator, who introduced himself as Jake Garrold, asked people to take their seats. He was a plump, stubby man in his early forties wearing a large and ornate turquoise and silver bolo tie, and his grating voice was softened by a slight drawl. "Let us pray," he said before beginning a short prayer informing God we were "good Christian men" and asking for his assistance: "We seek your help in truly understanding your message for us and all men." Then Jake introduced Junior and me to the fellowship, explaining that we'd give a brief statement as to why we had sought out the study group. (I was favorably impressed with Jake's marked emphasis on the word "brief.")

Junior stood up and walked to the lectern at the front of the room. He looked strikingly collected, and I felt a twinge of almost fatherly pride in him. George W. Bush was sitting near the front. The chairs fanned out in crescent-shaped rows rather than straight lines, and I could observe his impassive face.

"I came here today because I feel only Jesus understands my situation," Junior began. "For a long time I've felt estranged from my father.

You see, I'm the oldest son, first born, like Jesus. And like Jesus, I followed in my father's footsteps and went into the family business." There were a few titters from the audience, but Junior waited for them to settle down, and his earnest patience made the men resume listening. George was focused on Junior.

"But my father looks down on me just as Jesus's father looked down on him. We forget that Jesus didn't have it easy; his father was the second-guesser in the sky, always looking over his shoulder. Jesus was the son of God, but in some people's eyes that just made him God Junior." I was afraid Junior might have gone too far, but he never paused for a laugh and his face appeared almost stern. He spoke slowly, as if this was something that had weighed upon him for a long time.

"We forget that Jesus was a man, like us. He had to constantly prove himself because people had no faith in him when he first started out. His father was well known, loved and respected, and Jesus had some big shoes to fill when he walked on water. Jesus's father was a war hero who brought down the walls of Jericho for the Israelites while his son—God Junior—refused to fight, not because his son was a coward, as people said, but because he was a man of peace. The Lamb of God who demonstrated the courage it takes not to fight now, not because you're afraid, but because you have great battles to fight in the future."

George gazed at Junior as if he'd found a new savior.

"My heart goes out to Jesus. It's not easy having a father who's above criticism while your enemies crucify you—God Junior—here on Earth. His father created the lion and the lamb, while God Junior created loaves and fishes. 'Good,' people said, 'but not as good as his father.' His father led the Jews out of Egypt, while God Junior led twelve disciples around the desert. 'Good,' people said, 'but not as good as his father.' His father was an overnight success who created the world in seven days, but God Junior wandered in the wilderness for forty days and forty nights and could barely afford to pick up the tab for the last supper. 'Good,' people said, 'but not as good as his father.' When Jesus died he probably felt like a failure. His business of saving souls was a start-up, and everyone knows rendering unto Caesar can eat up your capital when you're just getting going. God Junior made mistakes, like all young businessmen do. He hired Judas. Not a smart move. He chased the merchants and moneychangers out of the temple, when he should have been networking with them and taking them out to lunch. Not a smart move. He performed miracles free of charge, when he could've charged top shekel for leper-care. Not a smart move. But it's hard to be all-knowing when you're trying to keep your business all-growing."

Jake kept trying to catch Junior's eye to indicate to him to wrap it up, but Junior avoided looking in his direction. George appeared concerned when Junior appeared to choke up.

"There are some days when, like Jesus, I just want to shout, 'Father, father, why hast thou forsaken me?'" He sniffled a bit. "But Jesus will have a second coming, a second chance to prove himself to his father. And I believe we all deserve a second chance to prove ourselves to our father."

Junior looked upward with a beatific smile, then gazed on us.

"Thank you."

There was an enthusiastic round of applause as Junior sat down, and Bush was among those clapping the loudest. Jake now looked at me and repeated with a renewed emphasis that I was going to give a "brief" statement. I walked to the lectern but felt nervous as I tried to follow Junior's lead as best as I could.

"My son has said his father has forsaken him, but I can assure him and all of you that his father can no more forsake him than Jesus's heavenly father could forsake him. But that doesn't mean a father and son can't have differences. It wouldn't surprise me if sometimes among his disciples Jesus referred to his father as 'my Old Man.'" There were smiles and nodding heads in the audience.

"And I'm sure Jesus's Old Man was old school and didn't care for his son's long hair and beard, but his Old Man held his tongue. And I'm sure Jesus's Old Man thought, 'You're thirty-three years old and it's time to settle down,' but his Old Man held his tongue. And I'm sure Jesus's Old Man worried about his son riding a donkey late at night after drinking wine with his fishing buddies, but his Old Man held his tongue."

I was winging it and worried that I sounded ridiculous, but the men in the crowd were raptly attentive.

"And I'm sure his Old Man would've taken one look at Judas and said, 'Son, you don't need the Tree of Knowledge to tell that he's one bad apple,' but his Old Man held his tongue. And you can bet Jesus's Old Man wasn't crazy that the one single woman in his son's life was Mary Magdalene, a well-known sinner who needed to have seven demons cast out of her, when his son could have had his pick of nice girls with only five or six demons inside them. But his Old Man held his tongue there too."

I don't know where the seven demons came from, but I'd always found certain Bible stories memorable in my after-school Roman Catholic catechism classes.

"You see, Jesus's Old Man loved his son and wanted him to succeed. He didn't want to meddle in his son's business, and it took every ounce of willpower for Jesus's Old Man not to interfere. When Jesus was arrested, his heavenly father could have bailed him out, but sometimes a father has to show his son tough love and let his son carry his own cross. I know every father here knows that when your son makes a mistake it's the father who feels crucified. But I'm here tonight because I love my son and want him to know all is forgiven."

The moderator caught my eye and pointed at his watch.

"Thank you."

It must have gone over well. I also received a strong round of applause, and when my eyes met Bush's he grinned at me. For an instant, I actually felt a connection with him as another man struggling to figure out his life.

Jake stood up and resumed his place behind the podium. "Thank you for such an . . . an interesting profession of faith," he said briskly. "Now this week's Bible lesson is the Miracle at Cana. I know some of you didn't do your homework, which means you're going to hell, but

I'm going to be merciful and clue you in—in case you're not familiar with this miracle."

I'd heard about Jesus's major miracles: raising the dead, walking on water, the loaves and fishes, but wasn't familiar with the Miracle at Cana. I'd always thought there'd be plenty of time to read the Bible in the afterlife.

"You see, Jesus and his mother were guests at a nice family wedding at Cana, a suburb of Nazareth," Jake explained. "Well, during the reception Jesus's mother told her son they were running short of wine. Now this was a social calamity in both BC and AD. What to do? They needed vino pronto. But there were no Wal-Marts or pickup trucks back then. By the time you rode a donkey to the wine merchant and back, the honeymoon would be over and the bride would be due any day now. Jesus's mother knew this, and she looked at her son with a mama's steely eyes. Jesus felt his mother was pressuring him to be the Savior of the party. His mother guilted him into performing a miracle, and he turned six jars of water into wine. And not just any wine either. The Chateau de la Manger was delectably sippable—carrying oaky signs of the cross without being woody, displaying subtle top-notes of frankincense and myrrh—leading the master of the banquet to commend the bridegroom for saving the best for last."

Jake cleared his throat. It sounded like he was trying to dislodge a badger from its burrow. "What can we learn from this story?"

There was an expectant silence as everyone waited for someone else to supply the answer.

"A good Christian will always offer to do a beer run," a heavy-set man suggested, prompting chuckles from the group.

"Drink deep because Jesus is buying," a wizened man wearing a John Deere cap offered.

Jake nudged the room into a more serious discourse. "When some-one buys a round for the bar, isn't his love and generosity unconditional? Well, Jesus was saying, 'drinks are on me.' And his tab is still open. What other things does this story reveal about Jesus?"

Other voices piped in from around the room.

"Jesus didn't want to end a good time."

"He cares for our happiness."

"We're never to give up hope."

Bush raised his hand and Jake acknowledged him with a nod. "Jesus never closes down the bar, proving that his love for us has no last call."

"Amen," cried several members of the audience. "Christ is my drinking buddy" and "He's my designated driver to heaven" were precepts that every man in the room embraced.

The study group met for a little over an hour. After Jake concluded the meeting with a hymn, several men headed straight for the door, while others broke into conversational huddles. A few men came up and welcomed me to the group, and I chatted with them while trying to keep Bush in sight. George spoke briefly with a few men but kept moving steadily toward the door. I caught Junior's eyes and excused myself before George departed. We discreetly tailed him out to the street. The rear end of his car leaned into the curb. "Shit!" he exclaimed as he examined the flat tire. He looked up and caught my eye.

"Damn," I said as we stopped on the sidewalk. I couldn't remember using "Damn" as a curse word before, but I've since discovered that when visiting the South, your mouth will soon sound like it's aching for a harmonica or corncob pipe.

George slammed the hood of his car. "That's the last time I buy Fat Fuck French tires. Those are only six months old and I don't have a goddamned spare."

"I just bought one," Junior said.

I tried to think of something to say to George, but the first thing that came to mind was screaming "You've killed more Americans than bin Laden!" Then I remembered I was supposed to behave like Junior's father and said to George, "I told him not to buy it."

"You tell me everything I do is wrong," Junior said.

"No, I don't."

"So I'm wrong about that too?"

George laughed and shook his head. "I have to remember that, next time my dad calls."

Introductions were made, and when he said, "George . . . George Bush," I had to suppress the urge to ask if he was related to that other George Bush asshole. Junior followed up by asking, "Are you related to the vice president?"

A smirk appeared on his face. After six years his signature expression still gave me the creeps. His lips slithered around like snakes trying to find a warm place on a rock.

"I am."

I put what felt like an equally bogus smile on my face to feign pleasure at hearing his identity. Junior grinned. "Cool," he said before crossing the street to our car. There was a moment of silence before Bush spoke. "You've got a good boy there."

"Yes. But he still has a lot to learn."

"He will. Look how he jumped in to help. Not everyone would."

"That's true. But he jumps before he thinks. He thinks with his gut without planning beforehand or asking for advice. He makes up his mind without considering how things could go wrong. Then when things do go wrong, he refuses to admit he was wrong."

"A smart man is never wrong; he's just not right, right now."

"Yeah, but if you make a mess of things, tell somebody."

"You don't want him crying wolf every time he's barking up the wrong tree."

I searched his grayish-blue eyes for outward signs of intelligence but they were as lifeless as car lights; I could see they were on, but I had absolutely no sense that a brain lurked behind their gleaming.

"He learned to drive without crashing my car," I said. "He can learn to run my business without wrecking it."

"That's it," George said. "If you go for broke, sometimes you end up there. Some of us prefer to take our learning curves at a hundred and twenty rather than putt-putting along. I say if you can't stand the heat, crank up the AC."

It was spooky. Nothing he said made sense, but his relaxed posture gave him the cocksure air of a sage. It was the perfect set of attributes for a Republican presidential candidate.

"I take it," he said, "that your wallet's been fucked harder than a whore with a pension?"

I nodded grimly. "My son John made a bad deal and lost a bundle. It almost sank us. He's taking it harder than I am."

"Well, that's good. The sooner you feel bad, the sooner you're done with it."

I should have responded that that skill would come in handy when twenty-five hundred American soldiers come home in body bags from Iraq, but I didn't. George had a disarming ability to talk away hostility. He was convinced of his inherent likeability, proving that in America, the delusion that's caused the most harm is the heterosexual version of the Narcissus myth, where a guy sees his own reflection and doesn't fall in love, but thinks he's found his new best friend.

Junior returned carrying the spare tire while Taylor lugged the jack. Taylor was introduced as his younger brother.

"How come you weren't at the study group?" George asked.

"He doesn't have to study," Junior said. "He's the smart one." Then he glared at Taylor.

"Well, I'm smart enough to know how to change a tire," Taylor responded.

"And we're smart enough to let you do it," George said as he looked at Junior, signaling that he'd gotten off a good one. Junior gave him a thumbs-up, which I thought was excessively buddy-buddy. Taylor began to jack up the back of the car while we watched.

"How long you been in town?"

"We haven't moved yet," I said quickly when Junior seemed unsure of what to say. "We're looking to relocate and attended Bible study to get a sense of the place."

I explained that we lived in New York but thought Texas would be a better place to run our business. George talked up the virtues of Midland like a one-man chamber of commerce before asking what line of business we were in.

"Comic books," I said.

"Like Superman and Batman? There's money in that?"

"There is if you know what you're doing." I glanced at Junior. "But if you don't know what you're doing, there isn't."

Junior didn't respond immediately but continued moping. I was impressed with the maturity of his acting ability: he really knew how to play disgruntled. Taylor removed the tire and a little air leaked out with a hiss; if I didn't know better, I could've sworn the sound was coming from Junior.

"Sounds like we're both in mineral rights—I'm looking for oil and you're looking for Kryptonite." Bush's grin quavered. "Only I hope your business ain't as bad as mine." He explained that he ran an oil and gas company and was going to have to lay off workers. "It's bad. We're spending a dollar to make a dime."

"We're not doing so well either," I said. "We've had a few setbacks, which is why we're looking to move."

"You don't need to keep reminding me that I'm not as lucky as you are," Junior said. He looked at me with such ferocity that it unnerved me. It was almost like he really was angry.

"It wasn't all luck," I said.

Junior looked at George. "When Dad started out he had it easy. Twenty years ago, old ladies had attics and basements filled with comics that they just gave away. Now the easy money isn't easy. I have to dig to find something."

"I didn't have it easy," I said. "I had to schmooze those old ladies into letting me into their attics. Jesus, I had to compliment more fat cats. 'Oh, look at Mr. Whiskers, he's such a nice kitty.' And I'm allergic to cats."

Junior glowered at me.

Taylor lowered the jack and stood up. "That should do it."

I looked at Bush and said, "Mission accomplished." It was completely childish but I couldn't resist.

"That'll get you going." Taylor said. It was impressive how he'd finished the job in no time. I'd still be figuring out how to attach the jack to the car.

Bush looked down at the replaced tire. "Damn. That was fast. He is the smart one. Sorry, John." Bush winked at Junior.

I couldn't resist good-naturedly rubbing Taylor's hair. "Heck of a job, Brownie."

Taylor looked at me oddly but didn't say anything. No one else commented on my strange outburst, but I relished mocking Bush with his own Bartlett's quotations.

"I can't thank you guys enough."

It looked like Bush was going to take off—his car keys were in his hand—and Junior and Taylor kept glancing nervously at me. We still needed to have him meet Elena, have him fall for her, get him drunk, and then videotape him having sex with her. Jesus, this was going to be a long night. I was also hungry.

"We're looking for a good restaurant for dinner. Can you recommend some place?"

Bush's smile reappeared without any hint of smirk. "Dona Anita's. It's my favorite place in town. Everything's great, but I love the chimichangas."

Junior put on a look of mock supplication mixed with hero worship. "We'd be honored if you joined us."

"You're one of the first locals we've met," Taylor added.

Bush appeared flattered by the young men's invitation.

"I'm buying," I offered.

The smirk reappeared. It was such a clumsy smile that it looked like George's face was trying not to drop his lips. "Then I'm eating and drinking!" he shouted.

Bush gave us directions to Dona Anita's from the church, but before we said good-bye, Taylor held up his dirty and greasy hands. "Can we stop at the motel for a minute so I can clean up?"

We also needed to go there to see if Michael had arrived. Then I remembered we had to quickly convince Elena that I was Junior from the future. Even I thought that might take some time.

"You guys do that," Bush said. "I'll go ahead and get us a table. I've got to call my wife and tell her I won't be home for supper. She won't like it, but she'll be fine if I tell her it's business and bring her cigarettes. Some women love getting a dozen roses, but Laura lights up at a carton of Camels."

"It is business," I said. "You'd be helping us."

"Although, I like to mix business with a little pleasure," Junior said.

"Damn right," Bush said as he opened the door to his car.

I actually wanted to keep this a business meeting. I was horrified that anyone might think we were his friends.

13

WE KNOCKED ON THE DOOR of room 218. Elena opened it, and Michael, freshly showered, was getting dressed behind her. I was immediately struck by how little they had changed in twenty years. In 2006 Elena would still have the same buxom chest and narrow hips, short hair, and flawless skin, but she would develop a few lines around her eyes, evidence that the more of life you see, the more you need to squint. Michael's hair would recede slightly, but he'd still be fit. Although I'd soon notice his younger self possessed an unguarded effervescence lacking in the forty-four-year-old Michael. Elena stuck out her hand and said, "Nice to meet you again, John." Michael grinned with a sudden movement of his face that was as delightful as watching someone do a handstand. It made me think one of the chief infirmities of middle age is that your smile isn't as limber as it used to be.

Michael stared at Junior and then at me. "Wow," he said. "You look like . . . brothers."

"You can say it," I said. "Father and son."

Michael nodded. "That too."

Elena also examined both of our faces closely. "Well, I'm not going to fuck a stranger just on anyone's recommendation." She found two moles on Junior's neck and arm and seemed reassured when she found corresponding ones on my neck and arm. She pulled out an inkpad and then responded to our inquisitive looks. "We stopped at a stationery store." She ordered each of us to press our thumbs into the inky-blue cushion then press them next to each other on a blank sheet of paper. She compared the prints carefully before declaring, "They're a match." She sighed heavily. "I kind of hoped they wouldn't be." Her face crinkled abruptly, as if she smelled something awful. "I'm going to fuck a Republican. A Republican *man*. This will be the most disgusting thing I've ever done in bed."

We chuckled, but her forbidding expression stopped us. "I'm serious. Now tell me exactly why I'm doing this. I need to believe that my fucking him will save us all from a calamity." I briefly recounted Bush's political history, trying to give only the highlights of his incompetence and villainy, but Elena asked several pointed questions whenever I tried to condense his record of malfeasance. "Don't skip over anything," she said. "*You're* not the one sleeping with him." She appeared to be distraught and sat down on the edge of the bed. "I honestly don't know if I can go through with this."

I decided to tell her about our daughter. If I were about to attempt to have sex with Bush or Cheney, I'd need an especially compelling reason to overcome my revulsion. But I would do them for Isabella's sake. I sent Junior out of the room for a minute. He protested but split when I snapped, "We don't have time."

Elena seemed joyful, incredulous, and oddly serene when I told her about Isabella. She repeated Isabella's name in the most maternally tender manner, saying it as if she were caressing her. Suddenly she stared at me. "I have a baby by myself?"

"No, you'll do it with someone you meet . . ."

"Don't tell me!" she shouted before I could finish. "It's bad luck."

I smiled. Elena had dated some disastrous girlfriends before she met Sonia. Even I felt superstitiously cautious about talking about her future.

"Who's the father?"

"I am."

She looked carefully at me. "That makes sense."

To further our case, I explained how Bush would do absolutely nothing to combat global warming, and the consequences of his inaction would be borne by Isabella and her children; how he would waste a trillion dollars on an unnecessary war in Iraq, short-changing Isabella's generation; how he would torture people for the first time in U.S. history; and I harped briefly on his trying to drill in the Arctic National Wildlife Refuge, destroying something that should be preserved for Isabella, her children, and her grandchildren. "Oh, and he will also propose a constitutional amendment to limit marriage to a man and a woman, making Isabella's family constitutional outcasts."

Elena asked me several questions about marriage equality, happily surprised to hear something that had been inconceivable in 1986 would be close to unstoppable in the next twenty years.

I'd been having doubts about whether trying to prevent George W. Bush from becoming president was worth the effort, but telling Elena about Isabella reminded me once again how he had wantonly endangered my daughter's future happiness, and renewed my determination to stop him.

Elena checked her appearance in the mirror above the dresser, combed her lustrous hair, and pulled down the light pink blouse she was wearing. She looked terrific. I assumed any straight man would find her hard to resist. "Let's go or I'll change my mind."

Before we departed, Michael pointed out he would need an auditory signal from Elena to allow him time to head to the closet before she entered the room and then another signal to come out. "I'm not going to wait in the closet all night while you're having dinner and drinks." Elena promised that she would talk loudly and fumble with the key in the lock in order to give Michael time to hide in the closet. "And when I say, 'Oh, George, that's fantastic!' That's your signal to come out. And I'm praying that happens before I have to give him a blow job. My gag reflex isn't strong enough to swallow Republican dick."

Junior was waiting outside and wrapped his arm around Elena's shoulder and hugged her. "Ask not what your country can do for you, but who you can do for your country."

"Great. You're making me feel like Rosa Parks—only I'm letting someone sit on my face."

Dona Anita's was a short drive from our motel. Everyone was quiet while I gave Elena background information on George and sketched out a rough psychological profile: "He has a domineering mother and an overachieving-war-hero-oil-man-millionaire-before-he-turned-thirty father." I added that his father was the captain of the Yale baseball team but his son had only been a cheerleader at Andover. I summed Bush up with President Clinton's famous quote about him, "He doesn't know anything. He doesn't want to know anything. But he's not dumb." (I didn't attribute the quote to President Clinton. There wasn't time. I just claimed "a famous U.S. politician will say about Bush . . .") As we pulled into the restaurant's parking lot, I thought Elena had a tough job ahead of her, but she'd routinely handled hecklers and drunks in comedy clubs, and I was confident her improvisational abilities were capable of outwitting our least curious president.

I felt a palpable mournfulness as we walked to the entrance. It was distressing that the only way we could save our country was by a sordid, underhanded seduction. And I hated that I was asking one of the mothers of my daughter to be intimate with him. I tried to put those thoughts out of my head by thinking that we would all be much better off if he never became president. It didn't help. I just had to regard the situation as one of the paradoxes of modern medicine I'd learned from treating my cancer: the cure is often more nauseating than the illness.

We told the hostess we were meeting a friend. She smiled in recognition and led us to the back of the restaurant. Dona Anita's Mexican décor was surprisingly more Frida Kahlo and Diego Rivera than piñata donkeys dangling from the ceiling. George was seated at our table with an empty rocks glass rattling in his hand when he spotted us. He had arranged for a table for four, but seeing that we were five, he asked a busboy to add a two-top to give us more room. George smirked strenuously when Elena was introduced and then graciously pulled out the chair next to him for her.

"It's always nice to visit Texas," she said, "where there are still gentlemen."

"That's because ladies still visit us."

"I've heard about you," she said while shaking his hand. "You're the Texan who can't change a tire."

"Yeah," George admitted, "but my mother says the smartest man in the world always knows who to call."

"And I take it you're the smartest man in the world."

"No. But I got his number."

Elena laughed. "Well, my mama said there's those who fix and those who know what's busted. And sometimes it takes more brains to know what's busted."

"Your mama sounds like a wise woman."

"So does yours."

"She is." He flagged down our waitress by holding up his empty glass as she passed our table. "In our family, behind every successful man is an angry woman telling him, 'Don't be an idiot.'" He said this with a smile, but it sounded like one of those unintentionally revealing sentences punctuated by a spot of blood.

"Are we gonna order some drinks?" George asked us as the waitress stood with a pad and pen in her hands.

"You don't have a say in this," I said. "You're not buying so I'm the decider." I couldn't resist using his infamously idiotic word. "I'm the decider and we're having a round."

George turned to Elena. "He can be the decider if he's buying."

I wondered if George was on his second or third drink. I hardly expected a future president of the United States to make disparaging comments about his mother, but then I grasped that he wasn't famous yet, and no one in the entire country—including his parents—would have dreamed that someday he'd become president. It truly was an Age of Innocence.

George first asked Elena if she'd like something to drink, and she ordered a margarita on the rocks with no salt. He ordered a Jim Beam on the rocks. The drink orders continued around the table. I had to face that there was a chance I was about to drink alcohol for the first time in thirteen years. It made me uneasy. My sobriety had been exceedingly difficult to achieve. But there was no way to get George drunk if I practiced abstinence. I was going to try to covertly empty my drinks in a potted palm near our table when George wasn't looking, but in case I had to drink I considered ordering a Cosmo, my favorite cocktail in the day. Then I realized I didn't start drinking them until sometime in the '90s. The bartender would have no idea how to mix one. I decided to play it safe and order white zinfandel, a nauseatingly sweet wine that I hoped would ensure I didn't fall in love with drinking again.

"Now everything's good here," George said to the table. "But some things are better than others."

"Everything looks good to me," Elena said, looking directly at George. I thought she might be rushing things with him, but who was I to judge? My understanding of heterosexuality was as limited as my grasp of calculus; I'd studied both in school but made no effort to master the subjects, as I was absolutely certain I'd never use them.

"What do you recommend?" Elena asked George. He immediately leaned over and pointed to several items on the menu. A busboy brought chips and salsa to our table and we gorged on them in the same manner that the United States devoured most of Mexico in 1848. When the waitress returned with our drinks, she took our orders. After she left, I looked at the empty baskets on our tables and asked a busboy for more chips.

"What do you do?" George asked Elena.

"I'm a stand-up comic."

George's eyes widened. "Really? Do you make money at that?"

"Some," she said. "I'm starting to get work."

Elena would get plenty of work over the next twenty years. She'd have her own half-hour special on Comedy Central, host several television shows, and be regarded as one of the best stand-ups in North America. I considered telling her about her success but remembered that she told me once that the struggle of becoming a stand-up is how comics develop. It seemed dangerous to interfere with that process.

"Next month, a friend of mine is doing a show in New York at Comedy U," Elena announced. "I'm going to show my support."

She'd mentioned in the car that a friend of hers was planning on coming out as gay on stage at a straight comedy club in SoHo. I caught Junior's eye and tried to make him aware of my concern without alarming George. I didn't want him to realize he was hanging out with a bunch of queers. (I didn't consider that George might have found fucking a lesbian hot.) Junior picked up on my concern and shot back a dagger-eyed look that asked, Do I seem like an idiot?

"So you're the artsy type?" George asked, his interest seeming to flag.

Elena ignored the dismissive attitude behind his question and asked, "What do you do?"

"I'm in oil and gas."

"And how'd you get started in that?"

"It's in my blood," George replied.

Elena smiled at his choice of words and George picked up on that.

"Not literally," George added.

"I hope not. If your blood type is Texas Light Intermediate, your cholesterol would be out of control." She grinned. "Although you do seem sweet enough."

George appeared to be favorably impressed again. "How do you know about benchmark crude?"

"I have a very smart ass," she said.

I wasn't surprised that she knew the technical jargon of the petroleum industry. Elena's wide-ranging curiosity matched my own.

Junior chirped in. "Elena knows everything. She's the smartest person I know."

"I'm not the smartest person. Otherwise, I'd be having dinner at a fancier restaurant with fancier friends."

"She's the smartest ass," Junior said.

She glanced down appreciatively at her own butt.

"It's earned a BA?" George asked while making a humorous point of also checking it out.

"Actually, it has a master's."

"In what?"

"History."

George perked up again. "How's a master's in history help in stand-up?"

"I know what's what and who's who, and those are things every stand-up needs to know."

George dipped a chip in salsa before saying, "So your act isn't pie-in-the-face comedy?"

"My act is smart. It's more pi in the face." A look of incomprehension crossed George's face while he chewed. Picking up that she had to explain her joke, Elena added, "The mathematical symbol." George nodded and smiled, showing that he got it while Elena rummaged for a notebook and pen in her purse. "Somebody's probably already used this," she said before she wrote down "π in the face."

I was unable to say aloud what I thought: "π in the face" sounded like a perfect description of my experience of time travel. George watched Elena write with a strange look of amazement, as if he'd never seen a woman holding a pen before.

"I have to write things down or I forget them," she explained. "Now that I think about it, "π in the face" seems like a joke an eighth-grader would make in algebra. That's stand-up too. A lot of your ideas fizzle."

"We call them 'dry holes' or a 'duster' in my line of work." George became melancholy for a moment. "Lately that's all I've been drillin'."

"I'm sorry to hear that. It's hard to always be prospecting, then discover you've hit fool's gold instead of pay dirt." She suddenly seemed pleased. "Actually comedians *are* searching for fool's gold."

George took a sip of his bourbon. "I never realized comics were so serious about their work."

"Just because a job looks like fun doesn't mean there's not work involved. Do you think baseball players don't work?"

I was impressed by how craftily she turned the subject to baseball.

"No," George said. "They work hard developing their natural talent."

"All successful artists and businessman do that," she responded. "Doing stand-up is sort of like playing baseball. You don't become good without playing the game. You step up to the plate and either knock it out of the park or strike out. Only in stand-up, you actually need to bat close to a thousand, because if you're batting three hundred you stink."

The waitress arrived, carrying a tray and a tray stand. As she started serving our meals, I ordered another round and Elena asked George about his business.

"I founded my own company, Spectrum 7. Business is real bad now. The price of oil is lower than a centipede's balls." The smirk crawled out of its hole. "Pardon my Texan."

Elena's cheeks dimpled, signaling to him that she wasn't offended.

"I have a lot of respect for anyone who starts their own business. It takes guts."

"I have a lot of respect for someone who starts his own company and doesn't just follow in his father's footsteps," Junior said as he scowled at me. "Especially if you're not trying to follow your father *and* your brother." Then he glared at Taylor, who erupted as if he'd been brooding all night.

"Oh, it's my fault you didn't look through your purchase. You just saw some old comics and impulsively jumped, without checking them for missing pages. Instead of being pissed off at me and Dad, be pissed off at yourself. It's your job to know the business. I do. You fucked up."

"Taylor, drop it," I said. "We all make mistakes. That's life. You're down now but you'll be up later."

I don't know where these bromides were coming from, but it occasionally depressed me to think the majority of thoughts in our heads are hand-me-downs. Taylor still looked steamed and Junior appeared to be humiliated by his public slam. He took a healthy swallow of his margarita.

"I'd rather be the guy who jumps and misses than the guy who sits and pisses," George said before he winked at Junior.

"Look," I said to Junior and Taylor. "We had a setback, but what's most important is our family loyalty. No matter how tough we are on each other, our real enemies are other people."

I sounded insane and felt disloyal to my friends, who were as important in my life as my family. It made me question whether feigning selfishness could actually make me believe this bullshit. George raised his glass. "Let's toast to that. To family kicking ass," he said as we followed suit, raising and clinking our glasses as we repeated: "To family kicking ass."

Our waitress passed by, and I ordered another round. I'd already dumped two drinks in the potted palm and thought a third might kill it.

George said to me, "You're leading your team. That's what a good CEO does. That's where the phrase 'captains of industry' comes from. A successful boss doesn't have to know or do everything except cheer on his team. I was a cheerleader and know how to lead a team." He finished off his drink. He didn't sound drunk, but his reminiscing was starting to get wobbly. "And people think cheerleaders don't take it hard when you lose. Because we're not out on the field. We're standing on the sidelines. But let me tell you, I took every loss as hard as our players. And I risked my neck for our team. You ever try a backflip on lumpy turf? It ain't easy and it takes guts. When your team's losing and you're down thirty points, the cheerleader has to keep smiling and not let anyone see that he's down too. You have to boost your team when they fumble. You have to keep telling them they're going to win even when you know it's over. That's what makes a great leader."

As I listened to his pep talk I thought, He never stopped being a cheerleader. It made me more determined that we had to stop him from becoming president. He wasn't stupid, but he was a profoundly damaged man. He really was a tragic figure, if tragedy is defined by the pathos of your limitations.

"Your dad was an oilman, right?" Elena said.

George's face twisted once like a screw-top cap that turned partway but wouldn't budge further. I recognized that stubborn expression from my years of boozing. It was the look of a mean drunk.

"People think I got everything handed to me because of him. That's bullshit. It was my trust fund I tapped. My money I risked. He wasn't out there raising my capital. I earned every penny. He wasn't out there knocking on the door of every family friend. It was me and it was hard work. You spend six months sweet-talking money from millionaires and you won't be so sweet. I called in every favor, owed everyone big time. Put my reputation on the line. And we're down now but we won't be forever." He swallowed a mouthful of bourbon. "People think having friends with money makes life easy. I wish I had more friends without a dime. With rich friends, you have to compliment their pretty houses, compliment their not-so-pretty wives and say, 'Hey, looking good' to their fat kids. You have to talk money without sounding like you care about money. You have to blow hard with a gentle breeze."

The waitress brought him a new drink, and he lifted the glass and halved the contents.

"Just because your dad buys you a baseball team doesn't mean it's gonna win the Series. That's your job," George declared, setting his glass down before digging into his chimichanga with his fork.

We had two more rounds at Dona Anita's. When George got up to go to the men's room, all of us dumped our glasses into an empty beer pitcher that I grabbed from a nearby table that hadn't been bussed yet. After I paid the check, George offered to buy us a nightcap at a bar called Higgins.

I gingerly asked him if he was sure he was okay to drive.

George patted his pants' pockets, searching for his car keys. "Don't you know? In Texas it's not considered drunk driving if you can step on the gas without falling over."

Elena offered to drive him. She had stopped drinking after two margaritas and was probably the most sober of any of us. "I'm not worried about you driving," she assured him. "I'd just enjoy the company." She smiled at him flirtatiously. I was impressed by how good she was at pretending to be attracted to him. The one undeniable benefit of having spent some time in the closet is that it nurtures a talent that you can fall back on any time: lying convincingly. Sometimes I worried that queer kids in the twenty-first century coming out at twelve, or even younger, would never develop that valuable skill.

"Sounds great to me," George said. "I love riding with pretty ladies."

"You love riding pretty ladies?" Elena asked.

George laughed. "Oh, you're bad."

His leer was a promising sign that he wanted into her smarty-pants. We watched him toss his car keys to Elena, who caught them with a flick of her wrist. She waved to us as they pulled out of the parking lot.

Taylor drove our car and on the way to the bar, Junior asked, "Does he *really* become president?"

Part of me also found it hard to believe, which I admitted. "Yes," I said sourly.

"Jesus Christ," Taylor said and then sighed.

Confirming their doubts made me feel ashamed that somehow I and every other American alive in 2000 were responsible for letting him become president on our watch. Bush and Cheney were a reminder that the price of liberty is eternal vigilance; you're required to scream "You stupid asshole!" every time you spot one.

"He seems like a nice guy," Junior said, "but he comes off about as brainy as Mr. Ducker, my wood-shop teacher in junior high. I'd trust him with a band saw but not with running our country."

"What's weird is that he comes off as arrogant," Taylor said. "Like he's smarter than everyone else. That's like an amoeba thinking it's still the most intelligent species on the planet because it was the most intelligent species two billion years ago."

"We've gotta stop him," Junior said.

"Thank God he seems to be into Elena," Taylor observed.

Junior's statement made me angry. "There's no 'We' involved. She's the one who's going to stop him." I found our whole plan intolerably squalid. I hated that Elena was even driving with George Bush, let alone planning on sleeping with him. Was it our job to stop him by any means possible? I was starting to worry that changing history might change Elena, Junior, and Taylor more than it would alter the future of our country.

"If he's as bad for us and the world as you say he is," Taylor said, "isn't it our duty to stop him?"

Taylor seemed to have really turned against Bush. I was beginning to hope it might stick.

"You know, if I could sleep with him and stop him, I would in an instant," I said. "But I can't let her do this. It doesn't feel right. It's not right. I don't know how this will affect her, and I don't know how this will affect you."

"We'll be fine," Junior said dismissively.

"I don't think so," I said. "You just said that in a snotty know-it-all manner. I don't recall being like that when I was your age. It already might be ruining you. This smugness might just grow exponentially until you become Dick Cheney. We're traveling on untrodden ground here. I don't want you to save the world and lose your souls."

I knew I sounded demented, but I was feeling apprehensive about the whole thing in my gut. It wasn't simple fear, but that instinctual alarm that by middle age I'd learned to heed.

"No one's ever figured out a really nice way to fight evil," Taylor said. "There are always casualties."

"Yes," I said. "But I don't want the mother of my . . . child to be one of them." I'd almost slipped again and said "daughter."

There wasn't any rational reason to argue against following our plan except for my almost superstitious distaste for George W. Bush. He was bad luck. I didn't want anyone I cared about to get too close to him.

"At this point, George W. Bush is an innocent man," I said. "Do we have the right to stop evil by any means? All of a sudden I'm just not sure."

"If we really want to stop evil, maybe we should travel further back in time and bump off Adam and Eve," Junior suggested.

What if my not letting Elena sleep with Bush meant that Isabella's world tipped hopelessly into global warming? Our discussion made me vow to ask Elena if she wanted to reconsider her decision before it was too late.

We parked on the street and walked to Higgins, a fern bar with exposed brick walls and the fake Tiffany lamp chandeliers that were popular in the '80s. George pulled out a credit card and handed it to the bartender. "Whatever my friends are having," he said. I went to the men's room, and when I came back George was seated at the bar and the kids had pulled their bar stools close to him. "Don't ever sound too smart is my advice," he said. "It puts people off. If you speak dumbass, nobody expects you to kick butt."

With a flick of his eyes and a finger pointed at our empty glasses, George ordered another round. I'd carried my wine to the men's room, where I'd dumped it in the sink. George had to be drunk after putting away five or six bourbons, but he didn't sound drunk. He had become louder and more pugnacious, and from my experience a mean drunk who quits drinking and finds Jesus will spend the rest of his life turning nice into nasty. Tomorrow, with a hangover, he'd make everyone around him wish they had a drink.

"I'm realistic," he said. "I say good things happen and shit happens, but unfortunately most of the time that means good things happen to shits. And we want to be one of those shits." He looked at Elena. "Pardon my Texan."

I'd never realized that cynicism could be folksy; George was an aw-shucks Machiavelli who winked at you after saying a ruler should be scary rather than lovey-dovey.

George continued, "I've learned more about business in Bible study than I did at Harvard."

I'd forgotten that one of the most blinkered presidents in our history was a graduate of Yale *and* the Harvard Business School.

He took another sip of his drink. "If you think about it, Jesus took over a small local family business and went global. He reinvigorated the brand. He's an example of a successful team leader who knew how to delegate authority. His disciples were out in the field, and yet he's kept everything humming for two thousand years. And Jesus is on a first-name basis with everybody. People love that. He doesn't spend his time reading long reports and he hates long meetings; he checks in once a day by prayer and can figure out who's telling the truth by comparing stories. If you're on the ball, that's enough. Jesus judges everybody on his team by his or her character; he sizes them up like any good business-man. Then he either promotes them upstairs or fires them." George smiled at his play on words. "And this is most important: he keeps everything he hears confidential. There are no leaks from Jesus's office. That's real power."

Everyone listening to him appeared to be captivated. From the looks on our faces, I'd say the appearance of concentration is pretty much the same whether you're enthralled by a speaker's profundity or appalled by his banality.

Elena smiled at George before she whispered something in his ear. Junior immediately said, "Hey, no secrets."

George smirked. "Keeping secrets is the secret of success." He then announced that he had to get going but offered me his business card. "Call me if you have any questions about Midland. If I don't have the answer, I know somebody who does."

I looked to see if Elena was going with him, but she and Taylor were exchanging phone numbers. They had talked about going to Bandelier National Monument while he lived in Los Alamos. When George got off his bar stool, his cowboy boots met the floor with a slippery shuffle, and he teetered for a moment before steadying himself. He looked embarrassed but joked, "My feet are already in bed."

Elena also stood up, and neither of them said good-bye as they headed for the door.

We waited a short time before leaving. I didn't want to meet them in the parking lot. In the end, I didn't stop Elena and talk to her about my misgivings. I regretted it immediately and thought of trying to stop her by calling her on her cell, but then I became infuriated again that no one had cell phones in 1986. (It felt as if my entire civilization were built upon them.) We were all tired and some of us were slightly drunk—Taylor's eyes were half lidded—and the ride to the motel was quiet, almost as if we were trying not to disturb the couple's tryst. I felt sick to my stomach and couldn't decide if my nausea stemmed from the tiny sip of white zinfandel that touched my lips or disgust at embroiling Elena in our scheme. I was the grown-up and should have stopped Junior and Taylor when they first suggested it. But I refused to let die the dream of a world where George W. Bush never became president. It wasn't a utopian dream of a world without problems; it was a vision of a world with fewer stupid, self-inflicted problems. From the vantage point of 2006, that sounded like paradise.

George's car was parked in front of Elena's room. I tried not to imagine what was happening, but Michael had given Elena the cocaine he'd bought. I said goodnight to the boys in a whisper. Beforehand, we'd agreed that Michael would let us know when the deed was done and confirm that he had the videotape we needed. I was in my room, brushing my teeth, when there was a knock on my door. That was quick, I thought, but it made sense. Bush's botched invasion of Iraq reeked of premature ejaculation. I opened the door and was surprised to see Elena. "Are you okay?" I asked.

She entered my room, awkwardly avoiding eye contact before she sat down on the edge of one of the double beds. She petted Ravi without looking up.

"Where's George?"

She made a dismissive face as she batted her hand. "Passed out in my bed."

There was another knock on my door. Junior and Taylor whispered loudly, "It's us!" before I let them enter. Junior explained their appearance. "I left my room curtain half open and saw Elena walk by."

Elena appeared to be close to tears.

"Are you okay?" Taylor asked.

She shook her head no.

"I can't do this. I'm sorry. I've spent four hours listening to this guy, and I just don't believe anyone this mediocre will ever become president. I know you seem to be from the future, but something's not right here. Either you have to be lying, or the world will become more horrible than I want to imagine. I can't believe—and I don't want to believe— our country could ever put him in the White House."

I was overcome with relief. We'd tried, but obviously it wasn't meant to be. Then I was beset by two disemboweling fears. Perhaps it was impossible to change history and thus we would be unable to prevent Carol's suicide. And in twenty years, would Elena recall this decision and bitterly regret not stopping him? She would castigate herself for allowing six, soon to be eight, years of bad leadership by refusing to have thirty minutes of disagreeable sex. One body sacrificed to stop the thousands of bodies being sacrificed in Iraq. I voiced this new possibility to her.

"Make up your fucking mind," Junior said. "An hour ago you were saying fucking him might ruin us, and now you're saying not fucking him might ruin us. Which is it?"

"I don't know. That's the problem of existence. Everything's possible."

Elena smiled grimly. "Come on. Does he really become president?"

"Yes," I said. "I'm not lying."

I voiced a small hope. "Maybe his getting drunk with us tonight is enough of a flutter of the butterfly's wings to change the future. This didn't happen in my past so there's a chance that we've changed the future for the better."

It sounded like a pipedream, hearing it said aloud.

"Where's Michael?" Junior asked.

"Watching him," Elena said.

"Let's get him home," I said, thinking that if anyone had ever predicted it was my destiny to try to stop George W. Bush from becoming president, I would have laughed. It wasn't such an amusing idea right then.

We all moved toward the door, and when Junior opened it, powerful floodlights blinded us. The room was immediately filled with six men in black uniforms carrying assault rifles, and Ravi began barking. Junior immediately grabbed him by the collar. I could see red laser dots moving over my chest and Junior's. The soldiers wore black makeup on their faces and ordered us to freeze. We waited silent and motionless until two Dick Cheneys entered. It was the young Dick, the one from 1986, and old Dick. Young Dick stepped into the room first, blocking Old Dick's path. Old Dick's face curdled in frustration for a moment, and you could see him physically reining in his anger like a ringmaster cracking a whip at a growling lion. They were excessively courteous to each other, each Dick trying to leave standing room for the other. Old Dick's altered appearance disproved my theory that he'd made a deal with the devil, since he'd aged horribly in twenty years. It looked as if every artery in his fleshy body was as constricted as his smile. Young Dick skittered about like a newborn scorpion, hankering to sting something. "Not so fast," he said before closing the door to our room.

I tried to think of what we could do, but your options are limited when you can see on your body exactly where the first bullet will hit. Young Dick nodded at a soldier, and the soldier opened a briefcase and removed five metal cuffs. He placed one on each of our right wrists. The gay man in me noted the soldier's muscles bulging through his tight-fitting uniform, but the thought exasperated me as if my brain were incapable of being serious for even a moment.

"All right, here's what's going to happen," Old Dick declared. "You two and that Michael are going to his room." He indicated Junior and Taylor with a nod. "You're going to get your dicks hard and swing them in George's face. Elena, you'll go with them, and while they're waving their things at George, you'll be petting him, telling him to take a little nibble, making him think you're offering him one of your very nice tits." He lop-smiled at her. "George will open wide, and one of you guys will give him a mouthful of dick-titty. Once we get footage of George looking like a cocksucker, we'll call it a night."

"I still think four penises would be optimum," Young Dick said.

Old Dick became biblically wrathful for an instant—the word "smite" came to mind—but then resumed his general look of genocidal impatience: will everyone just die. "Look, we made a plan. Let's follow it."

"Four penises will imply that he was attending a gay orgy. It closes the deal."

Old Dick snarled, "We can't use his cock." There was an almost imperceptible nod in my direction.

"Why not?"

Old Dick impatiently pointed to Junior and me.

"These two share the same cock."

"Is anyone going to examine them that closely?"

Old Dick remained silent for a minute before speaking. When he resumed speaking, he sounded like a special education teacher at the end of a very long day.

"In twenty years, our image-analysis software will be able to count and match the number of pubic hairs in a verification procedure. We used it to prove alleged pornographic photos of Saddam were faked. If we have two penises that match up, we open ourselves to charges of falsification. The Bushes would be looking for that. They've always made a policy of having friends in intelligence; they'd figure that out and the tape would be worthless. You do understand that revealing time travel has never been on the table?"

Young Dick became angry but held it in check.

"You didn't tell me about the image-analysis software."

"Everything's revealed on a need-to-know basis."

"So you don't trust me?"

"You're inexperienced."

Young Dick looked crushed but didn't respond, making it appear that he agreed with Old Dick's assessment of him. Old Dick sighed.

"I expect you to do what you to have to do in 2006. You've been briefed. Don't forget that or we're fucked."

Young Dick nodded and then he ushered Elena, Junior, and Taylor out the door, accompanied by four black ops. "We'll wait here," Old

Dick said as he took a seat. Two black ops remained with us, their guns aimed at my chest. I also had to sit down. I was in a state of shock from learning that we were the reason Dick Cheney became vice president. It had been his plan from the start. Send me back in time where I'd try to stop George from becoming president, and our videotape would allow Cheney to blackmail him.

14

FOR THE FIRST FEW MINUTES, we stared at each other as Ravi growled in the bathroom. I had to lock him up to stop his barking. Looking into Dick Cheney's blue eyes and trying to figure out what he's thinking was like looking up and trying to figure out what the sky is thinking. He seemed at ease with long periods of silence, and almost appeared to relish the absence of conversation, as if his idea of nirvana was a world where he could have anyone bound and gagged. I couldn't stop thinking about what was going on in Elena's room. It made me sick that they were being forced to help Cheney. I assumed the videotape was the reason Cheney was able to choose himself to be Bush's vice presidential running mate. I imagined Cheney meeting with George privately. Old Dick would have him by the balls for cocksucking and then dictate his terms on how he'd be running the country after the election, or else the tape would be leaked to Fox News.

It seemed clear he had never been trying to kill us. He shot at us to get us out of New York and headed toward Midland. Though how had Cheney figured out our plan to stop Bush from becoming president? Did he wiretap our car when he was at my parents'? I was certain he didn't go near our car, but did he return later? Young Dick was certainly involved. He knew about the time machine. Perhaps we were followed after we left Buffalo. Maybe the car was bugged during the night we spent in St. Louis. After a few minutes of random conjecture, I decided to ask him. "How did you know we were in Midland? How did you know about our plan?" He didn't immediately respond to my questions, but I hadn't really expected him to answer me. With most people you observe some facial movement that suggests a decision-making process is occurring, an eyebrow wags or a lip curls, but not with Old Dick. His face remained resolutely stationary, as if a computer were processing my inquiry.

"You've been under constant surveillance since you left the Bronx. Your car was bugged, and I've received daily transcripts of your conversations."

Cheney gave me a cold, toothy grin—a grin that gave me the disturbing sensation that he got a sick thrill from flashing his skull.

"I'm curious," I said. "You've sworn to protect the Constitution against all enemies, foreign and domestic, and yet you torture suspects, jail people without trial, and illegally invade people's privacy."

"So."

"You can't defend the Constitution if you're undermining it."

"We haven't had a terrorist attack on U.S. soil since 9/11."

"So." I let the word linger for a moment. "But 9/11 happened because you did nothing after you were warned bin Laden was determined to attack. Specifically warned he might hijack airplanes. Maybe you could have given the airlines and airports and every passenger a yoo-hoo about that. It happened on your watch and wouldn't have if you'd warned the country. You failed to protect us then, but now you have the gall to claim that only you can protect the country."

"Intelligence briefings are notoriously speculative."

"You and Bush have an alibi. For intelligence briefings to work, the people hearing them need to be intelligent."

I wanted to hear him say, "Fuck you!" but he remained dispassionate, aloof as God.

"I have a master's in political science." His voice was unemotional; he sounded like a history teacher grading a student's paper, correcting an error in the text by writing a comment in the margin.

"Great. From an administration that doesn't believe in science."

"We believe in science. Science used politically."

I think Cheney was making a joke. His lips sidled to the right side of his face.

"You've ignored climate change. What are you going to tell your grandchildren when there are droughts and they can't grow enough food to feed themselves? 'I had other priorities'?"

He ignored my dig at his infamous "I had other priorities" comment, made when he was questioned about taking five draft deferments to avoid serving in Vietnam.

"We can't slap together a policy because Chicken Little thinks the earth is running a fever."

"Why not? You slapped together the invasion of Iraq."

He was preternaturally calm, and even though I kept trying to rile him, he remained placid, almost bored.

"At least we're not sitting on our cans bureaucrapping."

"No. You guys swing into action and don't accomplish anything. Instead of sending massive amounts of troops to Afghanistan to get bin Laden, you let him escape. When everyone in the country supported doing whatever it would take to get him."

"Oh, please, liberals don't have the stomach for war."

"Well, conservatives don't either if you two draft-dodgers are any example."

In their 2004 reelection campaign, it had nauseated me that Bush and Cheney claimed the mantle of being the indispensable protectors of our country, even though they'd skipped out on risking their own necks in Vietnam. It also made me pissed that conservatives assumed liberals lacked toughness and were irresolute.

"No, I didn't fight in Vietnam—only a dummy risks his neck fighting for a nation that no one in his right mind would even want to visit. That's why Americans eagerly fought in World War II. Every American would like to see Europe and the South Pacific. The reason why we haven't won any war since then is that we keep fighting for crap-on-the-map countries. Americans don't care about Korea, Vietnam, Afghanistan, or Iraq. Who wants to die for a place you'd never want to live?"

Cheney calmly twisted open a bottle of mineral water and took a swig. His voluble ease only goaded me to keep on attacking him.

"I'm surprised you haven't lost the support of the fundamentalist Christians," I said. "Because according to you, Jesus Christ wasn't crucified. He just underwent 'enhanced interrogation.'"

Cheney didn't respond to my remark. I wasn't even sure if he was actually listening to me.

"In Washington you're either a paper-pusher or a paper-rammer," Old Dick said. "I'll shove a report down your throat and out your ass to get things done. Done *my* way."

"How many grandchildren do you have?"

"Five now, but my daughter Mary's talking about starting a family."

"She's the lesbian?" I knew the answer to my question but wanted to see if he'd flinch hearing the L word. There wasn't any change of expression.

"You know that. Don't act as if we're both stupid."

"Aren't you concerned about their future? The future of their planet?"

"I'm an environmentalist," Old Dick said. "I keep saying to the president, 'What's wrong with biological warfare? They're Green Weapons—made from organic ingredients.'"

His attempt to be humorous was as successful as his invasion of Iraq and attempt to kill bin Laden. He became somber again, as I became angrier.

"Yeah, and thanks for trying to drill in the Arctic National Wildlife Refuge. It's a wildlife *refuge*, not a wildlife refinery."

The Republican-led votes to drill there had triggered a deep sense of hopelessness about our country, despair mixed with disgust that we'd become a savage nation that ate its national parks.

"I should have guessed you're a tree-hugger."

"A same-sex tree-hugger," I corrected.

"Now *that's* a fucking liberal," Cheney said.

To my lasting shame, his remark didn't make me laugh, but it did make me smile. The worst trait of Americans is our nation's faith in our almighty sense of humor, ignoring centuries of evidence that if the devil can cite scripture, he can also crack a joke.

"The planet isn't going anywhere. My grandkids will have to figure out their own lives. I won't be around. And I've always believed less government is better."

"You must be thrilled. You can't have any less government than one-man rule."

Cheney laughed. "That's good. I have to remember that."

I had meant my comment to be insulting, but he took it as a joke. He visibly relaxed, his perma-grimace softening into a scowl.

"I'm going fishing as soon as I'm done here," he said.

"You love the outdoors but you're against preserving it," I said.

He shot me a look that was the gestural equivalent of unloading a shotgun directly at my face.

"You need an intelligence briefing on my record. I voted for wilderness protection for Wyoming. Helped protect almost a million acres. Liberals never mention that."

I was unaware that Dick Cheney had done anything that could be considered environmental protection. Although I'd always had grudging respect that, unlike most Democratic politicians who were swishy about "gay marriage," Cheney had come out with a memorably blunt argument for marriage equality: "Freedom means freedom for everyone." This made me concerned that I'd end up bonding with him if we spent too much time together.

"Look," Cheney said, "for five years we've been trying to drill in ANWR." He pronounced it "Ann Wahr." "And we've failed. Why? Because you and your same-sex tree-huggers have made protecting ANWR your priority. If we can't beat *you*, then you should actually take it as a sign of hope."

I hadn't considered that, and a shudder of optimism ran down my spine.

Old Dick looked at his watch. "It's taking longer than I thought. If they're not back in five minutes . . ." His conversation trailed off, and he started cracking his knuckles. He rose from his chair, but his face contorted in frustration when he realized there was no room to pace and he was forced to sit down again.

"I should've supervised this myself," he said, "but I couldn't leave you with him."

"With Bush?" I asked, confused by what Old Dick could possibly think was dangerous about leaving me with George.

"No," he sneered. "Myself. He's an ambitious son of a bitch and would pump you dry for information about the future. If I left you with him he'd eat you alive."

You have to be one twisted fuck when you don't trust yourself, I thought. Even though Junior and I had our differences, I trusted him.

"What could I tell him?" I asked.

Cheney pondered my question before answering. "He's royally pissed that Ford never told him about the time machine—he was his chief of staff. But Gerry was right not to tell him. He's a loose cannon. Bored being a congressman and feeling ambitious. He wants back in the driver's seat. If he found out Clinton became president, he'd be tempted to trip him on his path to the White House. Back in the day I had a Wyoming-sized chip on my shoulder and could be mean and vindictive. I've mellowed with age."

"Yeah," I said. "Those prisoners in Guantanamo think of you as a big ol' softie."

Cheney chuckled at my sarcasm. "The only reason he's here is because I needed his help. He had to meet privately with Bush's father to tell him his son was in danger. Barbara's trained them well. With that family you can't do anything over the phone. It's face to face or no deal. Two hours after he met with Daddy Bush, presto: black ops." He shook his head in admiration. "Those CIA bastards never forget a friend."

I was impressed Old Dick actually double-crossed Bush's father into unwittingly using his CIA connections into helping ensure that Cheney would be able to blackmail Young George.

Old Dick looked at his watch again. "Jesus, how long does it take to get hard and stick your cock in someone's face? Let's see what's taking so long." He nodded to the guards, one of whom opened the door, stepped outside, looked both ways, and then nodded to Old Dick. "You'll have to come with me," Old Dick said to me, with a nod toward Elena's room.

We reached the door of her room just as Elena opened it. Junior and Taylor could be seen inside tucking in their shirts and buckling their belts, while Young Dick stood in the doorway holding a brick-sized cell phone in his hand. It was one of the early Motorola models. Michael and Elena appeared exhausted as they shouldered their overnight bags. "We gave him a shot of that CIA knock-out drug," Young Dick announced to Old Dick when he entered the room. George, naked, was passed out on the bed. Elena took the sheet and pulled it over him. "It's not right leaving him hanging out," she said.

Old Dick watched George sleep. "He'll have a hell of a hangover tomorrow. I feel sorry for whoever's working for him; he likes to think he's tough but doesn't handle pain well. One jogging bruise, and he's a son of a bitch for days."

"How do we know that he won't go to his father and tell him what happened?" Young Dick asked. "We could wake up tomorrow with a roomful of black ops."

"He'll never tell his father," Old Dick said. "It's too embarrassing."

Old Dick stared at Young Dick.

"Did you get what we need?"

Young Dick nodded. "Yes."

"Did you play it back?"

"I'm not an idiot."

"I'm just making sure we're covered. You're not always careful. You made that crack about Ronnie. "

"One slipup," Young Dick said. "It doesn't matter. It was at a Republican caucus."

"It could've caused problems. We've got two more years to go. People can't know Ronnie's losing it."

Oh my god, I thought. Did Reagan's Alzheimer's kick in during his second term? And did his administration cover it up? Then I considered why they would talk about this sensitive matter in front of us. My stomach churned when I concluded why they felt safe discussing state secrets in our presence: they knew we'd never be able to tell anyone. Guantanamo Bay had room for five more prisoners.

"I'm not comfortable leaving these five out of protective custody," Young Dick said.

A throbbing vein appeared on Old Dick's forehead. "We've gone over that. They can't be eliminated or locked up."

"Do you even hunt anymore?" Young Dick asked. "Because it sounds like you've gone catch-and-release on everything."

Old Dick looked as if his two lips were debating and the con side was winning.

"I've killed and locked up more people than you can even dream of!"

"You keep saying that. But you treat these five as if they call you 'Grampy.'"

"Look, hotshot, I've given orders to shoot down passenger jets and then five minutes later asked, 'What's for lunch?' No one's tougher than I am, including you. I'd love to lose these five at some undisclosed location, and my trigger finger's been itching hard for this one." He pointed at me. "So hard I'm tempted to use it to poke out his eyes. But if these five people disappear that's a huge disruption of the timeline. We think the system has some play but we don't know its tipping point. We can't get rid of them or we'll risk everything. What is it that you don't understand? It's like I'm working for Gerry Ford again. He needed a three-hour gab session with his advisors and his ass signed in triplicate before he could take a shit. It couldn't be clearer. In my time, all five of them are leading lives, which unfortunately means they've got to continue doing so."

Young Dick looked at his feet. "I'm just trying to be thorough."

"You've got to learn to relax or you're going to have another heart attack."

His comment bewildered Young Dick.

"Really?"

"Actually two more."

Young Dick looked as if he had chest pains.

"Two? Fuck."

"Ah, you'll be fine. I tell people heart attacks are like wives: once you've had four, they don't scare you anymore."

Old Dick's homemade folk saying put a smile on his face, but Young Dick still seemed distracted, almost as if he was trying to check his own pulse by listening hard.

"Can't you use this time machine to go into the future and secure us an artificial heart?"

"Done."

"Really?"

Old Dick patted his chest. "I had the I-Pump installed in 2098."

It was comforting to have confirmed what I'd always suspected: Dick Cheney was actually heartless.

"So you've gone into the future too?" I asked. "What were the effects of global warming?"

"I tried to find out, but they wouldn't allow me to learn anything. I was operated on at an undisclosed government location. Turns out they'd been waiting for me to arrive for almost a hundred years. They're afraid knowing anything about the future can be as disruptive to the timeline as changing the past. They put in my new ticker, but wouldn't answer any questions. I was impressed with their nondisclosure policies. After a month spent recuperating, I wanted to hire all of them to work on my staff."

I thought it odd that people in the future would want to help Dick Cheney. But then I thought that perhaps in a century people would look back and see that we needed the disaster of the Bush/Cheney administration for our country to make progress, just as Europe seemed to need World War II to finally bring a semblance of peace to that continent.

"So just let them go?" Young Dick asked.

"Why not?" Old Dick said. "Even if they talk, no one will believe their story. We've actually got a leak planned that will cover this. Shirley MacLaine's going to talk about men from the future trying to change history on *The Tonight Show* tomorrow night. After that, anyone who talks about time travel will be seen as a dingbat."

"All right," Young Dick replied. "But it seems risky to me."

"You can't see the big picture," Old Dick said. "But I've got your back."

His soothing comments just seemed to tantalize Young Dick further. His body visibly wrenched, giving the impression that if a cobra bit him, it would die from his venom.

"I never thought I'd turn into a wuss."

"Please," Old Dick said. "You're a Girl Scout compared to me."

Young Dick stepped back from him, slightly cowed by his accusation.

"I do appreciate your help in this." Old Dick held out his arm with an open hand and waited. Young Dick smiled menacingly and gripped his cell phone more tightly.

"I'll keep it safe," he said.

"No. You'll receive it when you need it."

"That's not necessary."

Both men's jowls became steely.

Old Dick said, "I don't do negotiation."

"You think I do?" Young Dick nodded and the guards pointed their assault rifles on Old Dick. As soon as they moved, Old Dick pressed a button on his watch. Instantly, twenty-five women soldiers in camouflage uniforms surrounded us. They appeared out of the air and scared the bejesus out of us, including Young Dick, who squealed embarrassingly. They quickly proceeded to Taser the six original black ops, then injected them with something that made them pass out. I could smell the ozone from the Tasers, but it felt surreal, almost like we were modeling for the cover of a pulp adventure novel. The grim-faced women aimed their weapons at Young Dick. "Son of a bitch," he said. "Women soldiers. That's different."

Old Dick showed his teeth. "It was Mary's idea," he said. "She said, 'Dad, you should try women soldiers.' She was right. They're tougher than the guys and keep their yaps shut." Old Dick held out his hand. "I've got twenty years on you," he said. "Now hand over the tape."

Young Dick smirked. "The tape has been sent for safekeeping."

"Well, you're going to call and get it back," Old Dick said.

"No, I'm not."

"You'll do it now, or soon you'll be pissing your pants."

"What are you going to do? Kill me?" Young Dick grin-grimaced. "I guess you can't do that. That would alter the timeline."

Old Dick out-grimaced him. "You don't know who you're dealing with." He nodded at the commander. "Bind his legs and arms." Old Dick looked around the room. "We need something to tip him back on. Check the closet for an ironing board; that might work."

The soldiers did as they were told, and soon Young Dick was bound, hand and foot, to an ironing board. "I've always wanted to try this," Old Dick commented. "Lynne and I used to watch the videos but I've never seen it done live." Old Dick looked at Elena. "We're going to need your water bottle." She innocently handed him the two-liter bottle of spring water she had in her backpack. In 1986 only historians and ex-POWs were familiar with waterboarding. Old Dick gazed down at Young Dick, who appeared unconcerned but confused about what was going to be done to him. Old Dick fished a small cell phone out of his jacket pocket and offered it to Young Dick.

"Grab hold of this. When you're ready to give me my tape, drop it. Do you understand? We'll stop as soon as you drop it."

Young Dick seemed confused. "I need you to say that you understand," Old Dick said.

"I do."

"Good." Old Dick looked at the commander. "Bind his mouth, then get me a T-shirt."

The commander nodded and turned to the woman on his left. "Soldier, we need your T-shirt." As the commander gagged Young Dick, the soldier unzipped her black fatigues and removed her black T-shirt. She had an elite-force trained body and looked impressive in her camouflage bra. Old Dick took her T-shirt and instructed two other soldiers on how to cover Young Dick's face. Once that was done, Old Dick poured water on the T-shirt to wet it. Young Dick squirmed.

"I think this is how it's done. Well, here goes." Old Dick poured water into Young Dick's nose, and his body immediately pulled against his restraints and muffled cries could be heard over the sound of water being poured. Young Dick thrashed like a fish out of water.

Elena shouted, "Stop!" and stepped forward, but a soldier grabbed her, preventing her from interfering. Junior, Taylor, and Michael also lunged at Old Dick.

"You're torturing him!" Taylor yelled. He froze when two soldiers aimed their rifles at him. Junior and Michael were also restrained and warned not to try anything. Old Dick glanced at them, shook his head, and chuckled.

"The future's not for sissies," he said before pouring more water in Young Dick's nose.

We heard the cell phone hit the floor. Old Dick signaled for a soldier to remove the mouth restraint. Young Dick spluttered for a second and then said, "I'm not telling you anything." Old Dick seemed fine with that and with a nod of his head signaled for him to be gagged again. He raised the water bottle again and said, "This hurts me more than it hurts you."

Old Dick calmly refilled the bottle in the bathroom as he waterboarded Young Dick eight times before he caved. It was horrible to watch. Elena began crying uncontrollably when Young Dick pissed himself. Junior and Michael asked if they could sit down. On the sixth try, Taylor vomited into a wastebasket. I forgot how sensitive he was to animal suffering. Taylor always teared up when Bartleby yelped in response to our kindly vet putting medicine in his ears. Old Dick appeared to be satisfied but sounded disappointed. "That was quick. We had to do that 183 times with one guy. I thought I was tougher than that."

Old Dick ordered them to remove Young Dick's mouth restraint. "You ready to talk?"

"Yes." He asked for his cell phone, and Old Dick nodded and a soldier handed the brick to him.

"Don't even think about double-crossing me," Old Dick warned. "I know you've already made copies of the tape. I want them and the original. With this time machine, I can find you anywhere. And if you fuck with me in any way, I'll come back here and lock you up with enough spiders to make the skin crawl right off your fucking cock. Do you understand?"

Young Dick trembled as he nodded. He called on his cell phone and gave some orders and what sounded like a series of code words: "Alpha-Hardass," "Foureyes360," and "Sureshot." As we waited, Young Dick asked, "How does taking these tapes to 2006 help us? Don't you need them earlier?"

Old Dick truly smiled. "I'm two steps ahead of you. I'll be stopping in 1999 and leaving these at an undisclosed location."

Young Dick beamed at Old Dick.

A short time later, we heard a helicopter land in the parking lot. I wondered what the other guests thought about that at two a.m., imagining a vending machine distributor being pissed about being woken up when he has a big meeting at nine with the head of Midland's bus depot. A soldier then knocked on the door and handed a briefcase to Young Dick. Old Dick opened it and looked inside. "That's everything," Young Dick said. "The original and all six copies."

Old Dick half smiled. "And people keep telling me torture doesn't work. They keep saying you get false information." He spoke to Young Dick. "Can you believe it?"

"Oh, it works," Young Dick replied, rubbing the back of his head. "You've made a believer out of me."

I was mortified. Had we caused the chain of the events that ensured

Dick Cheney would become America's leading cheerleader for torture, or had we merely underscored what was already in Cheney's heart?

"See you in twenty," Old Dick said to his Junior before pressing the button on his watch. He and the women soldiers disappeared, although surprisingly we didn't.

"I thought he was returning us to my time," I said to no one in particular.

Young Dick smiled. "So did he, but two can play double cross. We haven't figured out how your bracelets work but we did figure out how to disable them. He'll have to come back, because I have you. He'll learn to negotiate." I imagined Old Dick returning in the next minute with a thousand soldiers and decided we had to get the hell out of there. I immediately grabbed Young Dick and twisted his arm behind his back. "Give those soldiers more of that knock-out stuff before they wake up," I shouted. Everyone appeared stunned and unsure of what to do. "Do it! He'll lock us up and throw away the key!" Michael grabbed one of the soldiers' supply bags and found a case containing thirty fully loaded syringes. He proceeded to administer a half dose to each of the six soldiers and a full dose to Young Dick.

"I'll track you down," Young Dick threatened. "You can't hide . . ." He didn't finish his sentence as he passed out. I ordered everyone to tie up their hands and feet and bind their mouths, and then tried to think of what we should do.

I needed just one day with Carol, one day to convince her that her life was in danger. I scrambled to think of what we could do to give me the time I needed. It would take a full day to drive to Crescent City and then one day to speak with her. Two days, I told myself, as if adding one plus one under pressure was a daring feat of logistical reasoning. "I'm not exactly sure what we should do with them," I admitted. "But we should move them inside."

We each grabbed one end of a soldier and carried them to my room, which was the closest to Elena's. As Junior dropped Young Dick onto the floor, he said, "Why not just leave them in one of our motel rooms, then pay for the rooms ahead of time and hang a Do Not Disturb sign on the door? Then call the front desk in two days." He shrugged. "If they can handle torturing people, they can handle pissing themselves."

"Leaving them without food, water, or bathroom breaks for two days would be cruel," I said.

"We can't do that." Elena was still trying to catch her breath. She'd helped carry the smallest soldier, who was still a large man. "We've got to be better than them." She was right; there's no point in trying to save the world if the planet you replace it with is just as mean. Elena counter-proposed that she, Michael, and Taylor would stand guard over them for two days.

"I know you two need to see your sister," she said. Junior must have told her about our real mission.

I warned them that the black ops were probably trained to escape from situations like this and would kill their captors. "Do you really think you can handle this? It's not safe to untie any of them. Not even for a minute. They might head butt you or use martial arts moves if you get too close." A lifetime of watching James Bond movies made any secret agent derring-do imaginable.

I added, "You're going to have to stand guard and watch them at all times. Even when they go to the bathroom."

The three of them appeared to envision what bathroom duty might entail with men whose hands were tied.

"You should give them half shots to keep them drowsy for the next few days. Feed them milkshakes. Then after two days you can leave. Give yourself time to get away. Then go into hiding somewhere for the next week," I instructed. "After a week this will be settled, and it should be okay to come out."

"Are you sure we're not going to be arrested?" Michael asked.

"Yes. For once I believe Dick Cheney. Getting rid of you would change the timeline too much."

Michael and Elena stood to lose their jobs in Santa Fe if they stayed two more days in Midland, and I asked them if they were okay with that. They both had lousy make-money jobs that they weren't attached to, especially after I handed each of them a large roll of cash. Taylor was headed to Los Alamos, and it made sense for him to stay behind with Michael and Elena. Junior seemed upset when he heard they were being temporarily torn asunder. "You can see each other in the fall," I said, wondering how starting my relationship with Taylor five years early would change my timeline. We also discussed whether to take Ravi with us. I thought he should go to Santa Fe, but Junior frowned at my suggestion. I relented and said, "Bring him." Whatever happened to us, even I didn't think Cheney would be unkind to a dog.

I became sad thinking this would be the last time I would see any of them again. Bidding your youth good-bye is less heart-wrenching when it's more of an incremental metaphorical adieu and your baby-face doesn't actually hug you. When I hugged Taylor, I was disappointed that I wouldn't have a chance to manhandle his seductive flesh for a longer amount of time. His appealing youthful personality had softened my resolve to break up with him. It made me feel old. Perhaps I was more forgiving because I didn't have the stamina to be mean anymore? Although Dick Cheney disproved the idea that people grow nicer as they get older. I didn't even have time to ponder that thought. Junior and I needed to leave immediately for Crescent City.

As we packed the car, Elena apologized for doubting me. "What's to apologize for?" I asked. "It's easier to believe in a time machine than a Bozo president." I gave Michael a big hug and wished we had spent some one-on-one time together. But I also looked at him with pride in our long friendship. We'd grow middle-aged together, going through various boyfriends while remaining steadfast to each other. I'd never feel the young Michael ever left me; whenever we laughed together I could still hear him.

We left the motel at three in the morning, and Junior quickly fell asleep in the car. I drove without stopping until eight. Outside of Las Cruces, I pulled over at a convenience store to buy coffee and let Ravi pee in the parking lot. Junior set a package of chocolate chip cookies on the counter when I paid the cashier. "That's breakfast?" I asked. "Your appetite for junk food isn't doing either of us any favors." He smiled shyly. "I figure, if I'm going to end up looking like you anyway, I can pretty much eat what I want."

I was pleased with his approval but thought he wasn't giving me enough credit. "If I'm not a wreck it's because I started to watch what I eat at your age. I'm not going to be able to use this time machine again to come back and yank candy bars out of your mouth."

"Fine," he said. "This will be my last cookie."

We both knew that was a lie. Cookies are my weakness, my Achilles' meal. I'd always thought a characteristic difference between old- and new-world eating habits was that in Europe a writer eats one madeleine and recalls his past while Americans wolf down a package of Double Stuf Oreos to forget the present.

Junior offered to drive for the next several hours, and I gladly moved to the passenger side.

"So we're the reason Cheney becomes vice president?" Junior asked.

"It's worse than that. I think we're the reason Bush becomes president. I think he quits drinking because of last night. Once he sobered up, he got into politics."

"This is a disaster."

I agreed again. "Hey, at least we tried. We tried to stop Bush from becoming president instead of just talking about how bad he is."

I fell silent for a minute as I considered whether we'd failed to prevent Taylor from becoming a gay Republican. Bush would still be president on 9/11, but Taylor had witnessed Cheney-on-Cheney torture, and perhaps that memory would be enough to stop him from going Log Cabin.

"You regret not trying," I said. "You don't regret failing." On second thought, that sounded bogus. "Well, not as much."

"I guess." Junior stared ahead at the road.

"So do me—do us—a favor. Take those art lessons and try writing and drawing a graphic novel. I didn't do it and I should've and I regret not trying."

Junior didn't say anything for a few minutes as we entered the empty miles of New Mexico's boot heel.

"I'll think about it," he said finally. He still sounded doubtful, I thought, as I felt my eyelids closing.

I fell asleep and woke up south of Tucson.

"I love the West," Junior said as we passed through a section of low desert with mountains backdropped in the distance. "I love the sense of openness. You can see for miles." It took me a second to realize this was Junior's first trip in the American West, a year earlier than my visit to Santa Fe for the Harmonic Convergence. It made me feel happy that we were sharing this experience together. (Of course, we shared every experience together, but this was different.) It was raining up ahead on the highway, and I explained how the storm could be fifty miles away. Driving in the Southwest at the height of summer is one of the greatest delights in American life. Having grown up in the verdant East, my first trip west was a revelation. The sky lifts off your back and the sun stops looking over your shoulder, while the trees and shrubs quit crowding you. I'll admit I was initially unimpressed by low-desert vegetation; most of the time you can't tell whether the desiccated brown plants are half dead or half alive, but it was an aesthetic I began to truly appreciate once I became middle aged.

We stopped at a cafe and called the motel to check in on our crew in Midland. Taylor answered. He said Elena and Michael and everyone else were still sleeping. "So far, everything's fine," he said.

"Good," I said. "I'll call you again in a few hours to see how you're doing."

Once we hit the road again, Junior commented, "Imagine how amazing seeing this land for the first time had to be for European explorers."

I'd been time-traveling in my imagination ever since I was old enough to read. Although I've never decisively answered whether I'd prefer to be born in the year when I could see either passenger pigeons or penicillin, I did recall something else that Junior could look forward to. "You know how you say I'm always the bearer of bad news. Well, in eleven years you'll read a biography of Meriwether Lewis. Then you'll go on to read the original Lewis and Clark journals and discover the greatest works of American literature written by men with a shaky grasp of spelling. You'll become obsessed and read books on their relationship with Native Americans and their contributions to natural history. You'll even read a literary novel that's based upon the assumption Lewis was gay and in love with Clark. You'll fall in love with their story. Elena will also read the biography and love it. We've talked about visiting Pompey's Pillar." I explained it was a spot in Montana along the Yellowstone River where William Clark carved his name and the date "1806" on the side of a sandstone butte.

Junior turned down the volume on Depeche Mode's "Enjoy the Silence." "I know a little about them. What's the big attraction?"

"Their story reads like the most fantastic adventure novel ever written. Instead of follow the Yellow Brick Road it's follow the Yellowstone River. They describe a lost world where California condors nibble on beached whales in Oregon and flocks of Carolina Parakeets fly in Kansas. They see prairies covered with immense herds of bison, elk, and antelope. And the Native Americans they meet welcome them. Reading about their journey makes you feel the entire world was once an Eden that we kicked ourselves out of."

We were passing through an open vista that appeared not to have changed for two hundred years, except for the billboard promoting a water park in Phoenix.

"Why do you think Lewis was gay?"

"Well, for one thing his dog was named Seaman. Spelled S-E-A-M-A-N, but still."

"That must have been weird when he called his dog," Junior observed. "'Seaman, come! Seaman, come!' Even in 1804 people must have thought that was strange."

I hadn't considered that and agreed that it was a Freudian slip before Freud.

"It was also reported in the Lewis biography that one of the men selected for the Corps of Discovery boasted in his old age that his fine physique enabled him to pass the inspection that more than one hundred others had failed. So basically, Lewis carefully selected twenty-six hotties to accompany him."

"What's with 'hotties'? You've used it several times. Is it the new term for 'buff'?" It had never occurred to me that the word "hottie" came into general usage in the '90s or early twenty-first century, but clearly it had.

"I can't decide whether it's a permanent addition to the language or a word that will sound like 'Daddy-O' in fifty years," I responded.

We passed a sign announcing Blythe, California, 150 miles. After that, there was another two hours of California desert before we reached Palm Springs. The West seemed endless in a car; traveling in a covered wagon, you must have wanted to Donner Party your family just to break up the monotony.

Junior glanced at me. "I bet if I became Lewis's boyfriend, he would've named Montana 'Johntana' after me."

"That's a scary thought," I said. "The entire map of the American west would become gay geography. Bubblebutt Butte."

"Hothole Springs."

"Morning Wood National Forest."

"One-Eyed Snake River."

"The Down-Low River?" I said, my inspiration failing. Junior didn't get my reference. He assumed it had something to do with depression. I had to explain it to him. In 1986 the term "down-low" was on the down-low among white Americans.

"Actually," Junior said, "I'd try to talk Lewis into naming things that would sound campy."

"Cry Me a River?"

"Instead of the Black Hills, they'd be called 'The Hills Are Alive with the Sound of Music.' We'd claim it was a Sioux name."

Junior listened to the Smiths while I tried to doze as we made our way through Phoenix. In a few hours we passed through an area where saguaros grew near the northern limit of their range. The sun-seeking codger cactuses lived exclusively in south-sloped senior communities where the prime of life was 80 and old was pushing 150. Each saguaro looked lonely and miserable, plants too prickly to make friends and too mean to die. It's no surprise to learn they have no contact with their far-flung offspring.

"Do you still want to break up with Taylor?" Junior asked. His question had a forced, overly breezy inflection, suggesting he was trying to deflect any suspicion he'd been pondering it for hours.

"I don't know," I replied. "But can I spend the rest of my life with a Republican? I'm not sure about that."

I pictured us fighting into our old age and beyond.

"If I stay with a Republican all my life," I said, "when we're buried next to each other, I'll feel compelled to have 'I'm With Stupid' engraved on my tombstone. With an arrow pointing toward him."

"Really?" Junior said. "Because I like him. A lot."

I recognized the sound of my own anger. It was a tune I'd been humming since I was a kid. Junior was miffed that I didn't really want to discuss Taylor with him. I wanted to make up my own mind and not be influenced by myself.

"I like him now too, but in twenty years, he's going to support Cheney and Bush."

"Look, I don't like Republicans either. But sometimes I think, Is that really so important? It's so hard to find a guy you think is sexy and who you have any interests in common with. Is becoming a Republican enough of a reason to break up? Are you still attracted to him?"

"Yes. He'll still be physically attractive in twenty years, but he'll have ugly beliefs. I'm not doing this impulsively. It makes me very sad. I'm glad I met Taylor and happy we were together for almost fifteen years. But I have a child and the Republicans believe letting people suffer is the solution for every problem. People have to be tortured to protect our country; people have to lose their houses and die because government health care is supposedly bad."

Junior winced and shifted his legs as if he were uncomfortable from either sitting so long or from listening to me. I flashed momentarily on the thought that I was no better than Old Dick. I was torturing Junior, and part of me seemed eager to inflict pain.

"People are dying horribly of AIDS right now in 1986 because being gay is more evil than being uncharitable. It's been going on since Reagan got into office and will go on for another twenty years. I'm done with it. I'm tired of excusing these people. I don't believe the bullshit that it's just a difference of opinion and they have the best interests of the country at heart. They're heartless and vindictive and profess a philosophy of gluttony. All they want is more for themselves and their friends. In the twentieth century, communism will be overthrown and we'll see the supposed triumph of capitalism, but sixteen years later we'll discover that the invisible hand of capitalism, when left to itself, spends most of its time jerking off. And, as you know, I have nothing against masturbation, but its virtue is also its vice: while you're doing it you don't have to think about anyone but yourself. I might be fucking up my own life by breaking up with Taylor. But I'm not happy with him now because he's not the man I—we—fell in love with. I'm sorry to tell you this, but people change."

Junior stared out the window and I imagined him thinking, Yeah, tell me about it. I don't want to turn into you. I hated that he thought I was a loser, and seeing my life through Junior's eyes made me question many of the things I'd done, but now he was making me question whether I should break up with Taylor. We were compatible in most ways, but could I really love someone who supported the enemies of my daughter's happiness?

"Of course, if I don't break up with him, that would be one more thing that I started to do and never completed."

"You quit drinking," Junior said. "You completed that."

I never really regarded my sobriety as an accomplishment. It seemed to be fixing something that was broken rather than achieving a goal. But Junior made me see it as something to be proud of. It was something that our father never achieved.

Junior turned to face me.

"What's your definition of love?"

"The best definition is Dawn Powell's."

"Who's she?"

I recalled that twenty years ago she was a forgotten writer whose books were all out of print.

"She's a novelist. Her books are something else you can look forward to. I first read about her when Gore Vidal wrote an essay about her novels for the *New York Review of Books*. It was sometime in the late '80s. I can't remember when, but it must be coming up soon. I'd never heard about her. In fact, you should snap up her first editions this year. There will be a revival of her work, and her books will all come back into print. But her diaries are her masterpiece, and in them she gives the best definition of love that I've ever read. She was married to a man named Joe for over forty years, and after his death people asked her how she did it. She wrote, 'Whenever I ran into Joe on the street it was always a kick.' It's simple and gloriously specific to living in New York, but to me it sums up true love."

"And if you ran into Taylor on the street?"

I hadn't expected his question and at first considered whether I'd cross to the other side or walk past without saying a word, but decided that after spending time with him as a young man again I would be incapable of doing either of those things.

"I'd stop and talk."

Judging from his radiant grin, my answer pleased Junior, and to my astonishment the overpowering sense of bleakness that I'd previously felt about having failed in love seemed to no longer be reflected by the blasted land we were passing through. Low rocky hills and outcroppings were surrounded by expanses of stony ground. We were silent, and the only sound was the muffled whoosh of the strong winds beating against the car. It suddenly seemed remarkable that I had no idea what Junior might be thinking.

"Taylor might change," suggested Junior. "He did throw up. Maybe that might be enough to stop him from becoming a Republican."

"It's nice to think so, but I wonder."

"Are you giving up on Carol, too?"

"No, I'm not giving up on anyone. Even you."

"There's not much you can do to change things when things choose to go from bad to worse," he said.

His comment worried me. My great fear was that everything I'd revealed to Junior about his future would make him pessimistically cynical.

"That's not always true. Gay people live better now than they did twenty years ago, and they'll live better twenty years from now. In twenty years same-sex marriage will be legal in Massachusetts and in all of Canada."

Junior's optimism was temporarily roused, but after he asked a few questions, he slouched back into his seat.

"It's okay to be skeptical but it's never okay to be cynical," I said. "What's bad in your life can sometimes turn out to be strangely great or at least interesting."

He exhaled sharply. "Tell me one thing that's like that."

I couldn't think of anything offhand and tried to recall something. Then I thought we should stop at the next gas station to call and find out how Michael, Elena, and Taylor were doing. Thinking of Michael reminded me of something, and while I wasn't confident it proved my thesis, it was all I had.

"Milton's party was probably the worst party you ever went to, but imagine now how disappointed you'd be if you'd missed it."

On Christmas Day in 1985, Michael and I went to our next-door neighbor Milton's open house, thinking it would be a sophisticated New York soiree. Instead, we found chunks of cheddar on saltines and a house full of bickering queens who served up every remark on a skewer. At one point, I tapped Michael on the shoulder. "Can you believe this?" I whispered. Michael lost it. He began to laugh, and watching him struggle to suppress his laughter made me laugh. Soon Michael was bent over in paroxysms of hysteria as people stared at us. Michael told me later that he knew what I had to be thinking since we entered the house, and my comment unleashed a gusher of merriment that had been building since we arrived.

"The party was a disaster," I said. "But in some ways it was the most memorable party I ever went to in New York. Michael and I still laugh about our ungracious behavior on that day. It's a shared experience that the two of us treasure. And I've tried to think why it resonated with us. I believe it was because we'd become such close friends that it was the first time we can both recall when we knew, without a doubt, exactly what the other one was thinking."

"I guess if you look at life through the prism of Camp, almost anything bad can be considered good," Junior said.

"Not really. Camp doesn't work at some point. No one ever says, 'My life is so bad—so unbelievably horrible—that it's great.'"

There was a moment of silence as we drove through the long stretch of California desert between Blythe and Chuckwalla. Junior cleared his throat and said almost apologetically, "I was thinking about Carol."

"Me too," I admitted. It reminded me that the things I shared with Junior outweighed our differences. My thoughts had been vaguely mournful without pinning down any specific memories, almost as if sadness were a smell or taste. Sometimes my head feels like a storage unit for sad things; I forget what I have buried in there until something or someone reminds me.

"What makes her life so bad?" Junior asked. "So bad that she wants to kill herself."

It had been five years since her death and I still had doubts about why Carol killed herself.

"I'm not sure anyone solves a suicide," I said. "It's like a detective trying to solve a crime where the only witness was also the murder victim. People write suicide notes, but to really explain why someone kills himself I think you'd have to write a suicide novel."

The thought of trying to read those depressing, unreadable books made me almost grateful that most suicides remain a mystery. "For most people, wanting to kill yourself is unimaginable," I added, "and yet the survivors try to piece together a story."

"You must have some idea."

"Yes," I said. "But we'll never know the whole story."

"Sounds like life."

His comment sounded cynical, but I don't think he meant it to be. It might have been a fantasy, but I decided to think of it as a sign of wisdom.

15

WE STOPPED AT A GAS STATION near Palm Springs, and I regretted not being able to show Junior the Big Morongo Nature Preserve, owned by the Nature Conservancy. "It's a must-visit place," I said. "If you go in May, you're guaranteed to see vermilion flycatchers. They're a small spectacular gray and . . . vermilion bird."

"What's with all the interest in birds? Don't tell me I become a birdwatcher. That would be the most depressing news you've told me yet."

"Well, then I have some really bad news . . ."

Junior shook his head. "That's one aspect of your life that should stay closeted."

"Too late," I said. "I'm a gay birdwatcher—outdoors and proud."

I used the pay phone to call Midland and learned that Michael had a black eye and Taylor had a bloody nose. When they gave one of the black ops a bathroom break, he'd almost overpowered them, even though his hands were tied. They'd barely managed to regain control, and Elena still sounded shaken up. She asked how much longer we had until we reached Crescent City, and I estimated another fourteen hours.

"Well, step on it," she said. "I'm scared, and the longer we stay with them the scarier it gets."

We did step on it, although we still needed to stop periodically to let Ravi out. When I explained how upset Elena sounded, Junior amiably offered to drive if I was tired. I was exhausted, and for the rest of the trip we basically took three hours on and three hours off. Junior could sleep in the car, but I couldn't any longer. I closed my eyes, but my mind wouldn't shut down, as I worried about the three of them back in Midland. I also worried about how we would convince Carol that she might kill herself in fifteen years and also whether knowledge of that event would dissuade her from ending her life. Perhaps some new reason to kill herself would appear in place of the justification she'd relied on previously. And I was still concerned that I might be implanting the idea in her mind.

As we headed north, there were long stretches where neither of us talked. I'd traveled a lot in California and thought of the state as a condensed continent with drive-through restaurants and drive-through trees, where the never-ending Gold Rush was stuck in traffic. I'd once considered moving there. Its climate was luminous, its cities sophisticated, and its natural beauties made my eyes feel they'd struck the mother lode. Springtime has never been expressed more magically than by an entire horizon filled with neon orange California poppies. But I couldn't imagine living in Los Angeles, put off by the thought of people with sequoia-sized egos whose major achievements in life were producing lucrative game shows. And I ruled out San Francisco at the thought of living with people who took overweening pride in the accomplishment of moving to San Francisco. I was happier living in New York, where people move with big dreams and then spend the rest of their lives proving the truism that no one's interested in hearing about anyone's dreams.

While driving in the dark up Highway 101, I worried about Junior. Traffic had almost disappeared entirely once we passed Santa Rosa, and the occasional headlights of oncoming cars illuminated his handsome face as he slept. His head rested against the window and his lips were slightly parted, but no sound issued from them. It gnawed at me that I'd altered his life in ways that neither of us would discover until I returned to 2006.

The sun was rising when we reached Eureka. When Junior awoke, he went from drowsy to goggle-eyed, checking out both sides of the road. He'd never seen redwoods before. I half-apologized that most of the trees were second-growth. Shortly before the car was cast into shadow, we passed through a grove of trees thick enough to make round dining tables that could seat twelve. "Wow," he gushed appropriately. It was thrilling to observe myself witnessing something stupendous for the first time; it was almost like reenacting a memory, even though my first encounter with redwoods had been at Muir Woods just north of San Francisco.

"Carol's been telling me I'd like it out here," he said, craning his neck to look up through the windshield, attempting to see the crowns of the trees. "But I'd just moved to New York and didn't have the money to visit."

For my first two years in New York, I thought traveling anywhere outside New York—not counting Fire Island and New Hope—was unnecessary; where was I going to go? I already lived in the city I most wanted to visit. In due time, I went to London, Paris, Florence, Venice, Santa Fe, and St. Petersburg and decided that New Yorkers didn't have a monopoly on cool. And seeing the natural glories of Alaska, Australia, and the Galapagos forced me to concede that Central Park's woodsy splendor is provincial by comparison.

Redwoods are skyscrapers that turn even sophisticates from Manhattan into gawking tourists. For a few years, after I became a New Yorker, Carol and I talked infrequently, catching up during our annual Christmas visits to Buffalo or our summer boat trips on the Niagara River. When I finally did visit Crescent City in August 1988, I was bowled over by the redwood forests and fantasized about buying a cabin there.

"Redwoods are on my 'Short List of Things That Won't Disappoint You,'" I said.

Junior smiled. It shouldn't have surprised me, but I was pleased that he liked my idea as much as I did.

"You know," Junior said, "Carol told me when Mom visited her out here, they were walking through the redwoods and Mom said, 'Nature is beautiful. It's the best thing about life. Everything else is a mess.'"

"It sounds like an entry in Thoreau's journals," I suggested. "If Thoreau had been a tough broad from Buffalo."

"What else is on your list?" Junior asked.

"Um, whales."

"I've never seen a whale."

I'd see my first whales with Taylor on a whale-watching tour off Provincetown in the early '90s. We had beginner's luck and for hours watched humpbacks breaching right next to the boat. After that spectacular introduction to cetaceans, I encouraged friends to come whale-watching with me the following week, and all we saw were a few dorsal fins.

"After seeing a whale, I can promise that you'll never say, 'That stunk!' Well, you could, but you'd have to be the most unbearable person on earth."

Junior took a sip from his coffee. We'd stopped in the middle of nowhere at a combination convenience/general store stocked with dusty canned goods, freezer-burned ice cream, and ancient cold cuts that sent a chill up your spine at the thought of eating them.

"What else?"

"Seeing a comet in the sky with your naked eye. That's amazing."

"Really?" Junior made a sour face. "In April we drove out of the city with some friends to try to see Halley's comet. We wanted to get away from the light pollution, but it was a washout. We went to the beach but couldn't find the comet. Turned out it was low in the sky, and the mist on the ocean obscured the view."

I'd completely forgotten about that night. A group of my pals had wanted to see Halley's comet. We'd driven out to Long Beach on Long Island on a very cold spring night and had been unable to find the comet. Our search might have been impeded because we were a bit blurred after smoking quite a bit of pot—but I had to give us credit for at least trying to see this once-in-a-lifetime wonder.

"Well, you're still young. There might be other comets that will come along."

"I hope so. But they don't seem that common."

The comet I'd been thinking about was Hale-Bopp. I told Junior how it would hang in the sky for months; thrilling me each time I saw it. When friends mentioned they hadn't seen it yet, it was incredibly satisfying to just point a finger in the air and then listen to their exclamations. "You know it was discovered by amateur astronomers; if we discover it first, it could be the Sherkston comet."

Junior seemed to be enjoying the game. "What else won't be a letdown?"

"The Channel Islands, off California." Junior raised his eyebrows as if he'd never heard of them. "They're like visiting California two hundred years ago. And you must go to the Galapagos."

"You've been?"

I nodded. "When you see a giant tortoise grazing in a field, it will amaze you. I think it's the only place on Earth where you can snorkel with sea turtles *and* penguins."

I was also thinking as we drove that the far northern coast of California was one of my favorite places. It still felt remote and unspoiled compared to the rest of the continental United States.

"You also have to see the three canyons: the Grand Canyon, Chaco Canyon, and Canyon de Chelly."

"I've seen the Grand Canyon from the air," Junior said. "I was flying out to visit Alan in LA." Alan was one of our brothers. "It was my first trip to the West Coast and the pilot announced that passengers on the right-hand side of the plane could see the Grand Canyon. I had a window seat on the right-hand side but noticed the guy in front of me made no effort to look. He kept reading the *Wall Street Journal*. I never want to be that guy."

I had no memory of that moment and wondered what else I'd forgotten about my life.

"No one does," I said. "*He* probably doesn't want to be that guy."

"I'd put maple syrup on your list," Junior said.

"Hmmm. You're right about that." I made another suggestion. "Perfectly ripe pineapple."

"How about maple syrup on pineapple?"

"Broiled. That could be dangerous; you might not want to eat anything else."

He grinned adorably, and I thought gay men in New York were idiots for not scooping him up.

"What about books?"

"Is there any book that won't disappoint somebody?" I asked. "Think of any classic book and you can always find someone who can't stand it. Mark Twain hated Jane Austen."

"You're probably right." Junior's face suddenly brightened. "What about *Green Eggs and Ham*?"

"Orthodox Jews and Muslims."

Junior laughed. I was glad to see that he got my jokes, but then thought, If you can't make yourself laugh, you should give up conversation entirely.

"The same goes for films," Junior said. "One man's favorite is another man's flop."

"What about *The Wizard of Oz*?" I suggested. "It's kind of the perfect film. It's beloved because everything's great: the script, the songs, the performances, the sets, and the costumes."

"I'd put that on my list; but you know there's someone somewhere who thinks it's overrated."

"That person should be forced to wear a sign. So everyone can avoid him."

"What about works of art?" Junior asked. "What do I have to see?"

"Michelangelo's *David* is the obvious one. At least for Western art. I'd also include Stonehenge and the Parthenon. Oh, and the cave paintings of Lascaux and Chauvet."

"I know about Lascaux, but I don't know Chauvet."

I was silent for a second. The Chauvet cave wasn't discovered until 1994.

"It's a cave in southern France." I explained how Chauvet was equally as spectacular as Lascaux and its discovery would be front-page news. I briefly explained my wild fantasy of the two of us flying to France and discovering the cave ourselves. And while we were in Europe, we could stop in the Alps and dig out the prehistoric iceman, and then fly to Indonesia and, in an archaeological triple play, discover Homo floresiensis, the "hobbit" people on the island of Flores. God, it was tempting. "We could make three major scientific discoveries, and Taylor would have only one."

"All of those are overseas. I've never been." Junior sounded ashamed.

Later that year he would go with Michael to Europe for the first time, but I decided not to tell him. Planning the trip and working doubles to pay for it had been part of the fun.

"You're hardly art deprived; you live in New York."

Junior chuckled. "It's never enough; New Yorkers always want more!"

Over the next ten years, I'd visit Crescent City many times and come to understand that northern California at the height of summer is like Buffalo in July: it's a seductive whore who shows you a good time but doesn't mention those rainy and snowy winter months that hang on like an untreated dose of the clap.

We entered Crescent City with the harbor to our left and a strip of fast food restaurants and cheap motels on our right. "A tsunami wiped out the town after the Anchorage earthquake in '64," I explained. "It's all been rebuilt."

"The town needs another tsunami," Junior said, his head swiveling as he eyed the downtown. "It's like every building is wearing a velour jogging outfit."

The idiosyncrasies of architecture give a town its character, and Crescent City's business district looked depressingly monotonous, with rows of flat-roofed clapboard-covered boxes painted varying shades of drab. Local histories record Crescent City had once been charmingly funky, a mixture of post–Gold Rush era, late Victorian, and early twentieth century bungalows, but the rebuilt city had become a village of the architecturally damned where every building shared an unsettling, uncanny resemblance.

The motels made me think of our friends in Texas. "Let's call Midland to tell them to get out of there," I proposed.

"Good idea," Junior said.

We stopped at the next pay phone we saw, outside of a bar called the Dram-Buoy. After dialing a zillion numbers to pay with a credit card, the desk clerk at the motel picked up. When I asked for room 342, she said, "They just checked out an hour ago." I asked her who had checked out. She described a middle-aged man wearing eyeglasses. I asked how his mood was. Without any hesitation, she replied, "Nasty as piss."

I felt sick. It had to be Young Dick. Cheney should have been tied up in Elena's room for another five hours. I became concerned for our friends and hoped no one had been hurt. I wished again that we hadn't tried to prevent Bush from becoming president, especially since it seemed we were directly responsible for putting him in office. If any of my friends back in 2006 discover my culpability in making him our commander-in-chief, I will rightfully be shunned, I thought. And New Yorkers are always willing to put their cold shoulders to the wheel to let an idiot know that no one can stand him.

I hung up the phone. Junior glanced at my face. "What's wrong?"

"No one's there."

"Did they leave?"

"I'm not sure. Cheney dropped off the room key."

Junior started to chew a thumbnail, and I tried to think of what to do next. Taylor knew where we were headed, and I had no doubt Young Dick would now be as amenable to getting information by "enhanced interrogation" as he would be as vice president. We didn't have much time. He could be in Crescent City in a few hours. I looked around to see if we were being watched as we got back in the car.

Carol and her husband, Ed, lived on the northern edge of town in a small development filled with three-bedroom ranch-style saltboxes. I

immediately recognized Carol's old '50s Chevy pickup parked in her driveway and felt that I was dreaming. I was going to see Carol again and was overcome with sensations of happiness, anxiety, and physical exhaustion, but the mix made me feel strangely numb. She'd bought her truck after high school, repainted it copper, recovered the bench-style front seat, then learned from our father how to maintain the engine. She used to pick up our eighty-year-old grandmother, who had to climb up to hop in the cab, and run errands with her. Carol was the one who informed me that our grandmother, who never learned to drive a car, did know how to drive a tractor, since she grew up on a farm in Canada.

I knew Ed was at work. He was an auto mechanic who started at seven, and his vocation had immediately endeared him to our father. We heard a dog barking from inside the house as we walked to the front door. I'd forgotten about her plump, hors d'oeuvre–sized mutt, Casey, who was part Chihuahua and part chorizo. He looked like a pig in a blanket skewered on four toothpicks.

We rang the doorbell and heard Carol saying, "Casey, who's that? Who's that?" inciting him to bark more furiously. She opened the screen door, and Casey shot out, racing down the sidewalk and then circling back to wag his tail, bark incessantly, and scoot between Junior's and my legs. Then he spotted Ravi and raced around him, occasionally leaping up to lick his face. Ravi stood still, patiently enduring the commotion.

"Casey, calm down," she said while following him out the door. She was back from the dead and this miracle left me in a state of incredulous gratitude. I felt remorseful that I'd almost forgotten she had once been a lovely young woman—tall, slim, and happy. She wore her long, straight brown hair parted in the middle, and her ever-present smile seemed as indelible as a birthmark. In her right hand were her truck keys, and she wore our father's black satin bowling jacket. "Tom" was embroidered on the front, with "Niagara Lanes" on the back. My memories of her were of a time when she was forty pounds heavier and her smile was always a feint, an attempt to momentarily distract you from suspecting the depth of her misery.

I waited on the sidewalk and watched Junior and Carol's reunion. He hugged and kissed her on the cheek and then looked back and waved me forward. "Carol, this is Kurt." She smiled warmly and shook my hand as she watched Casey go berserk.

"If I let him," she said, "he'll run in circles until he literally gets dizzy."

"Nice to meet you," I said, feeling unsure how to behave. Having foreknowledge of Carol's death made me feel deceitful. Suddenly I understood why God's not much of a talker; if you're concealing that you know when someone's going to die, most likely you'll come off as a total phony.

They immediately started conversing with the natural ease of two people who love each other, where every sentence feels as unremarkable as breathing. Carol asked, "How's Mom?" and Junior told her about how she had suspected the brown unbleached coffee filters looked liked the white ones after they're used. She laughed appreciatively and beamed at him. "How was the drive?" she asked before bending down to scoop Casey into her arms. Junior launched into how he loved the West, and Carol listened attentively. Until that moment, I never fully appreciated how glad Carol always was to see me. I was fond of telling a recent anecdote about my daughter Isabella. On my last visit to Santa Fe, when we went to pick her up at her preschool, she had been sitting on the steps. When she saw me, she became wide-eyed, stood up, and yelled, "John!" and then ran over and hugged my leg and wouldn't let go. I said until then I'd never truly been welcomed before. I was wrong. Carol's welcomes were the same—she didn't cling to my thigh, but she did hang on to my every word.

"And Dad?" she asked.

"The same. Still disappointed he's never been abducted by aliens."

"I can see Dad with little green men," she said. "Within an hour, he'd be looking under the hood of the flying saucer and asking to fire their ray guns."

"Yeah," Junior agreed, "and Mom would tolerate his friendship with them, but occasionally reveal her distaste by remarking, 'Who wears clothes made out of aluminum foil? They look like baked potatoes.'"

"Dad told me he's trying to see if he can postpone his retirement," Carol said. "He's even talked to the police commissioner in Albany about it."

A spasm of concern crossed Junior's face, but Carol was trying to get the squirming dog to settle down in her arms and she missed it.

They discussed his chances of succeeding, which Carol admitted were small. "The rule's the same for everyone. Out at fifty-seven." She added jokingly, "I think he's worried about being with Mom full time. I'm not sure I could handle that."

Observing Junior's natural delight in talking to Carol—the matter-of-fact familiarity, shared jokes, sudden tangents into a serious subject, discussed and then glossed over by an acerbic remark—made me conscious of how different I was from him. The disparity wasn't our ages. Taylor had changed after 9/11, and now I could see that I had also changed after Carol's death. Junior lacked my overall sense of hopelessness. There was no sign in him of the deep, mournful, unappeasable rage that consciously and probably unconsciously suffused every thought I had after her death, an anger taken out on the universe, Taylor, myself, and probably even on George W. Bush and Dick Cheney. Grief had turned my heart into an urn filled with ashes.

Carol pointed out several recent improvements she'd made to her front yard. We followed her tour, and Junior appreciatively approved her paint color choices of a mossy gray for the house and forest green for the shutters. "It's so damp up here," Carol said, "that I decided everything should match the mildew." The last thing she showed us was a small redwood tree she'd planted in the middle of the lawn. Junior looked skeptically at the evergreen stick stuck in a circle of dirt. "That's impressive," he commented. "That's the tallest twig I've ever seen."

Carol smiled at his sarcasm. "After I'm gone," she said, "I want to leave something behind that the new owners will resent. For the next thousand years."

The sun was trying to burn off the morning fog, but her comment made our smiles as misty as the air.

"I've got to run to the supermarket," she said. "I should've done it last night after work, but I was too tired. You can go in the house and wait; it won't take long."

"We'll come with you," I said. Junior yawned, making him look as exhausted as I felt, but I couldn't wait for her in her house. We'd been given an unprecedented chance to spend time with someone whose death would shatter us; it was inconceivable that we would leave her side. I thought Junior might resent my volunteering him to tag along, but I recalled he hadn't seen her for over a year. He chatted nonstop about how awesome the redwoods were as we piled into the front seat of her pickup. Pulling out of the driveway, she stopped and looked at me closely and then looked again at Junior. "If I didn't know better, I'd swear you two were related."

Junior blushed and seemed at a loss for words. "We get that a lot," I said.

"I told him he's welcome to try to join our family," Junior said, "but our standards are high."

"That's true," Carol said as we headed down her street. "Do you drink too much and never turn down a bong hit?"

"I'm a recovering alcoholic, although I almost fell off the wagon yesterday."

"That's not good," she said. "Long-term recovery automatically gets you blackballed. And you're in too good of shape for a middle-aged man in our family."

"Yeah, but I'm gay. Shouldn't that count as a separate category?"

"We treat the gays just like everyone else," she replied. "We expect you to be just as fucked up, although we do also expect you to be photogenic when you're busted for DUIs."

"That's a double standard."

Carol stared at me as if I were a simpleton.

"Ask a woman with a big chin if life's fair."

She assumed an air of grave solemnity. "This answer will decide it. So consider your response carefully." She paused dramatically. "Are you mental?"

"Completely."

"You're in."

Junior commented on how foggy and cold it was for June in California. "It'll burn off later," Carol responded, shifting gears.

He asked her how she liked living in Crescent City.

"I love the summers," she said while pulling into the parking lot of a Safeway. "But it's hard to think every cloud has a silver lining when the sky's gray for six months of the year."

Junior nodded sympathetically. "New Yorkers complain about their winters, but their winters are sunny and mild compared to Buffalo's frost-bite-you-in-the-ass winters."

Carol grabbed her purse and before opening the door said, "For the first time in my life I understand that the best barometer for my mood is actually a barometer."

She'd said it flippantly, but I found her remark chilling. I'd always thought the perpetually overcast winter climate of coastal northern California contributed to the onset of her depression. Then she moved to New Jersey and she was doomed.

Once inside the supermarket, Carol quickly filled a shopping cart and then got in line at a register with two carts ahead of us, instead of the register where there was only one customer waiting. "It's shorter over here," Junior said, pointing toward the other checkout lane. Carol shook her head vigorously and put a finger to her lips to shush him. "I know what I'm doing," she whispered. She removed a thick stack of shopping coupons bound by a yellow rubber band from her handbag. I noticed a six-dollar diaper coupon topped the bundle, which was strange. Carol didn't have any children.

The cashier was a sullen, lanky, teenage boy with a greasy mop of dark hair. His wispy, unattractive mustache made it hard to believe he had deliberately cultivated facial hair, although it was equally hard to suppose he'd missed shaving the same spot three days in a row. Carol handed him the stack of coupons. "Do you go by Josh or Joshua?" she asked cheerfully. His nametag said "Joshua."

"Josh," he replied as he rang up the coupons.

"How long have you worked for Safeway?"

"Not long."

"Are you still in high school?"

"No."

"Were you on the football team?"

"No."

He didn't have the build to play badminton, let alone football, I thought.

"Do you have a girlfriend?"

"No."

Each of her questions received a curt response, and I wondered why she persisted in trying to converse with someone who clearly didn't want to talk to anyone.

"Nineteen eighty-seven," he said after ringing up her order and subtracting the value of the coupons. We had eight bags of groceries and a case of beer to carry out to the truck. I tried to figure out if spending twenty dollars for that amount of groceries was a good deal back in 1986.

Once we were out the door of the supermarket, Carol was ecstatic. "I'm glad you didn't say anything. We got over a hundred dollars of groceries for less than twenty! You see, Safeway gives double coupons, and I use every coupon I find in the paper. I always shop either very early in the day or late at night, and I always have my order rung up by a male cashier. They hate their jobs. No man can take pride in being a cashier, and early in the morning or late at night they're tired and they just ring up every coupon because they don't give a shit. And I always ask them questions. The last thing they want to do is talk about themselves; they want to just disappear rather than bring any attention to their lives. So they ring me up fast because they want to get rid of me."

"That's brilliant," Junior said. "I saw the diaper coupon and thought, Why the hell did she cut that out?"

"It's worth twelve dollars with double coupons," Carol said as we loaded up the truck.

"What was your scam with Lane Bryant?" Junior asked.

I had no memory of what he was talking about and was curious to hear how she ripped off the women's plus-size fashion store. One of the benefits of time travel is that it makes you appreciate that if Proust's *In Search of Lost Time* is seven volumes, that means our entire life must be a seventy-volume opus because we only remember a tenth of what happens. In ten years, you won't remember the day the ink ran out on your pen when you were paying the electric bill. You won't remember when exactly you left your keys in the apartment and had to buzz your neighbor to let you in. You won't remember that on March 7, 1994, you ordered a tuna sandwich at a deli and they gave you toasted wheat even though you'd ordered rye. You won't remember that on August 9, 2005, you saw a woman on the street with a large port-wine birthmark on her face and quickly averted your eyes to avoid embarrassing her. You won't remember the shirt or socks you wore on April 9, 1998, and whether you had sex of any sort on February 22, 1977. By the time each of us dies, our lives have already been mostly forgotten, but each of us still authors a story we believe is nonfiction.

Of course, Carol was different from me and remembered everything. She grinned nostalgically. "I used to carry a big bag and wear lots of baggy sweatshirts. I'd never smile and always try to look sad and ashamed when I asked the salesperson if they had this blouse in a size sixteen." Carol whispered "sixteen" to indicate her show of mortification. "I'd try on several blouses and sweaters and wear them out of the store and return them for cash later. At Lane Bryant, no one would ever question a customer leaving a dressing room looking heavier than when she entered. It's the best place to shoplift, because the sales people are so sympathetic."

Junior appeared to be thoroughly amused by her tale of larceny. I used to think Carol's white-collar crimes were fun and games, a symptom of her restless intelligence, grifting suckers for a bit of fun. But after her death, Carol's scheming seemed more troubling; the material gains from her swindles were never large enough to change the circumstances of her life, and they appeared to be desperate exercises to try to find a focus for a mind that was too intelligent for any job she ever worked. She almost seemed to be trying to outwit her own life.

At Carol's house, we carried in the groceries, and she asked if we wanted breakfast. I was hungry, and so was Junior, and she offered to make us pancakes. Junior and I sat down on the large powder blue sofa while Carol made a pot of coffee and brought Junior a tall glass of orange juice. I looked around the immaculate room. There was a big TV along one wall with a recliner and sofa facing it. At the other end of the room were a small dining room table and six chairs. A framed poster from an Albright-Knox retrospective of Milton Avery hung in the dining area. Carol purchased it only after I encouraged her to buy it. One wall was covered with family photographs. I noticed both of our grandmothers were prominently featured. On a side table was the small hammered-copper picture frame I'd bought Carol for her eighteenth birthday. I'd found it at an antiques shop in Buffalo. The small round easel-style frame was an intricate arts and crafts design, more Wiener Werkstatte than Roycroft, made by Karl Kipp for his Tookay Shop in East Aurora in either 1914 or 1915. I thought it was the perfect gift for Carol. It was beautiful and had also been made in western New York. It had cost fifty dollars, which was a lot of money for me back then. Carol had placed a photograph of Buddy, our last family dog, in the frame. Buddy was wearing a pair of our father's eyeglasses perched on his nose. When Carol died, her husband, Ed, had given it back to me.

We needed to get on with trying to save Carol, but now that the moment had arrived, I didn't know where to begin.

"Carol, we need to talk to you." I used that ponderous tone of voice that sounds the alarm that something unpleasant is sure to follow. Junior appeared to be confused and irritated.

"Shouldn't we wait a little?"

"We might not have time. Either Cheney could show up."

Junior acquiesced but began to nervously rub the back of his neck. "This will sound unbelievable," I warned before commencing the whole Junior = Me time-traveling story. It was a sign of how exhausted I was that I honestly couldn't tell if my tale sounded more or less believable each time I told it. I skipped over explaining who Dick Cheney and George W. Bush were, since I knew Carol would refuse to believe that two men she wouldn't have hired at any of her jobs would someday lead our country. Carol listened attentively without betraying either credence or skepticism. When I finished, she raised her eyebrows and smirked. "I hope my other relatives don't start doubling up. I can't handle two moms."

Junior's body relaxed but his face was a question mark. "You believe us?"

Carol looked at me and frowned. "You might actually be too mental for our family." She shook her head, stood up, and began to walk toward the kitchen.

"I know it sounds crazy, but I believe him," Junior said.

"And I don't," she snapped.

"Why not?"

"If you're gonna claim to be the Easter Bunny, I need more proof than carrot-stained lips."

Carol's comment was bemused rather than hostile. Since high school, she'd always used her mastery of ridicule as a means of making friends. As a social strategy, her sharp tongue should have created legions of enemies, but her witty needling worked like an acupuncture treatment; the recipients ended up feeling rejuvenated after undergoing a session with her.

"Do either of you want to shower?" she asked. "I caught a whiff of one of you, and I don't want to prove you're the same guy by discovering you share matching B.O."

I tried to secretly breathe deeply a few times to check out whether I was stinking up the place. I didn't smell anything and decided it had to be Junior. We got up and followed Carol into the kitchen as she prepared and cooked the pancakes.

After flipping the first batch, Carol turned toward me and abruptly asked, "What do I call Uncle Dave and Aunt Debbie?"

I immediately understood that even Junior's testimony wasn't enough to confirm my identity.

"Druncle Dave and Aunt Phetamine."

Carol had bestowed those nicknames on our uncle and aunt because every breath they took was under the influence of some mind-altering substance. My answer didn't appear to elicit any reaction from Carol.

"What is Mom not allowed to talk about?"

It took me a second to figure out the correct answer.

"Quit talking about that cake!" I screeched, impersonating a Lily Tomlin character. In college, I'd bought Lily Tomlin's album of her first Broadway show, *Appearing Nightly*, and Carol and I had repeatedly listened to a sketch called "Lud and Marie Meet Dracula's Daughter." A bratty teenage girl enters the house, and her mother asks, "Is that you?" "No, it's Dracula's daughter!" She heads up to her bedroom and slams the door, but can't shut out her parents' inane bickering about which cake—the yellow or the chocolate—the father ate the week before. Finally, the girl opens her bedroom door and screams, "Quit talking about that cake!" Whenever our mother began to harp on some pet subject—our brothers' inability to get along, a neighbor's irritating habit of parking his car in front of our house ("They have a driveway!"), or a paean to why Buffalo-made Sahlen's hot dogs are superior to other hot dogs—Carol used to yell, "Quit talking about that cake!" It always made me laugh, and I'd laugh even harder when our mother would earnestly ask, "Who's talking about cake?"

"When you were in college, what TV show did we watch every night at six and eleven?

"*Mary Tyler Moore*."

When the show went off the air in 1977, channel 29 ran reruns twice a day. I'd basically stopped watching television in college until I rediscovered the brilliant *Mary Tyler Moore Show*. I spent my nights lying on the couch reading assigned books by Matthew Arnold, Charles Dickens, or William Butler Yeats, but I'd start and end the evening watching *The Mary Tyler Moore Show*.

Carol put the mixing bowl in the sink and ran the water. "You're good," she said. "But I still think this sounds like a hoax."

"How would he know all those things?" Junior asked. "I didn't tell him."

"I'm a good liar too," she replied.

"I'm not lying," I said, an admission that only invites suspicion.

"Great," she said, turning to me. "So we're supposed to believe something that has never ever happened before in history is suddenly happening to us."

"Haven't you just described every day of our lives?" I asked.

Carol's brown eyes glowed for an instant, a sign that I'd gotten off a good one.

"There's a reason we're here," I added.

Junior's blinking eyes registered his distress upon hearing my ominous intonation.

"Should we do this now?" he asked.

I might have been exasperated with Junior if he hadn't looked abjectly miserable. He bit the nail on his index finger. I felt sorry for him and for Carol.

"We can't wait," I responded.

"What's wrong?" Carol asked gruffly.

Junior's eyes moistened, which made me falter. In order to save Carol's life, we'd have to completely disillusion her. What if I was taking away the few years of real happiness she had without changing the outcome of her fate? It was a possibility, but not doing anything was unthinkable. I avoided looking at Junior, trying to steel myself, but still felt rubbery when I blurted out, "In fifteen years, you're going to kill yourself."

Carol laughed. "Not that crazy dream again." She addressed Junior: "You have to stop worrying about it. Or see a shrink."

"It's not a dream," he said. "You're going to become severely depressed and shoot yourself. It's a gradual unraveling of your life. I'm not making this up. It will happen."

"Oh, God!" She was livid and turned toward me. "I don't know what hold you have over my brother but I will break it if I have to kill you."

I didn't know what to say. After you predict someone's death, you've effectively killed the conversation.

"What was I supposed to do?" Junior asked. "He told me this. I wasn't going to blow it off."

"The next time someone tells you he's from the future, call me."

"Check out our fingerprints," I said. "They're the same."

"That's the first thing I'd figure out to fake if I were trying to con someone into believing I'm from the future," Carol replied.

"It's not just that," Junior said. "He does what I do. In Arizona we ordered hamburgers, and his came with pickles and he picked them off just like I would have. He sleeps on his side like I do. He bites his nails like I do. And it's really made me reconsider that habit because it looks disgusting. He's pee-shy like I am. He checks out the same guys I'm attracted to. He hates celery and onions. We laugh at the same things, and a couple of times we've even thought of the same joke at the same time. He's read the same books I've read, and when he mentions books I haven't read yet, he quotes things from them that make me want to read them. He buys the same Freshmint flavor Trident gum I always buy. He likes the same music I like—not similar, but the same songs. His signature is mine with just enough changes to make it believable that he's from my future. He smells like me, and when we sucked face, he tasted like me."

Carol crinkled her nose after his last remark.

"It's too many coincidental details for anyone to fake. I can't explain it, and I know it makes no sense. I wouldn't believe us either if I were you. But he's me. I know myself."

They both stared at me. I was chewing on a thumbnail. I pulled my hand away from my mouth abruptly.

"You two are fucking yourselves? That's great."

"We've slept in the same bed," I said, "but we're not sleeping together. He kissed me before he knew."

"So you don't even have a good relationship with yourself."

"Our relationship is better than yours will be with yourself," Junior retorted. "We haven't tried to kill each other."

"Although at times we've wanted to," I added.

She asked us to set the table as she carried a platter of pancakes into the dining room. After bringing in plates, utensils, butter, and real maple syrup, we carried in our drink glasses and sat down.

"Carol," I began, feeling uncertain how we could convince her we were telling the truth, "there's a reason why you become suicidal. In eight years Ed will have a car accident and hurt his back. He'll have an operation to fix it that will only make it worse. He'll end up on disability and become a prescription drug addict and you'll become one also. You'll move to this tiny dark condo in New Jersey, and you'll feel you can't divorce Ed because he's disabled, but you'll also feel you can't live like that anymore. You'll think the only way out is by shooting yourself."

She smiled hesitantly and shook her head no. "We're doing great. Ed likes his job. We're talking about starting a family. We bought this house. I'm even liking my job." Carol had told us about her new job at an auto parts store. The staff was impressed that she actually knew how to build a starter. "Things are good."

I didn't say it outright, but thought, Things change.

Over Carol's shoulder was a picture of our mother. Again, I thought about how our mother had consoled my brothers and me after Carol's death. I didn't feel confident I would ever get through to Carol. It didn't help that I felt worn out, incapable of thinking clearly, unable to muster the arguments I needed. I was so tired I began to ramble.

"After your death, Mom came to visit me. She was reading a book called *Life after Suicide*. When she was leaving for the airport, she said, 'I'll read this on the plane; that way no one will talk to me.'"

Junior and Carol put down their forks.

"Then a few weeks later I was in Buffalo and Mom was sitting in Dad's chair in the living room reading another book about suicide. Mom was chewing gum, blowing and snapping bubbles while tears streamed down her cheeks. It was typical of Mom: genuine mourning without losing her zest for life. Later she explained what she gained from reading books about suicide: 'The whole world's wacky. I read that this one poor guy was feeling suicidal and he was seeing a therapist and he called to make an appointment. A woman answered the phone and said, "Oh, you can't make an appointment." He jumped off the Golden Gate Bridge. Go figure that one out. You just have to not think about it and keep going.'"

Other memories came back to me.

"That night we were watching Eyewitness News and the announcer said, 'It's eleven o'clock. Do you know where your children are?' Mom repeated the phrase to herself: 'Do you know where your children are?' I was walking to the kitchen and said, 'Yeah, Forest Lawn.'"

It was completely wrong for me to say that, but I've always instinctually known how to make my mother laugh. My mouth was dry and I took a sip of coffee. As I swallowed it struck me that while my mother and Carol shared a disposition toward depression, they also were both delightedly irreverent toward everything. Their tragedy was that they could never see the resemblance.

"Mom and I both cracked up," I continued, "but I remember it didn't cheer me up. It was the first time laughter had ever failed to do that. Later I said, 'Mom, they say not to watch the news before you go to bed. It puts bad thoughts in your head.' She replied, 'I watch the news every night before I go to bed and sleep like a log.' Then she cackled. There goes another crackpot New Age theory, I thought."

Carol and I had been telling stories about our mother to each other since we were children, and I was too fuzzy-minded to notice that she and Junior weren't laughing as I would have expected. I thought of something else.

"One time she said, 'I wish Carol had talked to me. I know about depression. I know the anguish of what she felt. What it's like to be severely depressed. I couldn't take care of myself. I couldn't take care of my children. I felt useless and hopeless. Nothing could bring me happiness.' I remember thinking it was strange to hear Mom say the word 'anguish.' It was a word that I'd never heard her use before."

My pancakes were getting cold but I'd lost my appetite. "Driving to your funeral, Mom said, 'I don't know why you have to kill yourself to hurt people when there are so many ways to hurt people while you're alive.' She also started talking about heaven: 'I hope we don't fight up there,' she said. 'That's all I need, to be miserable up there too.' At the cemetery, the hearse stalled out and they couldn't get it restarted, and while we waited Mom said, 'Carol could fix it.' The saddest thing she said was when we were driving home after your burial. She muttered to herself, 'Now she's in the friggin' ground.'"

Carol and Junior appeared to be stunned. Neither of them had said a word, but there were tears in their eyes. I was dead tired, but sensed something had changed among us. I felt as if I'd unburdened myself of what I'd needed to say to her since her death.

Carol cleared her throat. "Only Mom would say those things." Her mouth opened and closed silently. "You really are telling the truth." I'd accidentally stumbled on the one thing that no one could invent, the one thing that could convince Carol of her own death: our mother's inimitable way with words. I started to cry, and so did Carol and Junior.

"I'm sorry," she said, through her tears. "It just seemed so far-fetched."

We stood up from the table. Junior hugged Carol and then she hugged me. The squall of tears was short-lived, and suddenly I was overcome with exhaustion and couldn't keep my eyes open any longer. I didn't care if both Cheneys came to get me now. Carol knew we were telling her the truth. She could change her fate.

As she led us to the guest room, I warned her that the Young Dick Cheney might show up at her door. Like my mother, Carol had no problem believing in a homicidal congressman who would later become a homicidal vice president. No wonder the women in my family were prone to depression, I thought; they really have no illusions about men. I showered first. It felt good to be clean and feel for the first time in days that I wasn't in a rush anymore. Carol had a chance and maybe Taylor did too. Junior seemed as happy as I did and all his hostility toward me was gone.

"I think she gets it," he said as he pulled back the comforter on his bed.

"I do too," I said while adjusting my blanket.

Junior fluffed his pillow before getting into bed. "Do you think we changed things?"

I didn't know, but I thought of Taylor's theory that history might be unchangeable since six plus three or two plus seven both equal nine. But I didn't want Junior to lose hope over the next fifteen years. "We don't know, but we'll never feel that we didn't try. You should feel good about that because I do."

"I feel good about it too," he muttered as his eyes began to close.

We soon were asleep, until the sounds of hinges breaking, boots pounding the floor, and commands being shouted woke us up. Camouflaged soldiers pushed us at gunpoint into the living room, where Young Dick cowered as Carol pointed a pistol toward his head. Casey was growling and Ravi was chewing on Young Dick's pants leg. I'd never seen Ravi bite anyone before.

"I'm going to kick this dog," Young Dick threatened, "if he doesn't lay off."

"You do and you'll say hello to a Colt police revolver," Carol responded. She then yelled at the dogs. "Casey! Ravi! Stop! John grab them!" Junior ran over and scooped up the barking bundle. I pulled off Ravi, who continued to growl.

"The house is completely surrounded," Young Dick said. "There are a hundred troops out there."

Carol cocked the trigger. It was the pistol she killed herself with, and seeing it was like taking a bullet. "Well, we have your brain surrounded," she said.

Young Dick ordered the soldiers to put down their weapons.

I couldn't figure out how Carol had gotten the jump on Cheney. He was smart and wouldn't allow himself to be outfoxed twice.

"Carol, how did you do this?" I asked, pointing to Cheney.

"The last time Dad was out here, he installed a high-tech security system. It was supposed to look for Bigfoot and flying saucers, but it can also detect helicopters. I just had time to grab my gun before this guy waltzed in."

It made sense. Before the war, Cheney was notoriously overconfident and predicted how easy conquering Iraq would be. I guessed he thought his home invasion to capture a woman and two queers would be even simpler.

"Now what do we do?" Junior asked.

"I just need him," Cheney replied, with a nod toward me. "If he comes with me, you two are free to go."

Junior and I had accomplished what we set out to do: convince Carol that she'd kill herself. I also wanted to extricate them from any further dealings with Cheney.

"I think I should go with him," I said.

"Are you crazy?" Carol asked. "This guy would give a corpse the creeps."

There was no reaction from Young Dick, almost as if he took her remark as a compliment. I turned to him. "If I go with you, will you let them go?"

His lips aped a smile. "Sure. We just need you."

While we had Young Dick at gunpoint, I asked what had happened to Elena, Michael, and Taylor.

"Nothing. We let them go."

I believed him. Obviously, he'd released Taylor. Otherwise there wouldn't be a time machine, and we wouldn't be having this discussion at gunpoint.

"You let them all go?" Junior asked, clearly thinking about Taylor.

"That's what I was ordered to do. I didn't want to, but I also didn't want another sinus bath."

No wonder Cheney's so unflappable, I thought. He's the only man on Earth who can claim with complete confidence that he is his own worst enemy.

"I don't think this is a good idea," Junior said. "You can't trust him."

"Actually, in this case we can," I responded. "If he changes history, he might not become vice president, or maybe his next heart attack will kill him."

On "heart attack" there was a noticeable intake of breath from Young Dick.

Junior and Carol looked as if they just realized they would never see me again, and I was glad they seemed unhappy about it. It made me heartsick to say good-bye to them, but I was also alarmed. Was I saying farewell to Carol again forever? I felt tears lapping against their break-walls. "I don't want to say good-bye to either of you," I said.

"I think we'll meet again," Junior deadpanned, which made me smile. It vanished when I faced Carol.

"Will we meet again?"

Carol gave a little shrug. "I honestly don't know. I hope so. I don't want to meet you next in hell."

Junior and I stared at her, confused by her last remark.

"You're gay, I'm a suicide, and according to the loving Roman Catholic Church we were brought up in that means we'll end up downstairs." Carol glanced at Cheney. "With him! That would be an everlasting punishment."

She avoided answering my question by joking. It seemed apparent that that characteristic family trait was impervious to being changed by any time traveler.

"I need to know that you can do this." I glanced at Junior also. "Both of you."

Junior didn't say anything, but Carol said, "How do we know? How does anyone know what the future holds?"

My face must have betrayed my doubt that we'd changed anything.

"But there is one thing I know," she said. "I know my brothers love me and would do anything to help me. Drive cross-country nonstop. Battle insane vice presidents."

"Travel through fucking time," Junior added.

They were right. I had no doubt that in the same situation my brothers, Kevin and Alan, would have done the same thing Junior and I did.

She tipped the gun toward Young Dick. "And I want to live just so I can vote against this asshole twice. Tracking in mud on our new carpet."

Junior chuckled. "That sounds like something Mom would say."

Carol gave a hint of a smile. "It does." She looked at me and said, "And I'll never forget what you told me she said."

Junior pursed his lips. "I owe you an apology," he said to me. "You're not a loser. You did this. You made a vow to get this done and you followed through."

We were both moved by his statement, but like most men kept our feelings to ourselves as if we were hoarders whose heads were stuffed to the rafters with every emotion we'd ever owned.

Carol rolled her eyes and sighed. "What he's saying is that he's proud to be you. Right?"

"Yeah," Junior answered.

"Jesus, was that so hard? No wonder men die of heart attacks. You can't even express nice feelings."

For the first time since Carol's death, I felt a glimmer of optimism. It was like a lone firefly flashing on and off on a summer night. There wasn't enough light to end the darkness, but it was exciting.

"Thank you both for all your help," I said. "Don't forget what I told you. You're both very special and can do anything. And I love you."

They both said, "I love you" back, although the sentimentality of the moment was undercut by having to profess our love in front of fifty soldiers and a power-mad congressman.

"Do we have a deal?" Young Dick asked.

"On one condition," I responded, as I thought of something else that needed to be done. "When she gives you that gun, don't give it back to her. Ever. Got that?"

"It's Dad's," Carol said.

I just stared at her.

"Oh," she said, transfixed by the gun.

Young Dick appeared to be relieved by my easy-to-comply-with demand. "No problem."

"Put down the gun," I commanded. She reluctantly placed the weapon on the floor, and a soldier immediately bent down to retrieve it. The rest of the black ops picked up their weapons, and Cheney ordered them to get me out of the house.

Outside was an army of soldiers. I could see people staring out their windows in the houses across the street and entire families standing in driveways or on front lawns. I had no doubt this would be topic A at the next meeting of the neighborhood watch group. A helicopter sat on the street and I was led to it. The pilot looked vaguely familiar, even though he wore a helmet and mirrored sunglasses that covered most of his face. Then I noticed his thick forearms, which were unmistakable. Taylor shook his head almost imperceptibly, and I pretended not to recognize him as I sat beside him. I'd been waiting to be rescued by Taylor and had begun to doubt it would ever happen. Dawn Powell was right. Seeing him unexpectedly again was a kick. I still loved Taylor.

"Do you know how to fly this?" I whispered.

"I've been taking lessons since you left."

"I've only been gone six days."

"You've been gone six months in our time."

I was confused. "We had a hard time tracking you down," he explained. "But we can show up at any time in the past. So, what seems like one minute to you might be ten years to someone in the future."

The helicopter slowly lifted off the ground. I could see Carol and Junior down on the front lawn standing inside a circle of rifle-toting soldiers. The two of them waved to me.

"How did you find me?"

Taylor didn't reply as we ascended, allowing us a view of the coast and the redwoods. He headed north past the Smith River, then landed in a field. He handed me a time travel bracelet and told me to put it on. Then he said, "Push the button on the underside on the count of three."

I did, and we reappeared in the living room of our apartment. It was disorienting to be back, and I stared at Taylor. We were both older, but the passage of time didn't seem depressing any longer: it seemed commendable, as if every liver spot and wrinkle were medals and ribbons awarded for extraordinary valor. That fantasy lasted for all of five seconds, but it was encouraging while it persisted. Bartleby loped over, wagging his tail. While I petted him, he reminded me that a loving dog's welcome never loses its potency.

"Welcome back, John," Taylor said before we hugged and kissed.

I'd thought that once I was in the present again, my mind would immediately be flooded with all the new memories that Junior had experienced. But my memories were indistinct, almost as if my new set of memories had been laser-printed over my old memories, making everything illegible and difficult to make out. I only captured fleeting moments, an image, a taste, or a smell, but I wasn't sure of their veracity. It seemed my father didn't die of alcoholism but had died of a heart attack a few years after he would have died from drinking, but I wasn't confident of either memory. And I recalled the cover of a graphic novel I'd written called *In Time This Will Seem Funny* about a group of time-traveling gay and lesbian superheroes. But I couldn't remember the story, making me wonder if it was something real or something I once imagined. I could see several covers for *Dark Cloud* but sadly nothing after issue #6. There was also a horrifying memory of a drunken George W. Bush putting his mouth around my . . . I quickly tried to squelch that thought and pretend that it didn't happen.

I had a million questions, but the first thing I asked Taylor was: "Are you Republican? Do you support Bush and Cheney?"

He glared at me. "Are you mental?" he asked. "I've never supported them." I looked at him closely. He appeared to be genuinely insulted. But I thought, If he wasn't a Republican, then why did he build a time machine for Bush and Cheney? Then it dawned on me. He built the time machine to give me a chance to save Carol. I gave him the hottest kiss we'd had in years.

Then I reached inside my jacket and fished my cell phone out of the inside pocket. The cell phone that still had Carol's number listed. I was impatient to know and afraid to find out. I sat down in a chair for a minute and looked over at Taylor. He nodded his head. I turned it on and waited for the screen to appear. I scrolled down and pressed "Contacts." I quickly scrolled down to the Cs. There it was: Carol. No last name was required. There had been only one Carol in my life. I became so anxious that I almost dropped the phone and fumbled pressing her name before hitting talk. It rang three times before someone answered.

"Hi, Groovy."

Acknowledgments

The first person I want to thank is Michael Carroll, who read a time-travel short story I'd written and told me, "I think this should be a novel."

I also want to thank all my friends who've given me invaluable advice and support: Christopher Bram, Draper Shreeve, Patrick Ryan, Fred Blair, David McConnell, Darrell Crawford, David Rakoff, Edmund White, Eddie Sarfaty, Court Stroud, Tim Miller, Alastair McCartney, Chris Shirley, Joe Radoccia, Brian Baxter, Jaffe Cohen, Maggie Cadman, Keith McDermott, Jackie Haught, Phyllis Bloom, Jeremy Adams, James Latus, John Arnold, Curt Bouton, Priscilla Gemmill, Elvira Kurt, Chloe Brushwood-Rose, Glenn Rosenblum, Mark Freeman, and especially Don Weise.

Of course, every aspect of this story has been run past my go-to guy on story and everything else: Michael Zam.

My editor Raphael Kadushin has been incredibly supportive and insightful. And I also want to thank the entire helpful and hardworking staff at the University of Wisconsin Press.

My biggest thank you is reserved for my agent and friend Rob Weisbach. Without him, this book wouldn't have happened.